HOOK

HOOK

Terry Brooks

Based on a Screenplay by
Jim V. Hart and
Malia Scotch Marmo

and Screen Story by
Jim V. Hart & Nick Castle

ARROW BOOKS

Published by Arrow Books Limited
20 Vauxhall Bridge Road, London SW1V 2SA

An imprint of the Random Century Group

London Melbourne Sydney Auckland Johannesburg
and agencies throughout the world

First published by arrangement with Ballantine Books,
a division of Random House Inc.

Arrow edition 1992

1 3 5 7 9 10 8 6 4 2

The right of Terry Brooks to be identified as the
author of this work has been asserted by him in
accordance with the Copyright, Designs and Patents
Act, 1988

Printed and bound in Great Britain by
Cox & Wyman Ltd, Reading

ISBN 0 09 911031 8

Contents

Author's Note

This is a story about Peter Pan. It is not the story everyone knows, the one written by J. M. Barrie and read by wise children and curious adults for more than eighty years. It is not even one of the lesser-known Pan stories. It is too new for that, having not come about until just recently and well after J. M. Barrie's time. This is its first formal telling.

This story is not just about Peter Pan either—no more so than any we know. It is about a good many things besides Peter himself, though he would be the last to admit that there were tales of any sort worth telling that did not concern themselves with him. The title, for instance, clearly indicates that the story is about someone other than just Peter. James Hook is central to the telling of any full-blown Pan tale, for every hero needs his villain. Prospective readers might also correctly point out that *Peter Pan* has already been used as a title and should not be pressed into service a second time simply to satisfy purists.

This story begins many years after the first, long after Wendy, John, and Michael returned from their first adventure in Neverland. It is not concerned with Peter Pan as a boy, for all those tales have long since been told. It considers instead what happened when the unthinkable came to pass—when Peter Pan grew up.

I relate this story to you as it was told to me, having tried the best I could to keep the details straight. I have embellished at times and commented when I could not make myself stay silent. All writers, I fear, have that failing.

My apologies to J. M. Barrie for taking license with his

vision and to others who have done so successfully before me.

This story is about children and grown-ups and the dangers that arise when the former become the latter.

It opens at a grade-school play.

TB

All Children, Except One, Grow Up

"Shhhh!"

The hushing rose in small bursts as the overhead lights clicked off, and the low din of voices engaged in idle conversation quickly died away. The members of the audience, young and old alike, straightened in their seats and faced uniformly toward the stage. There was activity behind the curtain, but it quickly faded into small squeaks and giggles. The curtain lifted slowly on a darkened setting, and the only light in the crowded multipurpose room of Franklin Elementary came from the green neon exit sign over the exterior wall door.

Moira Banning, elegant and poised, every strand of her short-cropped chestnut hair in place, glanced past eleven-year-old Jack toward the back of the room, a hint of irritation flashing in her green eyes. Still no sign of Peter.

Next to her, Jack Banning sat with his eyes facing front, waiting patiently for the play to begin. He was a small, elfin-featured boy with chocolate-brown hair and eyes and a tentative smile that suggested he was just a little doubtful about something.

Lights came up on the stage, and from behind the audience a spotlight. A cardboard replica of Big Ben was caught in the narrow beam, the Roman numerals of its face pasted rather crookedly into place. From off stage, a scratchy recording of deep, sonorous chimes began to play.

Bong. Bong. Bong . . .

Moira smiled and nudged her son, who squirmed away.

The chimes finished and a ticking began. Tick-tock, tick-tock. More stage lights came on, faintly illuminating a

1

bedroom in which children slept. Two beds with covers concealed the number of sleepers from those one or two in the audience who didn't already know the story of Peter Pan. A chest of toys, some bookshelves, and a bureau completed the set.

Then Peter Pan appeared, flying into view from off stage, suspended on a wire that shimmered like damp spider's webbing in the glare of the spotlight. Moira glanced past Jack once again, scanning the back of the room. Jack didn't need to ask who she was looking for or what the chances were of his dad being there.

On stage, the second-grader who had won the favor of the play director and been given the choice role of Peter landed in a stumbling run that ended with his legs folding and his body skidding a half-dozen feet. Laughter rose from the audience. He scrambled up hurriedly, cast a chagrined look in the direction of the laughter, and turned toward the bureau.

Immediately a flashlight beam directed from off stage darted erratically after him. Jack looked smug. Tinkerbell, of course. Peter rummaged through the bureau drawers and pulled out a piece of black cloth cut out in the shape of a boy. He held it up toward the audience so that no one would miss the significance of his discovery. Then he shut the bureau drawer behind him with the flashlight beam still darting about, and instantly the light winked out. Jack nodded solemnly. Tinkerbell was trapped. Just like in the book.

Peter sat down with his shadow, played around with it for a bit as if trying to fasten it on, then threw it down rather dramatically and burst into fake tears.

Jack rolled his eyes. Time for Maggie.

His sister popped up on cue, tossing aside the bed covers, her strawberry-blond hair bouncing, her eyes wide. She was wearing her favorite cream nightshirt with violet hearts. "Boy, why are you crying?" she called out loud enough to be heard in the next county. Only seven years old maybe, but no one was going to ignore her tonight!

"I'm not crying," Peter insisted.

Wendy, whom Maggie was playing, jumped down from the bed and rushed over to pick up the discarded shadow. Kneeling, she pretended to sew it back on. When she was done, she rose and stepped back expectantly.

Peter stood up and bowed politely from the waist, one hand crooked in front, one behind. A faerie greeting. Wendy immediately bowed back.

"What is your name?" Peter asked.

"Wendy Angela Moira Darling. What's yours?"

"Peter Pan."

"Where do you live?"

"Second to the right and straight on till morning. I live in Neverland with the Lost Boys. They are the children who fall out of their prams when their nurses aren't looking. I'm their captain."

Wendy beamed and clapped her hands. "What fun! Are there no girls?"

"Oh, no," replied Peter, shaking his head emphatically. "Girls are much too clever to fall out of their prams."

He moved back a step, spread his feet, and put his hands on his hips. The spotlight centered on him. He cocked his head back and crowed.

Jack grimaced. *Brother! Bring on the pirates!*

Suddenly a huge shadow passed into the light, casting itself onto the stage and swallowing up a now frightened Peter Pan. Heads swiveled curiously, a few anxiously. A man was making his way down the aisle, crouching now in an effort to escape the light, bumping into folding chairs and occupants as he went.

"Sorry, excuse me, pardon me," he whispered, bending and dipping and squinting into the dark.

Attorney-at-law Peter Banning caught his toe on a chair leg and nearly went sprawling. "Quiet!" and "Shh!" were whispered at every turn. His boyish face smiled apologetically, a mop of unruly brown hair falling down over his forehead, the skin at the corners of his startlingly blue eyes crinkling. He clutched a polished leather briefcase and a folded tan raincoat to his chest. Working his way clear of the spotlight, he let his eyes adjust momentarily, then caught sight of Moira waving to him from several rows farther down. Smoothing out the coat flaps of his dark blue business suit and tucking back his favorite yellow power tie, he eased past the irritated play watchers, stepped on more than a few toes, and arrived at Moira's side.

Jack smiled up at him expectantly, patting the open seat next to him. Peter smiled back, then motioned him to switch with Moira. Jack gave his father a pointed look, then stomped past his mother and threw himself into his chair.

"Down in front, please!" someone behind them hissed.

Peter settled himself next to Moira, the briefcase and the raincoat piled in his lap, and leaned over for a quick kiss. Moira obliged, her voice musical as she whispered hello.

"Sorry. It was 'the never-ending meeting.' You know the kind. And traffic was brutal." Peter grinned, leaning across his wife to Jack. "Hey, how was practice, Jackie? You working on hitting that curve for the big game tomorrow? Hey, tuck in your shirt."

Jack flinched and turned away sourly before doing so. Peter looked questioningly at Moira. "What's with him?"

Moira shook her head, then indicated the stage. "Your daughter's stealing the show."

On stage, Maggie as Wendy Darling was watching her costar being hoisted on the wire as if flying, her hands clasped, her face shining. Behind her, still in bed, the second-graders playing John and Michael were awake now as well and watching the show.

"Oh, you can fly!" she exclaimed loudly. "How lovely! But how do you do it?"

"You just think lovely, wonderful thoughts, and they lift you up into the air," answered Peter Pan, landing a bit more gracefully this time than before. "But first, I must blow faerie dust on you."

Tinkerbell reappeared, the flashlight beam dancing back into view. A jingling sound rose from off stage, and glitter rained down on Wendy and the boys. Michael was the first to fly, then John, and finally Wendy as well, all soaring about the stage like windblown kites. Applause rose from the audience.

Peter Banning looked shocked. "Moira!" He started to his feet, apoplectic at the sight of Maggie swinging on a wire, but Moira quickly pulled him back down again.

"She could fall, Moira!" he whispered frantically. "How could the school allow them to do something like this? It's too dangerous! Just watching makes me dizzy!"

"Oh, Dad!" Jack groaned, but the clapping drowned him out. Moira simply smiled at her husband, patted his arm reassuringly, and joined in the applause. Jack whistled, rather impressed that Maggie was doing so well, a bit envious that she was getting to fly.

Backstage, the jingling of bells mixed with the resonant tinkle of a xylophone as Peter Pan led Tinkerbell, John, and Michael out the window. After a moment's glance and a wave in the general direction of her parents, Maggie as Wendy followed and the curtain closed.

A low hum of voices and laughter rose from the audience as the children readied the stage for the next act. Peter straightened in his chair, finding it decidedly uncomfortable now that he had spent more than five minutes sitting in it. The voices and laughter faded expectantly.

Abruptly a ringing sounded, the high-pitched, annoying squeal of a cellular phone. Heads turned. Peter fumbled hurriedly with his raincoat and pulled the phone out of one pocket. Beside him, Moira sagged slightly, whispering, "Peter, please!" Jack, aware of the looks being cast in their direction, plugged his ears with his fingers and tried to pretend he was somewhere else.

"Brad, make this quick," Peter whispered into the phone. "I'm with my family."

The curtain drew back in front of him revealing a backdrop of Neverland in front of which were stationed seven brightly painted cardboard trees. Doors in each opened and seven Lost Boys appeared dressed in seven variations of old pajamas. Joining hands, they faced the audience and began to sing loudly, "We Never Want to Grow Up."

I'm a Toys "R" Us kid, thought Peter, trying to listen to the voice on the other end of the phone.

The Lost Boys finished singing, and the one playing Tootles turned to the others and declaimed, "I wish Peter would come back soon. I'm always afraid of pirates when he's not here to protect us."

From the right side of the stage, a band of pirates began dragging a raft on stage. Settled in the raft was the hefty-looking boy who had been given the part of Captain James Hook.

Peter Banning's attention was focused on the cellular phone. His voice rose. "Brad, that's why we have an ecologist on staff! That's why we're paying him all that money! Remind him he's not working for the Sierra Club anymore!"

From several rows in either direction, a scattering of boos and hisses were directed his way. He slid further down into his seat, curling protectively around the phone.

On stage, a Lost Boy raced about frantically, trying to escape the pirates. Smee, bespectacled and stripe-shirted, with padding for a belly, wiggled his cutlass threateningly.

"Shall I after him, Captain, and tickle him with Johnny Corkscrew?"

The boy playing Hook stood stiffly. "No, I want their captain, Peter Pan. It was he who cut off my arm and flung it to that crocodile."

Jack heard his father whisper into the phone. "Look, I leave for London with the family tomorrow night, Brad. So call a meeting in the A.M." Jack tried to protest, signaling frantically. *The game, Dad!* Peter glanced up. "My son's big game, don't forget. Gotta be there. So a short meeting. Quick and clean. Blow 'em out of the water."

He clicked the phone off and shoved it back in his pocket. Jack stared at him in dismay.

Tick, tick, tick, sounded from on stage. Smee and Hook cocked their heads in pretend fear.

"The crocodile!" exclaimed Hook. "Licking his lips for the rest of me! By lucky chance he swallowed a clock or I wouldn't hear him coming."

Kids in the audience joined in the ticking, Jack among

them. Peter Banning grimaced and put his hands over his ears. A crocodile composed of an old green blanket and two squirming children slithered on stage amid yells from the audience, sending Hook and Smee fleeing for safety.

Peter Banning sighed, frowned, folded his hands in his lap atop the raincoat and briefcase, and took a deep breath. There was something unsettling about this play.

The action continued, and Jack grew interested in spite of himself. By the time they got to the part where Hook and Pan face off for the final battle, he was completely absorbed. Wooden swords clicked together three times as the adversaries dueled before the rigging of the pirate ship.

"Pan, who and what art thou?" Hook exclaimed in dismay.

"I am youth. I am joy. I fly, I fight, I crow!" answered Peter Pan, and crowed loudly to prove his point.

The fight ended in Hook's defeat, the captain falling to the waiting jaws of the crocodile, who proceeded to chase him off stage. The sets shifted a final time, revealing again the nursery where things had begun. The boy in the old fur parka playing Nana barked loudly as the lights came up, and Mr. Darling paraded across the stage with the Lost Boys hanging gaily about his coattails along with John and Michael. Wendy and Mrs. Darling followed, slowing as they saw Peter Pan hovering at the window.

"Peter, let me adopt you, too," said Mrs. Darling.

Peter gave her his best stage frown. "Would you send me to school?"

"Yes, of course."

"And then to an office?"

"I suppose so."

"Soon I should be a man?"

"Yes, very soon."

Peter Pan shook his head. "I don't want to go to school and learn solemn things. No one is going to catch me and make me a man. I want always to be a little boy and have fun."

He blew into his wooden flute, the wire attached to his

belt hoisted him up, and off he flew. The lights dimmed with his departure and the stage emptied. The scratchy recording of Big Ben began to play.

In the audience, Peter Banning blinked wearily, wondering how much longer the play was going to last. At least Maggie wasn't being flung about through the air any longer. What idiot came up with that idea? He straightened his tie and adjusted his cuff links self-consciously. His suit was already rumpled beyond help. He needed sleep and a shower. He needed peace and quiet.

What was it about this play . . .?

He stared resolutely at the stage, frowning.

The stage lights came up, so faint they barely cut through the darkness, casting strange shadows everywhere. An older Wendy, dressed in a print dress and wearing reading glasses, was seated on the floor of the nursery close by a fire made of colored lights and tinfoil. A bed with a sleeping child was set to one side. Wendy was sewing, using the firelight to see. From somewhere outside, she heard a crowing sound and looked up expectantly.

Shutters blew open at the window and Peter Pan dropped to the floor.

"Peter," said Wendy, "are you expecting me to fly away with you?"

Peter grinned. "Of course. That is why I've come. Have you forgotten that this is spring-cleaning time?"

Wendy shook her head sadly. "I can't come, Peter. I have forgotten how to fly."

"I'll soon teach you again."

"Oh, Peter, don't waste the faerie dust on me."

She rose to face him.

"What is it?" he asked.

"I will turn up the lights, and then you can see for yourself."

"No," he said. "Don't turn up the lights. I don't want to see."

But she did, of course, and Peter Pan did see. Wendy was no longer young. She was an old lady. He cried out in shock. She went to comfort him, but he drew back sharply.

"What is it? What's happened to you?"

"I am old, Peter. I grew up a long time ago."

"But you promised not to."

"I couldn't help it. I'm a married woman, Peter."

He shook his head vigorously. "No, you're not!"

"Yes. And the little girl in the bed is my baby."

"No, she's not!"

He took a quick step toward the sleeping child, his dagger upraised threateningly. But he didn't strike. Instead, he sat down on the floor and began to sob. Wendy stared at him a moment, then ran out of the room. Wendy's child, Jane, awakened by the crying, sat up in the bed.

"Boy, why are you crying?" she asked.

Peter Pan jumped up and bowed to her. She rose and bowed back.

"Hullo," he said.

"Hullo."

"My name is Peter Pan."

She smiled. "Yes, I know."

Together, they dashed for the window, preparing to fly away. Wendy rushed into the room, hands outstretched. The lights dimmed, the curtain closed, and all the children came out together and sang, "We Never Want to Grow Up." Everyone in the audience applauded, and the children on stage laughed and bowed.

Wow! thought Jack. Charged with the play's excitement and joy, he gave his dad a glowing smile.

Thank goodness that's over! Peter Banning sighed, and missed the smile completely.

Pitches

Sunlight filtered down across the woodlands, bright and warm, filled with promise. The spruce and hemlock crowded together on the foothills, verdant and thick as they backed their way upward into the tall peaks of the mountains beyond, where snow glistened whitely. Rivers and streams ran down out of the mountains, wending their way through the trees toward a cluster of lakes and ponds. Here, to the right, a waterfall spilled out of the rocks. There, to the left, a meadow of wildflowers painted a slope in rainbow colors.

Almost looks real, thought Peter Banning, feeling pleased with himself.

He turned away momentarily to stare out the windows of his office high rise into the fog that hung in a pall across the San Francisco cityscape, then wheeled back again to confront the mock-up.

"We'll get the environmentalists off our case by convincing them that our clients won't develop the whole area all at once, that the project will be a gradual one, that we care about preserving the wildlife." His eyes snapped up. "You on that, Brad?"

Tall, sallow-faced Brad answered, "Ron's on that."

"I'm on that," Ron agreed. Short, round, and California tan, he was Brad's exact opposite in the looks department. What saved them both from corporate extinction was that they thought alike, and more to the point, they thought like Peter Banning.

Peter gave him a sharp look. "I hope so. In line with that, my suggestion is we start with this piece." He pointed to the meadow. "An open space so we get rid of the greenies and regulators right off the bat before they have time to build up enough steam to shut us down."

He reached across the table into a box that contained a series of plastic models and began snapping them down on the mock-up. Condos, ski runs, shops, and single-family homes. Lots of money to be made. He filled the meadow quickly, hesitated, then pulled up several dozen of the plastic trees. A resort complex replaced them, and at the very center of everything, a small plastic nature preserve that consisted of a park with trails.

"Good." Peter Banning shoved his hands into his suitcoat pockets momentarily, then conscious of the wrinkles he was causing, withdrew them. "Once the zoning is approved and everything is in place, after the Sierra Club boys and girls move on to another cause, we begin adding on. A piece at a time until this wilderness is converted into our client's dream resort."

He looked at Brad and Ron.

"That's . . ." one began.

". . . brilliant," the other finished.

Peter smiled. "I know. Let's just hope that between now and the close of this acquisition, no one throws us a curve."

His gaze fixed abruptly on the wall clock and a hint of panic surged through him. "Rats! I'm late for Jack's game!"

He wheeled away from the table and strode out through the conference-room doors.

It was a crisp, clear December day, and a brisk wind ruffled the rows of pennants that represented each team that played in the league. Across the top of the scoreboard from which they hung was a banner on which had been lettered in red: SANTA SERIES THIRD ANNUAL DATENUT LEAGUE WINTER TOURNAMENT.

Below, where things counted, the board read: 6TH INNING, HOME 2, VISITORS 5.

From where he crouched in center field, hands on his knees, ready and alert for the next batter, Jack scanned the stands. They were only wooden planks settled on iron

stanchions, and there weren't that many to begin with, so
his search didn't take long. Most of the seats were filled. He
could see his mother and Maggie in row three, yelling and
cheering. Between them, the extra red seat cushion was still
empty.

He better show, Jack thought determinedly.

The grass where he stood was green and lush from the
weekend's rain. Jack kicked at the earth, straightened, and
watched the next batter come to the plate. Kendall. Good
hit, no field. That was the book.

He glanced again at the scoreboard: 5 to 2, and time
running out.

He pounded his glove, thinking, *He better!*

The wind came up suddenly and stirred the infield dust,
causing a break in the action. The plate umpire raised his
hands to signal a stop. Jack sighed. All of the umpires were
wearing Santa Claus suits. They looked ridiculous.

The wind died and play resumed. Kendall took a strike
and two balls, then lofted a high fly toward Jack. Jack
shaded his eyes, watched the ball rise and fall, moved
beneath it, reached up, and snagged it easily. A cheer rose
from his teammates and fans. He threw the ball in, trotted
back to his position, and resumed his stance.

He risked a quick look back at the stands. Maggie and his
mother and the empty seat cushion. He spat.

He just better!

Peter Banning rushed ahead through mazelike corridors,
past secretarial cubicles, past closets and storerooms, past
doors that led nowhere he had ever been—or at least
remembered being. Posner, Nail & Banning occupied an
entire floor of the building. An entourage trailed in his
wake—Brad and Ron; their young associate Jim Paige; Dr.
Fields, the ecologist hired to advise the firm on the pending
development; a planning assistant whose name he could not
remember; and a receptionist whose name he had never
known.

Peter's mind raced. "Jerry, Jack, Jim." He could not
remember Paige's name. Tall, athletic, some sort of track-

and-field man at Yale, wasn't he? "Steve! Take the video camera. Go to the game ahead of me. Shoot what I miss."

"Can I say something?" Dr. Fields interjected, and was ignored.

Jim Paige moved up alongside him, waving a sheet of yellow-lined legal paper and a floppy disk.

"Your speech for your grandmother's tribute . . ."

Peter glanced over, still moving, turning the corner like an Indy driver on the final lap. "Will this be on cards?"

"Yes, sir, of course."

"Numbered? Who wrote this?"

"Ned Miller, sir."

Peter rolled his eyes. "Oh, wonderful. I couldn't put down his annual report. C'mon. Read it to me."

Paige cleared his throat. "Lord Whitehall, honored guests, et cetera, for the past seventy years the Wendy we honor tonight has given hope to and provided care for hundreds of homeless children, orphans of all—"

"That's great, very personal," Peter interrupted.

"Can I say something?" Dr. Fields tried again.

The receptionist pushed forward, breathless. "Mr. Banning, sir, please send my congratulations to your extraordinary grandmother. You must be so proud."

Peter smiled at her as if she were a candidate for shock therapy.

He rounded a corner and nearly bowled over his personal secretary, who was rushing to find him from the other direction. She gasped, recovered herself, and shoved a steaming cappuccino into his hands followed by an airline ticket folder.

"Amanda—my tickets, my tickets." He drained the cappuccino in one gulp, shoved the empty cup back in her hands, and resumed his charge down the office corridors. "Hurry, hurry, hurry,"

"Sir, there's been a terrible mistake," Amanda declared, rushing to keep up. "These tickets are coach."

"That's right. Rows fourteen and fifteen by the wing exits—statistically safest." They rounded yet another corridor. Building went on forever, Peter thought cryptically.

"Ron, have the four-oh-fours prepared before I return."

"Done," the other announced.

"Brad, the wetlands report."

"Done." Brad was breathing hard.

"Sierra Club report?"

Brad and Ron looked at each other. "Almost done," they muttered as one.

"Done, my foot! Nothing's done." Dr. Fields shoved to the fore. He was a small, wizened man of indeterminate age with thick glasses and gray hair that stuck out in all directions. He tapped Peter's shoulder. "You hired me as your environmental expert, and you've ignored my reports."

Peter glanced past him to Jim Paige. "Do you have more of the speech?"

His young associate peered down at the yellow sheets, trying to keep from tripping over Ron. "The addition of the Wendy Darling Foundling Wing guarantees that her work will never be forgotten and that a commitment to the future—"

"You're not listening to me," Fields interjected irritably. "You have to set aside acreage for a mating area."

"Dr. Fields, we have the designated mating area, right behind the ski lodge," piped up Brad.

"Two hundred acres . . . " began Ron.

"Designated mating area? Is that supposed to be some kind of a joke?" Fields was incensed. "You have no right to develop a piece of land without determining what the impact will be on the creatures living there. What if there are endangered species? Like, for instance, like . . ."

Peter reached over, still walking, and put his arm around the other's bony shoulders. "Like what, Dr Fields?"

"The three-toed speckled frog, the white-footed deer, any number of birds . . ."

Peter patted the environmentalist gently on the back, his voice as smooth as syrup. "We're all big boys here, Dr. Fields. Tell me, how much room do these creatures need to mate? For most of us, it's a matter of inches."

Everyone broke out in laughter, and Fields dropped back again, red-faced.

Peter glanced over at Paige. "Steve, you still here? Get going with that video!" Ahead, the elevator bank came into view. "Take the stairs! You're an athlete!"

Paige shoved the yellow sheets and disk into Amanda's hands and rushed away. "What was it he did at Yale?" Peter muttered to himself. "Mile, four-forty, broad jump?"

They reached the elevators, breathing hard. Peter was aware suddenly of how heavy he'd gotten. Not fat, mind you, but certainly heavy. He glanced down his sloping front side and could not see his shoes. Slowly, trying to not show what he was doing, he sucked in his stomach. Didn't help much.

Brad pressed the down button.

"I ordered flowers for your grandmother," Amanda announced, ticking off the list on her fingers. "I picked up your dry cleaning and put it in your car. Your hanging bag is in the trunk. . . ."

"Mr. Banning," Dr. Fields tried again, "it's just that there are people out there who believe, just as you might believe in some aspect of your own life, that the three-toed frogs of this world are what keep us all from going to hell in a hand basket."

"Yeah, people out there we have to protect ourselves from," muttered Brad over his shoulder.

"Oh, and here are your vitamins," Amanda continued. "And that file on Owens you were looking for." She shoved some slips of paper into his hands. "These are the messages you need to return on your car phone on the way to Jack's game."

"Jack's game," Peter reminded himself.

The elevator to the left arrived and the door opened. Peter started inside.

"Wait, boss!" yelled the nameless assistant. "Catch!"

Peter's holster phone flew through the air. He reached out and deftly snagged it. Not bad for an old guy. Blocking the elevator door with his foot, he strapped the holster on. Brad moved up to stand before him, pulled back his suitcoat flap to reveal a similar holster phone, and went into a gunfighter's crouch. Peter faced him, fingers twitching. As one, they reached for their phones and drew them out, holding them to their ears.

"I got a quicker dial tone, Brad," announced Peter. "You're dead."

Everyone laughed as they reholstered their weapons.

Peter waved. "Gotta fly."

"Don't worry—more people crash in cars than on planes," Brad called out.

"It's a lot safer than crossing the street!" added Ron.

"Just don't look down!" advised someone else.

"And don't let your arms get tired!" they all shouted and began flapping their arms. Dr. Fields was shaking his head and walking away.

"When it's your time to go, it's your time to go," Peter intoned solemnly, shot them his best boyish grin as they groaned in unison, and stepped into the elevator. The doors swished closed softly.

For a moment no one moved, facing the elevator bank wordlessly.

"All right," said Brad finally, turning to the assistant. "Frank, you fax the proposal for tomorrow's meeting to everyone coming." He shifted toward the receptionist. "Julie, get Ted on the phone. We have to deep-six that Sierra Club report. Amanda, find out . . ."

There was a ringing in their midst. Everyone looked around. Finally Brad realized it was his holster phone. He drew it out and clicked it on. "Yes? What?" His jaw dropped. "Peter, why are you breathing so hard? You sound like you're running a marathon or something. What's going on?"

At the end of the hallway, the stairway door burst open and Peter labored into view. The assembly in front of the elevator doors turned to stare.

"Never mind the phone!" Peter gasped, shoving his own back in its holster. He was gasping for breath. Gonna have a heart attack if I keep this up, he thought. "I need one more look at the interim reports before I head off to London. Only take a minute."

Brad swung into step beside him as he charged back up the hall. "Peter, you're late for your kid's game!"

"Don't worry," Peter assured him. "I know a shortcut to the ballpark. Plenty of time."

The others fell in behind him, wordless. The elevators disappeared from view.

"Hey, there's a joke I'd like to try out on you guys," Peter announced, trying to slow his breathing, smiling his boyish smile. "I read recently that they're now using lawyers as surrogate mothers. Know why?"

No one did.

Jack stood at the plate, bat cocked, chin tucked in against his shoulder, and watched ball two whiz by. Two and two. He took a deep breath and stepped back. His eyes lifted to find the scoreboard. 9TH INNING. HOME 8, VISITORS 9.

"Keep us alive, out there, Banning!" yelled his coach. "C'mon, hang in there!"

His teammates were yelling at him, screaming directions, encouragement, prayers. The sporting-goods logos provided by the team sponsors were jumping around like action toys on the front of their uniforms. Jack looked down at his shoes, then scuffed at the earth. He hadn't looked into the stands for almost two innings now, afraid of what he would find. Or wouldn't find. The game was almost over. Had his dad made it?

"C'mon, son, play ball," the Santa behind the plate said gruffly.

Jack took another deep breath and stepped back into the box. He took his practice swings, and while he was doing so and despite his resolve not to, he found himself looking into the stands.

His mother and Maggie were standing side by side, cheering. Next to them, directly over the red seat cushion, was a man with a video camera. Dad? Jack's heart leaped.

Then he saw that it wasn't his father, that it was somebody
else, a man he'd seen once or twice who worked at his
father's office.

Standing there where his father was supposed to be,
filming him with the camera.

Jack went numb. He faced the pitcher, cocked the bat,
and dug in—all without being aware of what he was doing.
He felt the catcher crouch behind him, watched the pitcher
nod, go into his windup, and throw. A huge, hanging curve.
It seemed to take forever to get there. Jack slashed at it with
no hope.

"Strike three!" roared the umpire.

Ecstatic yells erupted from the visiting team, groans of
disgust from his own. For a moment he could not move.
Then mechanically, dismally, fighting back the tears that
were building behind his eyes, he lowered the bat and began
the long walk back to the bench.

The sun had gone west and the late-afternoon chill stung
Peter's face as he exited the heated interior of his BMW and
started toward the ballfield in a rush, raincoat draped over
one arm, phone holster slapping on his hip. His eyes lifted
to the scoreboard: 9TH INNING. HOME 8, VISITORS 9. Still
time, he thought, running now, feeling heavier and slower
and older than ever. Gotta start working out.

He rounded the end of the bleachers and stopped short.

The stands were empty, the ballfield deserted. Even the
bases had been removed. All that remained were a few stray
candy wrappers and discarded cups. Peter waited for his
breathing to slow, trying to steady himself. He looked again
at the scoreboard and shook his head.

Jackie.

He felt foolish and ashamed.

He turned finally and walked back toward his car,
realizing for the first time how silent everything was.

He was almost there when the holster phone rang. He
pulled it out and clicked it on, listening.

"Oh, hi, Brad," he greeted woodenly. "Yeah, glad you
called."

To England

The muted roar of the 747 was a backdrop of white noise for the endless crying of a baby several rows back. Peter heard both without really being aware of either, his thoughts concentrated on the gleaming screen of the laptop computer settled on the lowered tray before him. In large block letters, the screen read:

GRANNY WENDY CALLS ME HER FAVORITE ORPHAN.
I DON'T KNOW WHY.

Peter stared at the screen, at the words he had typed, trying to fathom the riddle they posed. It was a secret from long ago, from a distant, lost past he could no longer clearly remember. Granny Wendy. Wendy Darling. His grandmother.

Why did the words stick with him? Why did they hang about like whispers of something he should understand and didn't?

He placed his finger carefully on the delete key. The flashing cursor began to move backward across the screen, gobbling up the letters of the riddle. One by one they disappeared until all were gone and nothing remained but a blank screen.

The 747 hit an air pocket that sent the computer skidding off the tray and into Peter's lap. Peter clutched the arms of his seat frantically, trying to balance the computer with his knees. The turbulence continued, sharp and unrelenting bumps that made him feel like he was on a sled racing down a rutted hill.

Seated next to him, closest to the window, Maggie
looked up. "I want a bigger bump."

Peter sat rigid. "That one was big enough for Daddy."

She grinned. "Just pretend it's a big, bouncing bus, and
you won't be scared."

Doubtful, Peter thought darkly, wishing he were anywhere else but cooped up on this airplane. He hated
airplanes. He hated flying. He hated anything at all that had
to do with heights, for that matter. He liked the ground—
good, old, solid terra firma. If man had been meant to fly,
he would have been given . . .

Maggie nudged him, and he looked over indulgently. His
daughter's blue eyes stared back. She had Magic Marker all
over her hands and face. Before her lay a sheet of paper that
the markers had transformed into a riotous collection of
colorful lines and squiggles.

She took the drawing and handed it to him. "It's a map
of my mind," she explained. "So I won't get lost in my
thoughts. See? This is our house in San Francisco, California. This is where Great-granny Wendy's house is in
London, England. This is the orphan hospital they're
naming after Granny."

Peter released his grip on one armrest long enough to take
the drawing from her. He pretended to study it, all the while
conscious of the airplane shaking beneath him. Another
heavy jolt sent the laptop sliding down his legs toward the
cabin floor. Dropping Maggie's drawing, he gripped the
armrest anew.

"Daddy, look what Jack drew," Maggie persisted,
shoving a second drawing at her father.

Reluctantly, Peter accepted it. In the picture an airplane
crashed earthward in flames. Moira, Jack, and Maggie were
parachuting to safety. Peter was falling headfirst beside
them.

"Where's my parachute?" Peter exclaimed.

He glanced over the seat top to where Jack and Moira sat
one row back. Moira was studying the back of a baseball
card. Jack was watching her from his window seat, his

hands closed protectively over the large stack of baseball cards resting on the tray in front of him. If he saw his father looking at him, he didn't let on.

"Okay, Mom, ask me another. Ask me another one."

Moira spent a further moment studying the back of the card she held, then said, "Give me the American League batting champion, 1985."

"That's *way* easy. Wade Boggs. He's probably the best third baseman ever. Why? Because after seven seasons in the majors, he has the third highest batting average ever. Did you ever see him play, Mom?"

Moira shook her head, glancing at Peter. "No, I never did. But I'll bet your father saw him. Ask him about Wade Boggs."

Jack seemed to consider the idea for a moment, intense dark eyes fixed on the cards before him, then said, "Ask me another one."

Moira's disappointment in the response was obvious. She brushed back her chestnut hair and handed back the card she was holding to Jack. "In a moment."

Jack accepted the card without comment, without looking at anything, and began flipping through the remainder of the cards with deliberate, forced interest.

The turbulence had eased now and the Fasten Seat Belt sign was off again. Moira rose, smoothed out her clothes, and stepped into the aisle, where she knelt next to Peter's seat. Her green eyes were intense.

"Peter . . ."

"Moira, you've got to help me with Granny Wendy's speech. It just doesn't sound right."

She put a hand on his arm. "Do me a favor first, Peter. Before we get there, will you please resolve this baseball business with Jack? He's still very, very upset."

As always, there was a faint hint of an English accent in her speech, a little of her heritage left over from the days before she married him and came to live in the United States. He liked the sound of her voice, the pleasant cadence it carried, different from anyone else's, distinct and resonant.

He nodded dutifully. "I will. Want to hear what I have so far?"

Her hand tightened. "You should have gone to the game, Peter."

Peter stared wordlessly at her, aware of his failure, uncomfortable with it. He knew he had let Jack down, had let them both down, by not coming to the game. He intended to make it up to Jack; he just hadn't figured out how to go about it yet.

Moira fixed him with a deliberate stare, then indicated Jack with her eyes. She reached down and retrieved the laptop computer. She waited. Peter sighed, rose, and moved back to the seat she had vacated, settling down beside his son.

Jack had put away the baseball cards and was tossing his ball in the air and catching it.

"Listen, Jackie . . . ."

"Jack," his son corrected, tossing the ball higher.

Peter took a deep breath, then reached for the armrests as the airplane hit a new series of bumps. The FASTEN SEAT BELT sign flashed on once more. Jack kept tossing his ball.

"You're going to hit a window," Peter warned, testy now.

Jack kept his attention fixed on what he was doing. "Yeah, well, it's probably the only time you'll ever see me play ball."

"How about if when we get to London we watch the tape of the game?"

"Oh, all twenty minutes of it? The part where I strike out and we lose?"

Peter's lips tightened. "I'll give you a few pointers on beating the curve."

There was no answer. Jack threw the baseball higher. It banged off the cabin ceiling. Passengers all about lifted their heads from their magazines and books. The baby was crying harder. Jack started to throw the ball up again, and this time Peter reached out and caught it.

"Stop acting like a child!" he snapped.

Jack snatched the ball back. "I am a child!"

Peter saw the anger in his eyes and visibly sagged. "I'm going to be there next season to see you play—I promise."

His son looked over at him in despair. "Dad—don't make any more promises, okay?"

"Six games, guaranteed!"

"Dad—I said, don't promise!"

"My word is my bond," Peter insisted, and reached up to cross his heart.

Jack looked away. "Sure." The anger in his face was palpable. "A junk bond."

He flung the ball at the ceiling, striking it so hard that the oxygen mask compartment dropped open and a tangle of masks and lines collapsed downward in front of Peter's face. Peter's hands gripped the armrests for dear life, and he closed his eyes tight.

Granny Wendy

Kensington Gardens offered rows of turreted, gabled Tudor homes built of painted boards and stone and brick, their cloistered domains gated and walled, their patchwork lawns drifted with snow, their gardens brilliant with cyclamen and holly. Tree limbs shadowed the homes with spiderweb designs, the trunks from which they branched old and stately columns bracketing the walkways and hedgerows. From out of shadowed alcoves and niches, lights burned like damp fireflies through the late-afternoon mist. Christmas decorations hung brightly from doors and windows and eaves.

Somewhere in the distance, Big Ben chimed the half hour and went still.

The cab pulled into the drive at number 14, and the Banning family, both exhausted and high-strung, piled out. The driver stepped clear and moved around to the trunk to remove their bags, wheezing from a cold he had been fighting for the better part of a month. Jack started to skip toward the front entry of his Great-granny Wendy's home, lank hair damp with moisture, dark eyes bright, but Moira reached out quickly to rein him in. Maggie, her face and hands washed clean now of Magic Marker, tugged at her mother's hand anxiously.

"Mom!" she kept saying. "I want to see Great-granny Wendy!"

Standing by the front passenger door of the cab, Peter was engrossed in resetting watches. He held his pocket watch, Moira's Rolex, and Maggie's Swatch.

"Just a minute, just a minute," he muttered to no one in particular.

"There you go, sir," the cabbie offered, after carrying the bags to the door. Peter paid him, counting the English money carefully so as not to overtip, and didn't bother to watch him drive away.

"Mom, is Great-granny Wendy really the real Wendy, the Wendy from *Peter Pan*?" Maggie asked suddenly.

"No," Peter replied wearily. "Not really."

"Yes, sort of," answered Moira at the same instant.

They stared at each other uncomfortably. Then Peter reached out and handed his wife her watch.

"Okay, everybody," he announced briskly, rubbing his hands to generate enthusiasm. "Let's look your best now. First impressions are the most important." He moved to arrange the children in formation behind Moira, Jack first, Maggie second. "Socks pulled up, shirts tucked in, stand up straight. We're in England, the land of good manners."

He marched them the few steps to the door, checked them a final time, and clanked the knocker—a heavy brass affair attached to a metal plate. They waited patiently. Finally the latch clicked, and the door swung open. A white-haired old man stood framed against the light, dressed in trousers and a plaid jacket with numerous pockets, all stuffed to overflowing. His face was slack and expressionless, and his eyes were rheumy. He seemed to look right through them to something beyond.

"Uncle Tootles," Peter greeted softly. "Hello . . ."

The old man fixed his watery eyes on Peter as if seeing him for the first time and slammed the door.

Jack and Maggie were in stitches, hanging on to each other gleefully.

Peter colored. "Jack, spit out your gum before you laugh."

The door opened a second time, and a sharp-faced, redheaded woman peeked around the edge. Then the door swung open all the way and out bounded a huge, shaggy English sheepdog. The dog went past Peter as if he wasn't

there, spinning him around in passing, heading for the
children. Peter cried out in warning, but the kids were
already embracing the huge beast, hugging it and shouting,
"Nana, Nana!"

The pinched face of the woman in the door reappeared—
Liza, the Irish maid, laughing and talking a mile a minute.
"Miz Moira! Hullo, now! Lookit 'eze adorable l'ttle
children! 'Darlings' down to their pins, they are! Welcome
home, welcome home!"

Moira enfolded her in a warm hug. "Liza, it's good to
see you."

"Ah, Mr. Peter." Liza looked at him almost pityingly.
"Poor Uncle Tootles. He's not hisself today—not most
days lately." She sighed. "Well, come in, now, come in."

They trooped in out of the weather, out of the gloom of
the misted dusk into the bright lights beyond, Liza and
Moira leading the way, Jack and Maggie following with
Nana. Peter stayed where he was a moment, brushing at the
dog hair that had attached itself to his suit pants, feeling
slightly out of place for no reason that he could immediately
identify. He paused on the threshold to look upward at the
old house, up past the rows of windows, most of them dark,
to the gabled eaves of the roof. It was a long way up, he
thought uneasily—and a long way down. He stood there,
unable to take his eyes away, a feeling of vertigo settling in.

Moira reappeared suddenly, took him firmly by the arm,
and marched him inside.

The door closed behind them. They stood in the entryway
of the old house, looking ahead into the living room, right
into the dining room, and left into the study. Polished oak
trim gleamed at every turn—from floors, cornices, and mop
boards, shelves and cabinets, beams and paneled doors.
Pieces of furniture that dated back three centuries crowded
one another for space, strange knickknacks and collectings
from antique stores and white elephant sales, beautiful and
wondrous or ugly and plain, depending on your point of
view. Bits of brass and iron glistened in the glow of the
Tiffany lamps and the chandeliers. Books lined the shelves,

musty and worn and well read. In the study, the lights of a
Christmas tree burned cheerfully.

Moira relieved Peter of his raincoat and hung it with the
children's coats on the unicorn-head rack. Following Liza
and Nana, they moved along the hallway toward the living
room. A stairway curved upward before them toward a
balcony and hall. Arched entries opened off the living room
in several directions. Peter glanced about, taking it all in,
remembering.

Through the opening leading into the dining room he
could see Uncle Tootles down on his hands and knees
searching for something.

"Lost my marbles," the old man was muttering to
himself. "Have to find 'em. Lost, lost, lost."

Tootles glanced up suddenly to see the others staring at
him. Crawling out from under the table, he rose to his knees
and smiled brightly at Maggie. She smiled back. He
beckoned, and she approached. Reaching into his pocket,
he drew out a crumpled paper flower, displaying it abruptly,
as if he had produced it by magic. He handed it to her, and
she giggled. Rising, he turned to Jack and made a modest
bow.

Jack backed away, feigning interest in a ceramic pot with
tigers painted on it.

"I thought he was back in a home," Peter whispered in
Liza's ear.

The maid shook her head. "Broke Miz Wendy's heart,
that. She couldn't stand it. After all, he was her first orphan,
wasn't he?"

Moira called to Peter. She was standing in front of an old,
well-preserved grandfather clock. The clock bore the face
of a smiling moon.

"The man in the moon, Peter," she said. "Remember?
He used to look down on me from so much higher up."

Peter stared at the clock, thinking of Uncle Tootles
instead, missing the warm look Moira gave him.

There was a movement on the stairs behind them, and
they turned. Granny Wendy was descending, slowly, re-

gally, her eyes sweeping past them all to fix on Peter. He straightened without realizing it, a puzzled look in his eyes, a hint of a smile or maybe a frown crossing his face. Granny Wendy was tall and slim, crow's-feet at the corners of her eyes and mouth, her hair gray, but her eyes so vital that she might have been any age and not the ninety-two years she had actually lived. She was wearing a comfortable white dressing gown belted at the waist, with purple ribbons at the sleeves and throat and a sprinkling of lace on her breast.

Jack and Moira stood wordlessly with Liza and stared up at her. She was conscious of them, of Moira as well, but she never took her eyes from Peter.

When she reached the bottom of the stairs, she stopped. "Hullo, boy," she whispered.

Peter took a step forward, trying to make himself taller, straighter, younger for her, trying to be things he had given up trying to be for anyone else a long time ago. "Hullo, Wendy," he whispered back.

Then suddenly he seemed to remember himself. "Gee, I'm sorry we're running so late. I'm up to my ears in this new deal, and, well, it's just one thing after the other and . . ." He was so flustered he could not seem to stop talking. He was aware of his children looking at him.

Wendy held out her arms. "Oh, never mind all that. Come here, Peter, and give me a squdge."

Peter went to her immediately, and they embraced. Her arms came about him and held him with a strength he did not expect she possessed. His own hug was tentative, uncertain.

"Oh, Granny. Gran. It's so good to see you," Moira greeted, and gave Wendy a hug of her own.

"My Moira." Wendy patted her granddaughter's slim back. She stepped away and looked down at the children. "Well. This lovely young lady can't be Maggie, can it?"

Maggie beamed. "Yes, it can. And know what, Great-grandma? I just played you at school in our play!"

Peter frowned, but Wendy smiled encouragingly. "And don't you look just the part, too." She turned to Jack, cocking her head slightly. "Can this giant fellow be Jack?"

Jack blushed, flustered and pleased all at once. "I'm s'pposed to congrat'late you on your orphan hospital, Great-granny." The words tripped coming out of his mouth, spilling in a jumble.

Wendy ruffled his hair gently. "Why, thank you, Jack." She brought both children together before her, a hand on the shoulder of each. "Now, mind you, there's one rule I insist be obeyed as long as you are in my house. No growing up. If you are, stop this very instant!"

Jack and Maggie laughed, charmed and relieved. Wendy bent to hug them both, laughing as well. She glanced up suddenly at Peter. "And that goes for you, too, Mr. Chairman of the Board Banning."

Peter smiled uncomfortably. "Sorry, too late."

Wendy broke from the children and came back to him, tucking his arm firmly under her own, wheeling him toward the living room. "Important businessman, are you? And just what are you doing these days that is so terribly important, Peter?"

Her bright eyes fixed and held him once more, mesmerizing, depthless. He found himself squirming to find a reply. "Well, you see, I, I, well . . ." He gave up and spat it out. "I'm doing acquisitions and mergers, and recently I've been dabbling in land development, ah, and . . ."

Behind him, Jack made a sound like a cannon being fired. "Yeah, Dad blows 'em right out of the water."

Wendy glanced down at the boy, then smiled at Peter. "So, Peter," she said softly, and her eyes were almost sad, "you've become a pirate."

In the Nursery

Night settled down about number 14 Kensington, a gradual darkening of the afternoon light, a quieting of sound into a restful hush, a fading of that day toward the beginning of the next. As Peter paused to stare out the hallway window thick flakes of snow shone like bits of silver in the glimmer of the streetlights.

He shuffled his feet on the worn carpet and stared down thoughtfully at his polished shoes. He could see them by bending forward a bit, he discovered. He pushed at his stomach and sighed.

He passed down the hall toward the sound of laughter coming from Granny Wendy's bedroom. Peeking in, he discovered Wendy dressed in an elegant silk gown of rose and mauve with lace sleeves and trim. She was seated at her dressing table, composed and smiling as Moira bent close to hook the buttons of her sleeves. With a glint of mischief in her eyes, she moved her arms just so, foiling Moira's attempts. Moira slapped her hands gently, and they both laughed. It was as if no time had passed since they had last been together, as if the bond between them was as strong today as it had been in Moira's childhood.

A new burst of activity rose from behind him, and Jack and Maggie came tearing down the hall with Nana in pursuit. Charging past their father, the children raced into Wendy's room, leaped from the bed to the love seat and back again. Nana, too large to gain the bed, raced around the carved wooden posts, barking.

Maggie caught sight of her father and called out, "Daddy, Daddy, come play with us!"

Peter smiled and began fumbling with his tie. "Later, sweetheart." He took a step into the room and caught Moira's eye. "Slippery shoes." He motioned down to them, scuffing at the floor. "You haven't seen my gold cuff link, have you?"

Moira gave him a look. "In here?"

"I think I might have dropped it earlier."

He moved into the room, searching, then bent down on his hands and knees to have a look underneath the bed. Instantly Maggie vaulted onto his back, yelling, "Giddyup, horsey! Ride, ride!"

Peter glanced up stoically. "Maggie, be of some help, please?"

Maggie leaped down and rushed away. Peter went back to looking, finding nothing beneath the trailing edges of the bed's quilted comforter, not even a dust bunny. He backed off and worked his way around the end of the bed and over to an easy chair.

As he peered around the chair he found himself face-to-face with Tootles, also down on his hands and knees, searching. They both drew up just in time to keep from bumping heads.

Tootles stared at Peter. His eyes were glassy pools. "Lost my marbles," he mumbled.

Peter nodded. "Lost a cuff link. I'm not dressed without my cuff links."

They stared at each other a moment longer, then separated and moved on, continuing to search.

After a minute Peter rose, feeling suddenly foolish. He brushed off his pants and departed the room. The pearl cuff links would have to do. Dratted nuisance, not being able to find the other. Kind of day it had turned out to be.

He worked his way down the corridor toward his own room. Through the windows he passed he could see the snow continuing to fall—huge, damp flakes, as still as midnight.

Midway along, he approached the children's nursery. Jack and Maggie had been given this room. He slowed. The door was cracked open, and he peeked inside. A small fire in the stone fireplace gave what light there was to the room, casting ghostly shadows in all directions. Jack and Maggie's luggage rested on two of the three small, ornate Victorian beds. Peter stared at the luggage for a moment, then glanced around at the room, peering to see into the shadows. Undecided, he hung on the door frame, drawn and repelled at the same time.

What was it about this room that affected him so?

From a darkened corner a cuckoo clock popped out and called six times. Peter released his grip on the door and stepped inside. One step, two, three.

And abruptly froze.

The room was just as it had once been, sometime long ago in a past it seemed he could almost remember, just as Wendy's mother, Mrs. Darling, had left it, the result of ''a loving heart and the scraping of her purse.'' The three beds, thick-quilted and comforting, sat two on the left (John's and Michael's) and one on the right (Wendy's). Coverlets made of white satin shimmered in the faint light. Above each bed on tiny shelves were china houses the size of bird's nests containing night-lights. The fireplace burned low and quiet, a faint hissing of sap buried in the wood echoing in the stillness. The mantel sheltering the hearth was supported by two straight-backed wooden soldiers, homemade, rough-hewn, begun once upon a time by Mr. Darling, subsequently finished by Mrs. Darling, and eventually repainted (rather unfortunately) by Mr. Darling.

The memories flashed in Peter's mind and disappeared. One moment he recognized it all; in the next the recognition was gone. He moved deeper into the room, touching this and that, pausing in foreign country that nevertheless was somehow quite familiar.

A ragged teddy bear sat with its back against a battered top hat on the mantel. Peter stepped up to the bear and brushed its fuzzy, worn nose with his fingers.

He saw Wendy's dollhouse then and peered down inside to see if anyone was living there. The bureau sat alone against one wall, and he moved to stand before it. His hands fastened on its smooth knobs and he jiggled it gently, trying to think what might be inside.

At last he found his way to the latticed French windows, latched now against the dark, their curtains drawn. He stepped onto the threshold, reached out tentatively, brushed back the curtains, undid the latch, and pulled the windows open. Thick snowflakes landed on his nose and mouth, and he licked them away. Carefully he stepped out on the tiny balcony to the wrought-iron railing and looked about, up first at the white-speckled skies, down then to the streets and rooftops below. His hands gripped the railing as he felt the earth fall away in a spin. Closing his eyes against the unsettling sensation, he ducked back inside.

The lace of the curtains brushed against his cheek, blown by the night wind, and he opened his eyes once more. There were scenes of some sort sewn into the lace, woven into patterns that backed up against one another like pictures hung on a wall. He bent closer, reaching out to hold the curtains still.

He saw a boy flying in a night sky with stars all about, the same boy standing with his hands on his hips and his head thrust back as he prepared to crow, and the boy again, engaged in battle with a pirate captain whose missing hand had been replaced by a hook.

Peter Pan.

Moira appeared suddenly in the doorway, flicking on the light. "Peter, Brad's on the line. He says it's urgent."

Peter turned abruptly and hurried from the room.

The room sat empty and silent then. But the windows had been left open, and the wind picked up suddenly, rustling the curtains. Moonlight broke through the clouds overhead momentarily and flooded the room. Its light was a strange, eerie color, and it cast new shadows that wavered and shimmered like ghosts.

Then the light crept along the floor and settled in the twin mirrored doors of a massive old armoire that rested far back in a corner, a dark wooden closet that might hold either dreams or nightmares.

*   *   *

Peter raced down the hall, already anticipating the worst. He'd brought the holster phone with him for emergencies. English phones were just too unreliable.

Granny Wendy walked past, twirling girlishly. "Like my dress, Peter?"

Peter went past without slowing, nodding perfunctorily. He charged into the guest bedroom where he and Moira had been settled and snatched up the phone from where it lay on the bed.

"Yeah? Brad? What do you mean, the Sierra Club report? I thought that was settled? A what? A Cozy Blue Owl?" His face had gone beet red. "Well, if they're endangered, maybe there's a good reason for it!"

Maggie appeared with Jack in pursuit. They rushed past him to the far side of the bed and disappeared. After a moment Maggie reappeared, shouting, laughing, "Daddy, save me! Save me!"

From behind the bed, Jack was making monster sounds. Peter ignored them, putting a finger in his ear to block out their noise.

"Since the dawn of time there have been all sorts of casualties in the evolutionary process!" he snapped. "Does anybody miss the Tyrannosaurus rex?"

"I do!" yelled Jack, and began to growl fiercely.

Peter whirled about. "Damn it, Jack, grow up! Maggie, get away! Moira!" He returned to the phone. "Ten inches high and has a mating radius of fifty miles? Well, why doesn't somebody just shoot me in the head?"

Maggie raced back around the bed, screaming with delight, and tried to climb up her father's back. Jack was in pursuit, growling and waving his arms.

"Everybody, just shut up!" snarled Peter, shaking them off. "All of you, shut up for one miserable moment! Moira, for God's sake, get them out of here—I'm on the phone call of my life!"

Moira appeared finally, took Jack and Maggie gently but firmly by the hand, called softly to Nana, and ushered them all out into the hall. Granny Wendy stood waiting, her hands outstretched to gather the children in, her bright eyes looking past them to the bedroom and Peter.

"You know, " she said softly, "when your father was a little boy, we used to stand by the window and blow out the stars."

Jack snorted. "Uh-huh."

Peter was off the phone by the time Moira reentered the bedroom, sitting disconsolately on the bed, his eyes vacant and staring.

"The deal is on fire." He ran his hands through his mop of brown hair. "I never should have left."

Moira stood there, not speaking. After a moment he lifted his eyes to find hers. He saw anger and disappointment reflected there. She was swallowing hard to keep from crying. They stared at each other in silence. Then he rose, started toward her, thought better of it, and stopped. He gestured futilely with his hands, tried to speak and couldn't.

He shook his head. "Moira, I'm sorry, I just, I just can't. . . ." The explanation he groped for wouldn't come. "I lost perspective, I guess, I don't know why."

Moira's voice was low and soft, but her eyes were suddenly hard. "You haven't been to Kensington Gardens for ten years, even though Granny asks you to come every year. I mean, Peter, how many broken promises . . ." She trailed off, fighting to stay calm. "You promised the kids real time here, and you haven't looked at them once except to examine them or yell at them. . . ."

The phone on the bed rang sharply, piercingly. Peter hesitated, then reached to pick it up.

"Give me that," his wife ordered.

Peter stared. "Come on, Moira, no."

"Just give me the phone, Peter."

"Please, Moira . . ."

Moira reached out and snatched the phone away. Striding deliberately to the open window, she tossed it through. Peter watched her in stunned silence.

Moira turned back again to face him. "I'm sorry about your deal."

"You hated the deal," mumbled Peter.

Moira nodded, brushing back her dark hair. "I hated the deal, but I'm sorry you feel so badly. Peter, your kids love you, they want to play with you. How long do you think that lasts? A lifetime? In three years Jack isn't even going to want you to come into his room. We have only a few special years with our children, when they're the ones who want us around. After that, you're going to be chasing them for a little attention. Listen to me, Peter. I'm home with them. I see them, I play with them. I know what you're missing, but I can't describe to you what that is because you have got to get down on the floor and play with them yourself in order to understand. Do you know how many times they say, 'Where's Daddy? When's Daddy coming home?' "

She took a deep breath. "Damn it, I'm just saying have fun, Peter! Enjoy them before it's too late!"

She tightened her lips and stared at him, waiting for his response. He stood there, staring back, unable to speak. Finally, she walked to the window and looked out, her face stricken, her eyes wet. She felt so sad for him.

"I didn't mean to throw your phone out the window," she said.

Peter's voice sounded hopeful. "You didn't?"

She turned back into the room, and their eyes met.

"Yes, I did," she whispered.

Nana pushed through the weather flap cut into the backdoor, the garbage bag held firmly in her mouth. The big sheepdog padded through the snow to the alley fence and dropped the bag into the can. She was coming back along the same path when she caught sight of Peter's holster phone. She stopped momentarily to sniff at it, then picked it up, carried it carefully to the flower garden, set it down momentarily, and began to dig. Snow and earth flew. In seconds, she had produced a sizable hole. She picked up the phone again and dropped it in.

Then she began to bury it.

The children's nursery was bathed in shadows. In the fireplace, the wood had burned itself down to red-hot coals that cast light the color of blood. Jack stood at the open windows, elbows resting on the balcony railing as he leaned out into the night, one hand fiddling with the dials and switches of his Walkman. The snow had stopped, and the air was crisp and clear. Jack wore his baseball nightshirt and had a bored look on his face.

"All children, except one, grow up."

Wendy's voice was low and compelling. She huddled with Maggie on the floor beneath a sheet that was serving as a tent, reading by flashlight from a ragged copy of *Peter and Wendy*. If Wendy remembered that she was dressed in her evening gown, she seemed not to care. Maggie listened intently, busily sewing ribbons along the hem of the sheet.

"You know where faeries come from, don't you, Margaret?" Wendy read. Then Maggie's voice joined in. "When the first baby laughed for the first time, the laugh broke into a thousand pieces and they all went skipping about—that was the beginning of faeries."

Wendy moved the beam of the flashlight to an illustration of the girl Wendy in her nightgown framed at the nursery window. "There," she whispered, "that was me, a long time ago."

Maggie looked at the drawing, then up at Wendy. "But Jack says you're not the really real Wendy."

Wendy snorted and pulled back the edges of the sheet. Together they peeked out at Jack, who pretended not to see.

A twinkle came into Wendy's eye. "And see where Jack is standing? That is the same window." She exchanged a meaningful look with Maggie. Neither saw Peter come through the door, resplendent in his tux, shuffling his speech notes nervously in his hands. "And this is the very room where we told stories about Peter Pan and Neverland and scary, old Captain Hook. Mr. Barrie, Sir James, our neighbor, took a fancy to the stories, so he wrote them down—dear me—over eighty years ago."

The rustle of Peter's notes caught their attention in the silence that followed. Maggie saw her dad and jumped up immediately. Grabbing the sheet off Wendy, she rushed over to present it.

"Daddy!" she cried. I made something for you. It's a para . . . a parachu . . . a hug! Next time you fly, you don't have to be scared!"

Peter patted Maggie's head, accepted the makeshift parachute, and carried it over and hung it on her bedpost. Returning, he reached down and helped Granny Wendy to her feet. Wendy smiled. She gave Maggie a hug, blew a kiss toward Jack, and walked over to turn on the night-lights.

As she was leaving she said softly, "Dear night-lights that protect my sleeping babes, burn clear and steadfast tonight and forever."

She paused momentarily at the door to look back, then disappeared into the hall.

For the first time Peter caught sight of Jack standing outside the bedroom windows. Striding over, he grabbed his son anxiously and drew him back inside. Pushing the windows shut behind, he slipped the latch in place.

In his haste, he had left his notes on the dresser near the window.

"Jack, what are you doing out there?" he asked. "Get away from there. We don't play near open windows. Do we have open windows at home?"

Jack pulled away. "No—our windows have bars on them."

He slouched his way over to the kiddie bed and threw himself down, clearly displeased. Reaching beneath his pillow, he pulled out his baseball glove. He slipped it on, thumped it, then groped under the pillow again. He frowned, lifted the pillow, and looked about.

"Hey—where's my ball? It was right here!"

Maggie's solemn eyes stole toward the windows. Her gaze was distant and fixed and her voice certain. "That scary man stole it," she said quietly.

Peter moved over to sit next to her. "There is no scary man. Now I want those windows locked for the rest of the visit."

Maggie looked at him doubtfully, then fumbled among her things and produced the paper flower. She handed it to Peter, who in turn tucked it into her hair.

"Tootles made it for me," she said. "It smells nice."

Peter smiled. "It's paper, honey." His face softened, and a strange calm settled through him. "Now slip yourself in the envelope of your sheets and mail yourself off to sleep."

Maggie squirmed down, pulling the sheets up to her chin. "Stamp me, mailman."

Peter bent and kissed her twice. "Special delivery."

He rose then and walked over to Jack. Reaching into his pocket, he pulled out his pocketwatch and held it out.

"Be in charge for me, Jack?" he asked. "We'll be home—two, three hours max, I promise."

Jack took the watch without replying. Moira appeared in the doorway. Her eyes met Peter's briefly and slipped away.

"Mommy," called Maggie softly. "Don't go out. Please?"

Moira moved over to sit on the edge of her daughter's bed and began stroking her hair. she glanced up at Peter, a pleading look in her dark eyes. "Why can't they just remain like this forever?" she asked—as if the answer might somehow settle all the questions that ever were.

Then she began a lullaby. Jack and Maggie lay back, and their eyes closed.

The Past Comes
Back to Haunt

From atop the dais, the polished wooden floor of Royal
Hall was submerged beneath a sea of white tablecloths. It
seemed as if no inch of space remained within its walls, the
whole of it given over to table after table of well-wishers,
more than a few of whom were direct recipients of the hard
work and unceasing efforts of the woman they had come to
honor. Crowded shoulder to shoulder, they sat turned in
their seats toward the front of the room and the dais on
which Peter Banning stood, speaking.

"And the confused traveler said, 'Where am I going to
find one?' "

The joke's punch line brought an eruption of laughter
from the audience that rolled across the length and breadth
of the great hall and echoed off its walls. Peter grinned and
glanced to his right momentarily, where Moira sat with
Granny Wendy. The table on the dais seated more than two
dozen people, all of whom he had been introduced to,
almost none of whom he could remember. Lord something-
or-other. Lady so-and-so. Most were members of the Great
Ormond Street Hospital board. Peter's eyes shifted away.
Crystal chandeliers hung from the hall's scalloped ceiling
like great prehistoric birds, the light dancing off their facets,
bathing the upturned faces below in a wash of gold. Jewels
glittered next to glassware and silver. Furs and tuxedos
kissed shoulders. Suits and ties and gowns of all descrip-
tions provided a backdrop of color and brightness.

Across the far end of the hall hung a banner that
proclaimed: SIR JAMES M. BARRIE FOUNDATION AND THE

GREAT ORMOND STREET HOSPITAL FOR CHILDREN HONOR
WENDY.

Dinner was concluded, a sumptuous affair, and the
speeches were begun. Peter's was the centerpiece of the
evening.

The laughter died away. Peter shifted his attention. "So,
please, ladies and gentlemen, bear with me from here,
remembering, if you will, that I'm used to addressing
shareholders."

The laughter returned, scattered, polite.

Peter reached into the breast pocket of his jacket for his
speech and found it missing. His hand moved quickly to
his other breast pocket, then to his side pockets and down to
his pants. A wave of panic swept through him. Where
was his speech? He hadn't bothered even to think about it
once they had left the house, determined to read it as it was
and the consequences be damned. He'd had it then; he
remembered having it. What had happened to it?

He glanced quickly at Moira, who was already searching
her purse. Her eyes lifted abruptly, and she shook her
head no.

Peter took a deep breath. "I apologize, I seem to have
misplaced my speech."

Silence greeted his announcement. He cleared his throat.
"Lord Whitehall, honored guests, ladies and gentlemen.
For more than seventy years Wendy Darling has given hope
to hundreds of homeless children. . . ."

That was all he could remember. He cleared his throat a
second time. "She has been a most significant asset to the
Great Ormond Street Hospital. . . ."

What else? What was the rest of it?

Below the dais, he could hear the sounds of people
shifting about uncomfortably, of shoes scraping, of coughs
and whispers. He kept going because he had no choice, not
sure what he was saying, sure only that he was beginning to
lose his audience.

He didn't dare look over at Moira or Wendy.

*   *   *

Darkness hung like a black curtain over 14 Kensington, deep and unfathomable. Although the snow had faded to a sprinkle of stray flakes, the clouds had closed tight again against the moon and stars, and the only light to be found came from the two distant street lamps as they glimmered gamely against a creeping of new mist. The peaks and gables of the aging roofs of Kensington's houses were stark and abrupt against the skyline, sharp edges cutting into the fabric of the night.

In the backyard, Nana lifted her head from between her paws and poked her wet nose out from beneath the covering of the porch. Liza had banished her almost an hour ago, miffed at some imagined wrong, and the faithful dog was awaiting the return of her true mistress for a righting of the matter. A length of chain secured her to a ground stake.

An unnatural movement in the sky had caught her attention, a reshaping of the clouds as they parted momentarily to let something through. A flash of wicked green light appeared and was gone.

Nana came to her feet with a growl.

In the nursery, Jack and Maggie were sleeping. Jack sprawled in a tangle of arms and legs beneath his covers; Maggie was curled into a tight ball with a blanket pulled over her head. Above them, the china-house night-lights glowed steadily, holding back the darkness, keeping the shadows at bay. The fire in the hearth had died out long ago, the embers turned to gray ash.

At the window, the curtains hung limp against the glass, the images of the adventures of Peter Pan lost in their folds.

Then suddenly the night-lights blazed brightly, as if the electricity that powered them had been increased twofold, then flared once and went out. The night pounced instantly, like an animal at hunt. In the darkness at the far corner of the room, the twin mirrors of the hulking armoire began to glow, faintly at first and then brighter—that wicked green light. Images appeared, indistinct, distant still, but growing clearer with the passing of each second, coming closer.

Jack stirred, mumbling.

Shadows crept up the wall, cast from nowhere, come out of nothing, fingers turned to claws, muzzles to teeth. The silhouette of something vast and sprawling rose up amid the sharpnesses, stretching from the mop boards up the wainscoting—jungle trees with their branches intertwined like spider webs, and jagged rocks from an island shoreline, damp with the ocean's spray.

In the mirrors of the armoire, the images took shape—a skull, its vacant eyes huge and staring, its bared teeth set in a chilling grin, and an ancient sailing ship, creaking and moaning as it strained against its anchor.

Lightning flashed suddenly across the toy ship in the bottle that sat atop the mantel, as if a storm had caught her unawares. Jack stirred again. The star mobile that hung over his head began to spin wildly. The old rocking horse settled comfortably by the toy chest began to buck, rope mane and tail whipping in a sudden burst of wind that came from nowhere. . . .

Down in the garden, Nana lunged against her chain, straining to break free, barking something that sounded like "Hoof, Hoof!"

In the study, Tootles stood before the ship models that lined the shelf, fascinated as the tiny masts began to shiver and the sails to fill with invisible wind. His wet, empty eyes stared at the swaying ships, and as he watched he swayed with them. When he heard Nana bark, he stepped back instantly, cocked his head, and whispered, "Danger."

Liza dozed in the kitchen, her head cradled in her arms. A scraping sound at the front door brought her instantly awake.

Wind whipped through the nursery, catching up the loose note cards of Peter's forgotten speech and scattering them. The light from the armoire had grown brighter, the images sharper. There were shouts, cries out of sleep and dreams, and the sound of something scraping sharply—iron on wood.

The blankets on the children flew off, torn away.

Blackness engulfed the room.

*   *   *

At the banquet hall, Peter labored on bravely.

But he was dying. Without his speech, he was a sailor lost at sea. The audience's restlessness was palpable. Desperation flooded through him. The entire evening was on the verge of becoming a shambles—Wendy's tribute, ruined. And it was all because of him.

He stopped abruptly in midsentence, threw caution to the winds, and straightened. The audience quieted slightly.

"Ladies and Gentlemen, I've given you enough rhetoric to chew on for one night. Let me just say one more thing about Wendy Darling. Wendy brought me in from the cold all those years ago, a foundling. She taught me to read and write when I could do neither. She found people who were willing to adopt me, to become my parents when I had none, and even then she never stopped worrying after me, caring about me, loving me."

There was dead silence now. Everyone was listening. "She has done so much. I married her granddaughter, my wife, Moira. My children love her. They think she can do anything. They even want her to teach them to fly. She's given me my life. And, my God, she has given life to so many children. That is her true achievement, the achievement we are here to honor tonight."

He paused. "So if Wendy means as much to you as she does to me, if she has helped you in your life as much as she has helped me in mine, will you stand up, please? Stand up, if your lives were changed by this wonderful woman." He motioned abruptly with his arms. "Stand up with me and salute her!"

They rose hesitantly, in ones and twos and then in whole groups until all were on their feet and applauding wildly. The hall came alive with the sound of it, a thunderous ovation, and Peter stood proudly at its center, his boyish face wreathed in a broad smile. His eyes met Moira's momentarily, and he was stunned by the depth of feeling he saw there.

Slowly Wendy Darling rose, tears in her eyes. She bowed

to the audience with a little, short nod, hands clasped tightly before her.

A cart set back against the wall behind the dais was wheeled to the front. On it sat a model of the proposed addition to Great Ormond Street Hospital and across its front was stretched a banner that read: THE WENDY DARLING FOUNDLING WING. Hands appeared to lift the banner above the model, and Peter went to Wendy's side to steer her into position for the ceremonial ribbon cutting. The applause intensified.

Then a gust of wind blew wide a set of tall, latticed windows behind them, sweeping down over the dais. Wendy stumbled with the force of it, and Peter reached quickly to steady her. Moira appeared with the scissors. The banner fluttered wildly in the wind. The chandeliers swayed.

With an uneasy glance over her shoulder at the windows, Wendy reached up with the scissors and cut the ribbon in half. Cheers rose from the audience, and the applause erupted anew. Peter smiled and hugged his grandmother, then turned and put his arms around Moira.

By doing so, he missed seeing the glint of fear that crept suddenly into Wendy's eyes.

Wendy's Tale

The Rolls plowed slowly, steadily through the night, snow turning to slush beneath its wheels. Peter laid his head back against the soft leather of his seat and closed his eyes. The evening had gone well. He was pleased with the speech he had given, the words coming from somewhere within, from a place he hadn't visited in a long, long time. He was surprised to discover that it was even still there.

"Home," Moira whispered in his ear.

He opened his eyes and straightened, finding the dwellings of Kensington Gardens all about, their gabled roofs and ivy-grown walls wrapped in the arms of the ancient trees, their draped and shuttered windows pinpricks of light shining through the snow. The Rolls pulled to a stop in front of number 14, snowflakes melting on the windshield. Peter opened the back passenger door and stepped out, stretching. Moira followed, her breath frosting the air, her face bright and very pretty. She shared a smile with Peter and touched his cheek.

Peter stepped around her and reached back to help Granny Wendy out. Wendy's face was drawn and worn by now, the excitement of the evening having finally caught up with her. Nevertheless, she smiled like a young girl.

"That wasn't so bad, Wendy Angela Moira Darling," Peter declared softly.

"For an old woman," she replied.

Peter shook his head and grinned. "Not you. You were wonderful."

"You weren't so bad yourself . . . boy."

He glanced sharply at her, but she was looking elsewhere,

her tired eyes distant. He took her arm and they began to walk, heads bent slightly against the mist, their feet squeaking softly in the new snow.

Moira leaned in from the other side. "I'm glad to see that you're finally enjoying yourself. . . ."

She stopped abruptly, her words trailing off. "Peter?"

Peter's eyes lifted. Before them, the front door stood wide open; a scattering of snow drifted across the threshold and into the hall. In the glow of the front porch lights, Peter could see a deep gouge in the heavy panels—as if someone had raked a screwdriver across the wood.

Granny Wendy glanced up, started, and caught her breath sharply. "The children!" she breathed.

Peter let go of her arm and charged through the door. The house was in blackness, cold and empty feeling. Behind him, he heard Moira flick the light switch without success. The power was gone.

"There, a candle, in the sconce beside you," Granny Wendy advised.

Peter groped along the wall, found it, produced a pocket lighter, and snapped it open. A flame sparked to life, and the candle's wick caught fire.

"Jack! Maggie!" Moira was calling out.

The candlelight chased the darkness far enough to reveal that the gouge in the door continued on along the entry hall and up the stairs, deep and ragged.

"What is going on here?" Peter muttered under his breath.

They made their way up the stairs, Peter leading with the candle held out before him, Moira and Granny Wendy following. From somewhere ahead, they could hear a scratching sound, and then Nana began to bark.

Peter rushed ahead and nearly tripped over Liza, who lay sprawled unconscious on the landing. Peter bent hurriedly over the maid, finding a discolored knot on her forehead where she had been struck. Her eyes flickered, and she gave a low moan.

"Call an ambulance," Peter ordered over his shoulder, and charged up the stairs and down the hall, his heart racing. What had happened here? Where were the children?

He saw Nana ahead, clawing frantically at the nursery door, barking and panting like a wild thing. A broken chain hung from her neck, and her coat was ragged and damp.

The gouge that had begun at the front door ended at the entrance to the nursery, without slowing, Peter charged in.

The room looked as if a hurricane had passed through. The beds were upended, their covers tossed away. Toys and books lay scattered everywhere. The rocking horse was on its side, and the windows were wide open, their lace curtains flapping.

There was no sign of Jack and Maggie.

The wind whipped past, and Peter's candle went out. He stood without moving, staring at nothing, trying to make sense of things. Nana padded past, sniffing anxiously, whining deep in her throat. She rushed to the bathroom and fastened her great jaws about the knob to open the door.

Moira appeared, her eyes moving from the gouge to the empty room. He could hear her gasp, hear the beginning of her sobs. Then she was past him, darting for the open windows.

"Jack! Maggie! Answer me!" she cried out.

Woodenly, Peter followed, stepping out on the balcony and leaning out over the railing. The yard below was white and deserted. He tracked the yards to either side and along the alleyway, choking back his fear, his growing sense of desperation.

"Jackkkk! Maggieeee!" he cried out.

"Peter!"

His name was spoken in a stifled cry. Granny Wendy stood at the door, staring at something. Slowly she reached up and removed a note pinned in place by a wicked-looking dagger. Woodenly, she carried the note to Peter.

Peter took the note from her and examined it. The writing was elegant, studied, some form of calligraphy scrolled by a sure and practiced hand.

It read:

> Dear Peter: Your presence is required at the
> request of your children.
> Kindest Personal Regards,
> JAS. Hook, Captain.

Peter repeated the words aloud, then stared at the note in disbelief and confusion. What in the heck was going on here?

A shrill, rasping voice cackled sharply behind him, causing him to jump in fright. He banged his head on a window frame as he wheeled about.

Tootles was crouched behind the dollhouse, wispy hair electric, hands clutched together like claws. There was a frantic look in his bright eyes and a twisting of his slack face.

"Have to fly!" he hissed. "Have to save Jack and Maggie!"

He caught his breath and held it. "Hooky's back!"

And abruptly Wendy's hand clutched for Peter, her eyes rolled back, and she collapsed to the floor.

Within a half hour, the police were there and the electricity restored. Liza sat in the kitchen with an ice pack on her forehead, telling two less-than-enthusiastic officers over and over again how she hadn't seen anything and would regret to her dying day her failure to do so. The ambulance was still parked in front as the attendants waited in vain to take her to thc hospital.

"Them l'tle uns be needin' me, right 'nuf, an' I plans on bein' 'ere for em! Take more an' a bump on the noggin to change that!"

Peter could hear her voice from where he stood by the front door, one arm about Moira as he stared out at the lights of the police cars and the neighbors' windows. Everyone was awake by now, peering out curiously. A ladder leaned against the Darling house where one officer had stood high up by the eaves to examine the outside of the nursery windows.

Inspector Good appeared at his elbow, pulling on his greatcoat. He was a plump, round-faced man with soft eyes and a weary voice. He smiled wanly as he faced them.

"Now then, Mr. and Mrs. Banning, we've done what we can. We've wired the phones should there be a call, and two of my best will stay close at hand should you need them." He shrugged the coat into place on his stooped shoulders. "No sign of forced entry. The locks are all in place. Nothing out of sorts anywhere except for that odd gouge and the dog's clawing. Even those upstairs windows are clean. They must have been opened from inside."

Peter shook his head stubbornly. "I locked the windows myself before I left."

"Well, sir, be that as it may." Good fished in his pocket and produced a plastic bag containing the note and dagger. "The chaps at the Yard will have a go at these. Might I ask, were you ever in the armed services? You don't remember anyone named J.A.S. Hook from there, do you?"

Peter shook his head doubtfully.

"Inspector," Moira said hesitantly. "This may be something from my family history. My grandmother is the Wendy on which Sir James Barrie based his stories."

Good stared at her. "Sir who? Run that by me again, missus."

"Sir James Barrie, Inspector. He wrote *Peter Pan*. He was an old friend of the family. When Granny was a little girl, he wrote stories for her about her imaginary adventures."

Good's nod was decidedly condescending. "Well, then, the note may refer to that, mightn't it? It would be nice to think that this is all a prank, someone's foolish playing about, reference your family history and all. But I don't think we should leave it to chance."

Behind him, the lights to the Christmas tree that had been placed in the study blazed unexpectedly to life. All three turned and stared wordlessly.

Inspector Good cleared his throat. "The season seems to come earlier each year, doesn't it?" he murmured, and was momentarily lost in thought. Then he smiled and touched the brim of his bowler. "Try to get some sleep. We'll need to talk with you again, come morning. Don't worry. We'll do our best."

He gave a short nod and went out the door, sweeping uniformed policemen up in his wake. Car doors slammed, and the revolving lights began to drive off. Peter pushed the door closed on the night and walked Moira slowly back into the study.

Tootles stood at the window next to the tree, staring at nothing. "I forgot how to fly," he was whispering. His voice was as dry as old leaves. "We all forgot. No more happy thoughts. All lost, lost, lost."

Moira moved woodenly out of Peter's embrace and began to tidy up the room, picking up bits and pieces of things, straightening presents, brushing off this and that.

"Moira," Peter called softly to her.

She didn't turn, still working at her meaningless task, her head bent determinedly. She was working her way along the bookshelves when suddenly she brushed against something and sent it crashing to the floor. Everyone jumped. Peter went to her as she collapsed in a chair, crying uncontrollably. "Peter, oh, Peter" she sobbed.

He smoothed her hair, fighting back his own tears, his sense of helplessness. He looked down at the floor. A ship in a bottle lay shattered at his feet. Transfixed, he reached down and picked it up.

It was a brigantine. On its mast was a tiny black flag that bore the skull and crossbones of a pirate ship.

A little later, Peter and Moira went up to Granny Wendy's room to check on her. They had put her to bed after she collapsed, telling Inspector Good he would have to wait until morning to speak with her. They made the journey in silence, lost in their separate thoughts. Peter was still trying to come to grips with the fact that something had actually happened to his children. It was just so inconceivable. All their lives, all the while they were growing up, he had done everything he knew to protect them, to keep them safe. And now this—this Peter Pan business. Some crackpot. Here, at Granny Wendy's home, the safest place in the world. How could he have foreseen such a thing happening?

He felt dead inside, and the feeling was the most frightening he had ever experienced.

They pushed open the door to Granny Wendy's bedroom and peeked inside. The old lady was sitting up in her bed, staring back at them.

"Are the police gone?" she asked quietly.

Moira nodded. "Yes," Peter breathed.

There was an awkward moment of silence.

"Come in, sit with me," she invited.

They moved into the room. It was lit by a single bedside lamp, the light softened by the frills of the cloth shade. Peter sat next to Wendy on the bed. Moira walked around and tucked the blankets carefully about the old lady before coming back to join him.

"This waiting is very unpleasant," Granny Wendy declared, fixing Peter with a sharp gaze.

"I know, Granny. Try not to . . ." He failed to find the right words and gave up. "There's nothing more to do tonight, nothing to do but . . ." He didn't want to say wait. "The police are doing everything they can."

"Which is nothing, Peter," Wendy said flatly. "There is nothing they can do."

"Gran, you can't believe . . ."

"Moira." Wendy looked away from him. "In times of crisis, we English do best with a cup of tea. Would you mind?"

Peter's wife smiled, her tears gone now, her face calm. "Yes, of course, Gran."

"And warm the pot. Peter, you stay with me, please."

Peter watched as Moira departed the room, slim, pretty, a hint of the old assuredness back in her stride. He reached up and ran his fingers through his mop of brown hair, and his boyish face crumpled with fatigue.

"Don't worry, Wendy. Gran. I won't leave you."

She fixed him with a fierce gaze, her eyes sharp and knowing. "Ah, Peter, but you always did. You don't remember, do you? Every year, you left me. And when you came back, you remembered nothing. And finally you forgot to come back at all.''

Her words were so harsh sounding that Peter immediately became defensive. "Take it easy, Gran, maybe you should try not to talk."

Her thin hands clasped before her. "I'm not raving, as you put it, Peter." She reached out and gripped his arm. "Listen to me carefully. What happened to your children has to do with who and what you are."

She took her hand away again and pointed to the worn copy of *Peter and Wendy* on the nightstand. "Hand me my book, please."

Peter hesitated. "I don't think . . . It would be better to rest now, Gran."

Her lips tightened as she faced him. "Do what I've asked, Peter. It's time to tell you something, time that you knew."

"Knew what? Tell me what?"

She waited wordlessly while he passed her the book. Then she opened it and began to read:

" 'All children, except one, grow up,' " she read. She looked up at him. "That is how Sir James began the story he wrote for me . . . such a long time ago. It was Christmas, yes, in the year 1910, and I was almost eleven. A girl becoming a woman, caught in between two chapters. How far back can you remember?"

Peter was immediately uneasy, shifting away from her on the bed, glancing about the shadowy room as if the answer lay there. He exhaled irritably. "I don't know. I remember the hospital on Great Ormond Street. . . ."

"But you were already twelve by then, nearly thirteen. And before that?"

Peter wished Moira would return. He glanced briefly at Wendy and away again. He tried to remember and couldn't.

"Before that, there's nothing."

Granny Wendy's hand closed on him again, tight, unyielding, a surprising amount of strength in her fingers. Despite himself, he turned to looked at her.

"Think hard," she urged.

Peter swallowed. "I was cold, alone. . . ." He stopped, angry now. "I can't remember! No one knows where I came from! You told me I was a foundling—"

"I found you," Wendy cut him short. "I did." She took a deep breath to steady herself. "Peter, you must listen to me now. And believe. You and I played together as children. We had wonderful adventures together. We laughed, we cried." She paused. "And we flew. But I didn't want to remain a child forever. I was so anxious to grow up and become a part of the real world. I wanted so much for you to grow up with me. But you wouldn't. Because you were afraid. And when you finally decided you were ready, it was fifty years too late for me . . . for us."

Her face crumpled into a sad, worn smile. "I was old, Peter. And you, you were just beginning to become a man."

Peter stared at her as if she had lost her mind—which, in truth, he thought she had. "Okay, just relax, Gran. I'll find some Valium. . . ."

But Wendy held him fast. "When I was young, no other girl held your favor the way I did. Oh, I half expected you to alight on the church and forbid my vows on the day I married. I wore a pink satin sash. But you didn't come. I couldn't have you."

Peter tried unsuccessfully to pull away. Something unpleasant was stirring inside him, something just beyond the reach of his memory. He wrestled with it, not quite certain if he was pulling or pushing.

"I was an old lady when you returned for the last time and I wrapped you in blankets, already Granny Wendy, with my thirteen-year-old granddaughter asleep in the nursery. Your Moira. And when you saw her, that was when you decided not to go back to Neverland."

Peter's eyes went wide. "What? Go back where?"

"To Neverland, Peter."

Peter nodded rapidly, his smile forced and entirely too quick. "I'm going to get Moira. Moira!" he called loudly.

Granny Wendy bent close, her face only inches from his own. "Peter, I tried to tell you so many times. But I could see you had forgotten. You would just think I was a silly old woman at the end of her life. But now you must know.''

She took the book and pressed it firmly into his hands. ''The stories are true. I swear it to you. I swear it by everything I adore. And now *he's* come back to seek revenge. The fight isn't over for him, Peter—he wants you back. He knows you'll follow Jack and Maggie to the ends of the earth and beyond, and by heaven, you must find a way to do so! Only you can save your children. Not the police. Not anyone else. Only you. Somehow you must find a way to go back. You must make yourself remember. Peter—don't you realize who you are?''

She released him then and pried open the book from between his fingers. She paged through it desperately and stopped. She tapped the page.

Peter Banning looked down. The book lay open to an illustration of Peter Pan, legs spread, hands on hips, head cocked back as he prepared to crow.

Wendy waited, searching his eyes in vain for some sign of recognition. There was none to be found.

Tink

Moira returned with Wendy's cup of tea, and Peter immediately rose and left the room. He departed in a rush, mumbling something about checking the house one more time, desperate to escape, barely giving either of the women a glance as he went. The urgency of his need surprised him. He felt as if he couldn't breathe, as if he were suffocating. It was all he could do to keep from running as he hastened down the hall, moving away from the light and into the darkness beyond.

Had everyone gone crazy?

It was bad enough that whoever had kidnapped his children—and he was pretty convinced by this time that it was a kidnapping—was obsessed in some way with that ridiculous Peter Pan story. But to have Granny Wendy believing in it, too, trying to make something out of family history and fairy tales—well, it was really too much to take. Wendy's mental state had fallen off more than he had realized during the past few years. Or perhaps it was simply the strain of what had happened.

Peter slowed in his flight, running his hands through his hair, across his face, and down his sides. Then he stopped altogether, leaned back against the paneled wall, and hugged himself as if it would keep him from falling apart.

Exactly what *had* happened? he asked himself. Who was responsible for this? It had to be a personal enemy, someone who knew him, someone who hated him. Otherwise the note would have been addressed to Moira as well, or to Mr. and Mrs. Banning or some such. Not to Peter. He grimaced. Some joke. JAS. Hook to Peter. He slammed his fist into his palm helplessly. It could be someone in competition with him, angry that he had gotten the contract, kidnapping his children to try to force him to withdraw.

He shivered. So what was he supposed to do now? What *could* he do?

He pushed himself off the wall and continued on, exhausted now both mentally and physically, worn-out from the strain of what had happened. Somewhere along the way he had discarded his tails. His waistcoat hung open and his shirt was unbuttoned. He knew he looked a wreck. He should get some sleep. He should go back to Moira and Granny Wendy and tell them everything was going to be all right.

He wished he could believe that.

He squeezed his eyes closed. Jack and Maggie—how could he ever forgive himself?

He found himself suddenly at the nursery door. He stood staring at it for a moment, at the gouge that traveled the length of the wall leading up, at the gash where the knife had pinned that infuriating note to the wooden panel. He reached out and touched the marks experimentally, as if by doing so he might discover the truth behind their origin.

Then he pushed the door open and stepped inside.

The room was as he had found it earlier, dark and empty and chill. The windows had been closed again, the rocking horse righted, the beds and their covers straightened. The night-lights were back on, their glow steady and certain once more against the shadows. Toys and books still lay scattered about. The children's luggage remained stacked by the bureau.

He stared vacantly at the room for a moment and then walked to the windows. He undid the latch and pulled them open to the night, feeling the breeze brush his face, watching the lace curtains dance. He stared up at the sky, the clouds broken and scattered now, the stars reappeared.

Peter found himself thinking suddenly of all the opportunities he had missed to be with Maggie and Jack, all the chances he had let slip through his fingers, all the times he had promised to do things with them and then failed to follow through. Jack's baseball game—he'd been too late, hadn't he? Maggie's play—he'd come, but how much attention had he paid to her? The times they'd wanted to roughhouse—hadn't he always been too busy?

If I could just have another chance, he thought dismally, if I could only have them back again . . .

Tears came to his eyes. He wiped at them futilely, then gave up trying and simply broke down and cried, his head lowered, his shoulders shaking, his hands gripping the window frames so hard they hurt.

Then the edge of the curtains grazed his face, teasing like a spider web. He brushed at them irritably, blinked back the tears, and lifted his head once more to stare out at the night.

That was when he saw the light.

The light was brilliant, a dancing brightness that hurtled out of the heavens toward earth. A shooting star, he thought—and then realized it was coming directly toward him. He stared in disbelief, then started to back away. It looked like a comet sweeping down from the Milky Way, white-hot head with a tail of fire. It kept coming, faster now, swifter than thought. Peter's eyes went wide.

Then abruptly the light exploded through the open windows, no comet this, too small by far to be anything so grand, but terrifying nevertheless, because it appeared to be alive. It caromed about the room wildly, knocking pictures from the wall, spinning this way and that, and then finally rocketed toward Peter. He saw it coming and backed away, brushing at it with his hands, crying "shoo, shoo," and searching at the same time for the door out. He caught sight of a stack of magazines and snatched one up, rolling it, then swatting at the light. Some sort of crazed firefly, he told himself, frantic now. Would it bite or sting? What else was going to happen to him before this night was over?

He was still retreating, the light dancing around now as if to taunt him, when he tripped over one of the fallen dolls and went down. He caught himself with his hands, losing his grip on the magazine as he did. Weaponless, he began skittering backward on all fours. The light darted and zipped away, back and forth, up and down, tireless in its pursuit.

Finally Peter backed himself into a corner, close by the rocking horse and the dollhouse, and there was nowhere else to go. He flattened himself against the wainscoting, gasping for breath.

The light darted in and away again, steadied, then settled slowly to the edge of the children's writing desk. As it did so it changed, gaining definition, taking shape. Peter found himself staring at a tiny creature no bigger than a minute. A woman, a girl, something of each? She wore clothes that might have been a mix of moonlight and morning dew and fall leaves. They glimmered as brightly as diamonds and clung to her like a glove to a hand. Her hair swept back from her pointed ears and was a mix of sunrise and sunset, both red and gold, and as bright as the summer sun at midday.

She straightened and began to walk about the desk, hopping over pencils and crayons, stepping lightly through an inkpad, then flitting down to land on Peter's knee. Peter stared, frozen as still as an ice statue. The little creature had wings! Tiny, gossamer wings! She walked down his leg, keeping perfect balance, and up the front of his rumpled white shirt, leaving tiny black footprints from the ink as she went. When she reached his chin, her wings fluttered and she rose in the air before him until they were nose to nose.

Bending delicately, she sniffed.

"Oh, it *is* you," she declared with some surprise. "It is. A big you. I wasn't at all sure. I guess it's not bad that you're big—you were always bigger than me anyway. Not this big, of course." She glanced down at his stomach. "Well, maybe this means you will be twice as much fun."

Peter's head was hunched down between his shoulders. He was trying both to breathe and not to breathe at the same time. His fear had paralyzed him.

"Moira?" he managed to whisper, hopeful that she would come.

The little creature was dancing about, not listening. "Oh, Peter, what fun we'll have—what times, what great games! Do you remember what it was like before?"

Peter made a supreme effort to collect himself. He took a

deep, steadying breath and swallowed down his fear.
"You're a . . . you're a fae . . . a fae . . ."

"A faerie, yes," she agreed, and brushed delightedly at
her shimmering hair.

"A pix . . ."

"Pixie." She gave an impish grin. "And if less is more,
there is no end to me, Peter Pan."

Peter paled. "Peter Banning," he corrected.

She squinched up her nose. "Pan."

"Banning."

"Pan."

"Banning."

She put her hands on her hips and stood there in midair,
sizing him up. "A fat, old Pan."

"Uh . . . a fat, old Banning." He managed a nervous
grin.

The faerie pursed her lips and thought the matter over.
"Well, whoever you are, you're still you. Only one person
has *that* smell."

Peter blinked indignantly. "What smell?"

The faerie's face went radiant with her smile. "The smell
of someone who's ridden the back of the wind. The smell of
a hundred summers of sleeping in trees, of adventures with
Indians and pirates. Oh, remember, Peter? The world was
ours and we could do whatever we chose. It was wonderful
because whatever we did could be anything at all and still it
was always us doing it!"

She darted forward to touch his face and flinched.
"Ouch! Bristly, sharp things!"

"Whiskers," Peter said dully. He laid his head back
against the wainscoting and closed his eyes. "It's finally
happened—I'm having a nervous breakdown."

A tug at his bow tie brought his eyes open again. The
faerie, possessing surprising strength for someone so tiny,
brought him to his feet and dragged him toward the open
windows.

"Follow me, Peter, and all will be well," she called
back.

Peter wasn't listening. "Or I've had a massive heart attack and I'm dying. I'm having an out-of-body experience. I'm floating toward the white light of . . . whatever. Look, I've left my body completely." He caught sight of the dollhouse behind him. "You see—there's Granny Wendy's house, number fourteen Kensington, way down there, way down. But wait a minute, those are my feet, aren't they, right there on the floor. Oh, my God. What's happening? Where are we going?"

The faerie laughed gaily. "To save your children, of course."

Peter's eyes snapped up. "Wait! How do you know about my kids?"

She laughed some more. "Everybody knows! Captain Hook has them, and now you've got to fight him to get them back. Let's fly, Peter Pan!"

She let go of him and flitted back across his face. As she passed she blew into her cupped hands and a sprinkling of silver dust scattered and settled over him. Peter brushed at it and then sneezed loudly, dropping back on his rump. The sneeze blew the faerie right through one of the tiny cellophane windows of the old dollhouse. Instantly the inside of the dollhouse lit up, as if a switch had been thrown and lamps brought to life in each little window. Peter crawled back across the floor and bent down, peering in.

"So it's true then, isn't it?" he heard her say from somewhere inside. "You did grow up. The Lost Boys told me, but I never believed it. I drank poison for you, you silly ass! Don't you remember anything? You used to call me Tink!"

She burst into tears, the sound of her crying echoing through the toy house.

Peter searched the windows. "Are you in there, little bug?" He opened the front door.

"I'm not a bug!" she declared, furious at him. "I'm a faerie!"

He tried to see up the toy staircase, his neck crinking as he laid his cheek to the floor. "I don't believe in faeries."

He heard her gasp. "Every time someone says 'I do not believe in faeries' there is a faerie somewhere who falls down dead!"

Peter's patience with himself and his out-of-body experience, which clearly wasn't anything of the sort, snapped. "I do not believe in faeries!" he screamed at the top of his lungs.

A loud crash sounded from within the dollhouse, and the faerie appeared at the top of the stairs, swooning. She clutched futilely at a wall, then toppled over, tumbling down the stairs to lie in a ragged heap at their foot.

Peter jerked erect, his face ashen. "Oh, God! I think I've killed it!" He fumbled with the hinged flap of the dollhouse side, swinging it open to have a better look.

The faerie's eyes fluttered. "Clap. Clap your hands, Peter. It is only way to save me. Clap, Peter, clap! Louder! Louder!"

Peter was clapping as loud as he could, aware suddenly of a ringing in his ears, like tiny silver bells, thousands of them. "I'm clapping, I'm clapping! What's that noise, that ringing? Are you doing that? Just stop it, okay? Hey, what are you . . . are you all right?"

She was standing again, ignoring him, pretending that she had forgotten him entirely. She brushed herself off and walked into the kitchen, where a Barbie doll was serving dinner from a stove top to a Ken doll seated at a table. With a frown the faerie switched the Ken doll and the Barbie doll around so that Ken was serving Barbie. She nodded and turned back to Peter.

"All right, now, who am I?"

Peter sighed hopelessly. "You're . . . ah, who knows?"

She put her hands on her hips and the wings ruffled faster. "You do! I know you do!"

Peter exhaled and shook his head. "All right." His lips went tight. "You're a psychosomatic manifestation of my suppressed sexual anxiety—a composite of all the girls and women in my life with whom I thought I was in love. That's who you are."

The faerie's light flared wildly, and she zipped from the

dollhouse as if catapulted, right past Peter's nose. He tumbled back and away from her, rising to his knees as she swung wide about the room and back again. He was just coming to his feet, hands outstretched, when she flashed down to the far end of the rug on which he was standing and gave it a mighty jerk. The rug was yanked from beneath Peter's feet, and he was sent tumbling backward head over heels across the room.

"Guess again!" snapped the faerie.

Peter rolled onto Maggie's discarded parachute, ribbons tangling in his arms and legs, and his head struck the baseboard of the wall with a thud. For a moment he blacked out. When he came awake again, everything was spinning.

"I see stars," he mumbled.

"That's right, Peter!" exclaimed the faerie jubilantly, flitting past his nose. "Second star to the right and straight on till morning! Neverland!"

She raced about, gathering up the makeshift parachute's ends, then lifted him up like the stork who delivers the baby in childhood stories. Straining against his weight, she flew toward the latticed windows and out into the night, the bundle that was Peter struggling weakly beneath, oblivious still of what was happening to him. Wind blew in chill gusts against the sack.

"Any bathrooms around here?" Peter mumbled.

The faerie tinkled like a bell. "Don't worry, we'll be over the ocean in a few minutes. Uhggg—you are so heavy!"

She jerked at the parachute roughly.

"Arghh, my head!" Peter groaned. "My back!"

They gained height, soaring out from the Darling house, up above its gables and over the roofs of the neighboring homes.

"Forget your back, Peter!" the faerie cried. "It's the back of the wind that matters now! We'll catch it, if we hurry!"

As they rose, the tiny stork and the huge baby, the faerie with her bundle of gripes and confusion, a fringed white head poked out of the back door, and eyes gone wide with

wonder and the remembrance of better times stared skyward. Tootles, clad in bright pajamas and a smile, watched
the faintly struggling Peter disappear from view.

Out across the city of London the faerie flew with Peter,
past houses and shops, down streets with rows of lamps
whose light reflected like silver on the carpet of new snow.
Below, in a shadowy park, a couple stood beneath one of
the lamps, kissing. The faerie swung past them, kicking
pixie dust loose from her tiny slippers. The couple rose
several feet into the air and hung suspended. They did not
look up, their arms coming tighter about each other.

"Straight on till morning," whispered the faerie with a
smile.

She began to rise, her bundle dragging clear of the light
until it had melted into the darkness.

Behind, distant and receding rapidly from view, Big Ben
chimed out the midnight hour.

Return to
Neverland

They flew until daybreak, out across the night sky, past
moon and stars, through the fabric of children's dreams and
the memories of childhood. Peter slept for the most part,
exhausted from the day's events and the emotional ordeal of
losing his children, dazed from the knock on the head he
had received when he had been tumbled by the upturned
carpet. Sometime during the night the faerie had harnessed
him into the makeshift parachute, but Peter remained
blissfully unaware of it all.

It was dawn when finally he began to come awake. He
was aware of a swaying motion, the rocking of the
parachute into which he had been bundled, and then of
daylight, soft and silver, penetrating the folds of his
cocoon. He did not realize yet where he was. In truth, he
thought he was back in his water bed at home, cradled in its
temperature-controlled embrace. He smelled the odd but
invigorating scent of brine and seaweed wafting on a gentle
morning breeze and smacked his lips.

He smiled and drifted back into sleep.

Had he awakened, he might have glimpsed what lay
below.

The ocean was all around, vast and depthless blue, its
cresting waves glittering like scattered diamonds in the new
day's sunlight. There was an island settled in the midst of
the azure waters, an odd, craggy atoll which possessed the
overall look and feel of a travel-magazine paradise, with
jutting peaks that scraped against the passing clouds,
patches of jungle nestled down within valleys and defiles,

coves into which the ocean rolled against white, sandy beaches and rocky cliffs.

Everywhere one looked, there was something wondrous to behold. Was that some massive, old sequoia on that rocky pinnacle just off the island's coast? Were those waterfalls tumbling down off the rocks at every turn? Was that some sort of town down below?

Was that a pirate ship at anchor?

Peter, alas, missed everything.

Abruptly he felt himself falling—not so rapidly as to be frightened by the sensation, but fast enough to be aware of it. Floating, that's what he was doing, he told himself, turning over in his bed. Odd, his bed seemed to lack definition. And where was Moira?

The descent grew more rapid. And was that someone grunting in a tiny voice? What was this business about being too heavy? Who was too heavy?

The descent ended in a jarring stop that tumbled Peter head over heels once more. He felt himself lurch awkwardly beneath his covers. He squinched his eyes shut as it all happened, grappling for his pillow, which had somehow disappeared.

When everything was still again, he slowly opened one eye, then the other.

Everything was blindly white.

Peter gulped. "I died," he whispered, terror-stricken. "I died."

But no, he was underneath his bed covers, that's all. He exhaled in relief. He was all right. He swallowed to clear his dry throat, pushed back the folds of the covers, and peeked out.

A huge eye was staring over at him.

"Moira?" he whispered hopefully.

He blinked away what remained of his sleep. The eye was still there. Worse, it was attached to what appeared to be a gigantic crocodile head. He squinted to get a better look. The crocodile head was attached to a crocodile body, and the body seemed to stretch on forever. It was standing directly in front of him.

He took a quick, panicked breath and held it. He squeezed his eyes shut and pulled the covers back in place. He knew he was dreaming. He just had to find a way to wake up.

Then a sudden movement in the folds of the bed sheet caught his eye. Something was crawling on top of him! He flailed wildly.

"Stop that!" a voice hissed.

A tiny dagger sliced a window through the chute, and the faerie peeked inside.

"Oh, no," Peter groaned. "Not you."

It was coming back to him now—the faerie's appearance at number 14 Kensington, the stuff about Peter Pan, Captain Hook, Neverland, and all that other nonsense.

He rubbed his head. "What's happened to me? Where am I?"

Her smile was dazzling. "You're in Neverland, Peter."

He sighed wearily. "Sure I am."

"Come over here." She beckoned to the window she had cut. "Take a look."

He did, peering first one way, then the other. Up beside him was the crocodile, its jaws open wide, its teeth gleaming. Between the teeth was a huge alarm clock with its hands askew and its numbered face cracked and broken. The crocodile sat in the center of a square that was settled on a broad stretch of beach. All about was a pirate town composed of the ravaged hulks of old ships. Ribs and struts stuck out everywhere like the bones of a dinosaur's rib cage. Gilt rails lined worn, sagging decks. From masts swayed signs offering services of all sorts in colorful language. DR. CHOP—LIMBS FITTED WHILE YOU WAIT. WENCHES & WINE—SERVED AT YOUR TABLE. ROOMS— BUNK YOUR JUNK. Shops and living quarters jumbled together in a mix of old wood and garish paint, like ragged cats in a litter, like a junkyard's discarded remains.

And there were pirates at every turn. They swaggered down boardwalks. They hung from doors and windows, calling out boldly. They clung to buxom women and hoisted glasses. They clung to each other. They carried pistols and swords, daggers and cutlasses. They wore tricorne hats and bandanas about their long hair, rings from their ears and on their fingers and through their noses, sashes of fine silk and boots of tough leather, greatcoats and striped shirts and pants as baggy as laundry sacks.

Peter stared, trying to figure it all out.

Then abruptly he did.

Mickey and Minnie!

It was almost more than he could stand. He groped for his cellular, but it wasn't there, of course. He looked down at himself. He was wearing the remains of his tuxedo—his pants, shirt, waistcoat, and bow tie. From last night, he remembered, the tribute to Wendy, the kidnapping, that confounded faerie . . .

He took a deep breath, righted himself, worked free of the remains of Maggie's parachute (he recognized it now), and staggered to his feet. He was only minimally surprised to find himself standing on a building ledge.

"What are you doing?" he heard the faerie call angrily. "Get back here!"

Peter paid no attention to her. Enough was enough. The crocodile stared over at him, its jaws frozen about the clock, its closest eye fastened on Peter. Peter blinked and shook his head to clear it. He took a couple of tentative steps and almost fell, catching himself at the last moment.

"I've got to get some Advil," he muttered to himself. "Maybe some V-8. Then find a pay phone."

Steadying himself, ignoring the cries of warning from the faerie, he moved toward a ladder leaning against the ledge, climbed carefully down, and stumbled away toward the door of the closest building—another wrecked ship, the back end, called the aft or something, wasn't it? He drew strength from the smell of food cooking and the sound of voices. Pirates wandered past him, a few turning to stare. He didn't notice.

He went through the door of the wreck. Inside, it was dark and smoky and implacably grim. Whoever had decorated it must have spent long hours reading Edgar Allan Poe. Kettles of stew or soup were suspended over open hearths. Pieces of meat and potatoes sat on long wooden tables cluttered with cooking implements. Pots and pans hung from racks. Candles set in sconces and crude chandeliers gave what light there was to the hazy den. Peter blinked. He must have wandered into some sort of low-end kitchen.

He became aware then that a handful of pirates had stopped what they were doing and were staring at him, their tasks forgotten. They did not look friendly. They looked annoyed.

"You don't happen to have . . . is there any kind of, uh . . . ?" he began, and trailed off.

A ratty toothless pirate came limping across the floor to face him, eyes squinting in a hard glint. Chewing tobacco formed a stain at the corners of his tight mouth, leaking out as his jaws worked diligently. Without a word, he reached up and tore off Peter's bow tie, eyeing it thoughtfully.

"Here, now!" Peter objected.

The pirate's eyes shifted back again. "I fancy them shiny shoes as well, mate."

Peter bristled. "Just a minute!"

Another pirate appeared from the haze and shoved the first aside. This one wore an eye patch and looked twice as mean. He grabbed Peter by his shirt and threw him against the wall. Peter careened into a collection of pots and pans, sent them flying in every direction, and ended up in the grasp of a barrel-chested pirate cook. The cook shoved him away. The pirate who had assaulted him first (Peter had already decided to press charges) came at him again, knocked him flat, reached down, and began pulling off his pants.

Peter kicked and yelled to no avail.

Then suddenly a familiar flash of light appeared, darting out of nowhere to snatch a candle from its sconce, whisk it to where Peter struggled, and shove it down the front of the attacking pirate's baggy trousers. The pirate reared back with a howl, beating at his pants. The light darted instantly to his eye patch, yanked it away from his grizzled face like a bowstring, then let go. The eye patch snapped back into place with a *whap* and the pirate went tumbling backward into a wall rack of cookware that released on top of him with a crash. He shuddered once and lay still.

Peter scrambled back to his feet, searching for a way out of this madhouse, but now the huge pirate cook was coming at him, wielding a battered butcher's knife. Peter moaned in dismay, backing against the wall. But the light zipped past once more and landed sharply on the curved end of a ladle sticking out of a soup pot. Out flipped the ladle, sending a spray of hot soup into the pirate cook's weathered face. The cook howled and staggered back, clawing at his eyes, then rushed forward blindly, lurched into the pot, knocked it askew, and brought the rest of the soup pouring down atop his head.

The kitchen was in chaos by now. The remaining pirates came at Peter, shouting and cursing, cutlasses drawn. Peter scrambled for the door, still reasonably convinced that he was dreaming, or if not, that this was some sort of movie stunt, but no longer willing to risk being wrong. He stumbled, and the pirates were almost on him. The light flashed by, cutting through a rope that secured the side of ribs curing overhead, and the ribs dropped squarely atop the pirates, knocking them cold.

Peter stood alone amid the debris, gasping for breath, groping for some measure of sanity. Down swept the light, landing on a wall strut inches from Peter's eyes. The light flared and dimmed, and the faerie from last night reappeared.

Peter laughed, certain he was crazy now. "Wow! You're fantastic, little bug! I can't believe my subconscious. I thought it would go for the demure type." He laughed giddily.

The faerie glowered at him dangerously. "Stop it, Peter! Stop it right now!"

She darted at him. He caught a glimpse of the tiny dagger's blade as she swept past his hand. He felt a sharp pain, and suddenly he was cut. He stared in disbelief at the back of his hand, watching the blood flow in a red ribbon from the wound.

His eyes went wide. "I can't believe you did that! I'm

bleeding! Look at me! What do . . . what is this . . .'' He shuddered, the truth of what the pain and the blood meant sinking in. "Oh, my God,'' he whispered.

The faerie landed again on the strut, emerging hastily from the light. "Are you okay?'' There was genuine concern in her voice. "Peter, are you all right?''

Peter Banning lifted his eyes to stare at her, no longer seeing a light or an image or some figment of his imagination. Gone in an instant's time was the misconception that he was in dreamland or anywhere else imaginary. Gone was the dizziness, the belief that he would wake from dreaming when his head cleared, the certainty that the world was as it had always been, as he had always known it to be.

He stared at the tiny faerie and knew that she was real.

He tried to breathe, and his chest constricted.

The faerie's face was pretty and bright with youth beneath the frown lines that etched her smooth forehead and the corners of her mouth. "Do you know where we are?'' she whispered to him.

He swallowed, then nodded. He couldn't speak.

"Who am I, Peter?''

He froze. If he said it, if he admitted it . . .

"Say it, Peter. You have to say it.''

He managed to shake his head. "I can't,'' he breathed. She bent close. "Why?''

"Because if I say it, if I . . .'' He swallowed. "If I say it, it will be . . .''

"What?''

"Real.''

The lines disappeared, and there was a strange new light in her pixie eyes. "Please,'' she whispered. "Peter, please. Say it.''

His face softened. The name was a feather on the wind. "Tinkerbell,'' he said.

"And I live in . . . ?''

"Neverland.''

He gasped at the enormity of what he had just admitted, jerked away, and ran to the window of the deserted kitchen to stare out into the pirate town. The crocodile tower loomed before him, facing out through the wrecks of the pirate ships toward the harbor beyond. Pirates jostled and shouted as they crossed the square and swaggered in and out of the buildings.

Peter swung back again toward Tinkerbell. "I can't accept this! It's not rational adult thinking! It's not possible!"

Tinkerbell darted from the shelf to land on his hand and began wrapping a handkerchief about the cut. "Listen to me, Peter. Jack and Maggie are here. And you've got to do battle with Captain Hook to free them. For that, you'll need the Lost Boys. And your sword. And you'll have to fly!"

Peter shook his head vehemently. "Just wait, just hold on one minute!" He steadied himself. "Whatever this is all about, whatever is happening here, I'm still me! I can't fly. I'm not going to fight anyone."

He spun away from her and strode toward the door. "Where are you going?" she called after him.

"To find James Hook, Captain, and get my kids back and go home!" he shouted back.

"No, Peter, it's too soon!" She flashed in front of him, trying to bring him to a halt. "Hook is waiting for you. It's a trap! He planned it this way—the kidnapping, the whole business. He'll kill you! You're not ready for him!"

Peter brushed past. He'd had enough of this nonsense. "I'm as ready as I need to be." He paused at the kitchen door. "Besides, my kids can't afford to miss any more school."

Tinkerbell stomped her foot on an imaginary floor, hands on hips. "Oh, Peter Pan!" she muttered. "You are as stubborn as ever!" She whipped past him as he tried to go out the doorway, seized hold of his shirt collar, and held him fast. "A look, then!" she hissed in his ear. "Just a look, though. Then you decide. But first let's dress you up a bit."

As he grunted irritably, she dragged him back inside.

Pirates, Pirates
Everywhere!

When Peter emerged again from the dingy kitchen, he was dressed in a hodgepodge of pirate garb—a scarlet cape across his shoulders, a black tricorne hat atop his head, and a black eye patch beneath his brow—all lifted from the unfortunate pirate cooks disposed of by Tinkerbell. He also wore a peg leg, laced to his kneecap by leather straps, his own good leg tied up behind him under the covering of his cape. A crutch supported him. His disguise might have been more comfortable if he had been willing to part with the remains of his tuxedo, but he couldn't quite bring himself to give up the last vestiges of the now departed real world, and he wore them still hidden underneath everything else.

Stepping out into the light, he gazed around tentatively. Pirates sauntered past without so much as a glance at him, engaged in their own activities. There were big pirates and little pirates, pirates with missing eyes and ears, with peg legs and empty sleeves, with scars that crisscrossed their faces and necks, with beards and mustaches and sideburns and muttonchops. There were dozens of them, all armed with flint pistols and sharpened blades, a whole arsenal of death-dealing weapons. Peter tried not to think too much about what that meant as he steeled himself for the task that lay ahead. Whatever this was all about, whichever world it was that he had been cast into—Neverland or dreamland or wherever—he was not leaving without Jack and Maggie.

He hobbled down into the pirate town, working his way carefully past its inhabitants, trying to act inconspicuous in his outlandish garb, hoping against hope that he looked like he belonged. The eye patch was a nice touch, but hard to get used to. Whenever he needed to see clearly, he found himself lifting the patch to do so. Shouts and laughter rose from every quarter—from within the many taverns and alehouses where glasses were being raised and purses lifted, from the blade shops where edges were being honed on whetstones, from the stables where horses were being shod and groomed, and from the streets themselves, where hands and arms were being linked in rough camaraderie.

Inside the tricorne hat, Tinkerbell bounced about, righted herself as best she could, and peered out through the hole cut for her in the brim.

"You don't act enough like a pirate!" she snapped at him irritably. "If you insist on seeing Hook and intend to stay alive in the bargain, then you have to do better than this! Let's practice. Do exactly as I say. Make your right arm limp. Pretend it is dead and useless. Let it hang by your side. Try it."

Peter grinned, amused by the idea. He let his arm hang limp. "How's that, little bug?"

She bristled. "Don't call me that! Call me by my name. Like you used to. Tink."

He shrugged. "Okay. Tink."

A pirate so hunched down he appeared to be searching for worms bumped into him drunkenly and careened away.

"Crack your mouth and drool," Tink ordered.

Peter twisted his mouth out of shape and let his tongue loll. Kind of fun.

"Now growl."

"Rwwlll."

"No, no! I said *growl*!"

She darted from his hat in a flash of light, dagger drawn, and jabbed at his posterior.

"Groooaahhh!" he howled.

A pair of fierce-looking pirates with blades strapped everywhere wheeled about. *"Grooooaahhh!"* they responded, and waved in greeting.

Down through the pirate town went Peter and Tink, past the jumbled hulks of the ships that had been cannibalized and turned to makeshift shops and shelters, past a group of shabby musicians playing fiddles and flutes who were fronted by a gnarled fellow in ragged knee-length pants and a jersey singing a pirate shanty.

They were passing a blacksmith standing over an anvil at his forge when Tink said, "Hsssstt! Look, Peter."

Peter stopped.

The blacksmith was holding up a metal hook, the end still glowing redly from where it had been resting in the forge's fire. Sunlight glinted off its point as it was turned this way and that for inspection.

Next to the blacksmith stood a stubby, bespectacled pirate in baggy sailor pants, soiled tunic, and a striped vest that looked like it had found its way onto its wearer's back off the streets of Tijuana. His nose was as blunt as a marlinspike's tip, and his eyebrows were as bushy as caterpillars. A broad, cheerful smile wreathed his weathered face, and a brimmed, feathered bosun's hat was perched rakishly atop his head.

Cautiously he reached up to touch the hook's point, then flinched away.

"Ohhh, sharp as a shark's front tooth!" he declared, sucking on his finger. "I think the captain will be pleased indeed."

"That's Smee!" whispered Tink in Peter's ear.

The blacksmith dunked the glowing hook in a pail of water, held it under while it steamed, and then brought it out again. He wiped it off carefully and handed it to Smee, who laid it carefully on a satin pillow.

"Good work, Blackie!" said Smee, tipped a hand to his cap, and was off.

"After him, Peter!" hissed Tink.

Down the wharf Peter limped, peg leg stubbing and dragging and chaffing mercilessly as he followed the bobbing feathers of Smee's cap through the crowds. From time to time they could see Smee loft the hook overhead, balancing it precariously on the satin pillow. He hummed and he whistled as he went, and pirates all around him called out.

"A floggin' good morning to ya, *Captain Smee*!" cried a

carpenter engaged in building what appeared to Peter to be a gallows.

"Any news of war, *Captain*?" asked another.

Smee smiled broadly, apparently missing the sarcasm in their voices, pushing on as if the greetings were not only sincere but his due. All the while the hook glinted and shone in the sun.

A group of women whose profession was unmistakable whistled as Smee went past.

"Put on your faces, girls," cried one. "Here comes Captain Smee!"

They darted out to greet him, dancing about, their skirts lifting rakishly.

"Look, look!" they chimed. "It's got to be the Captain's hook!"

"Hook's hook, right enough!"

"Well, girlie, you should know, shouldn't you, now?"

"It's 'is symbol of fortune and fame, yoho!"

"Keep the fame, it's the fortune for me!"

They spun and danced about Smee and back through the crowd, a dozen more appearing from nearby doorways to join in. Peter, anxious to keep Smee in view, had gotten too close and was suddenly swept up in the whirl of skirts and cheap perfume.

"James Hook, son of a sea cook!"

"Hey, that's not all, he's a son of a . . ."

"Jimmy Hook, our claim to fame."

"Him and few hundred more I could name!"

"Swordsman, poet, and debaucher! Sailing to plunder and torture!"

"James Hook, Captain Hook, the sharpest blade on the seven seas! Our Hook!"

They sang and danced away, leaving Smee flustered and smiling and Peter trying desperately to avoid being seen, even though he had ended up almost nose to nose with the pirate. But Smee seemed not to notice, turning away with a blissful sigh and continuing down the walk.

A moment later he veered into the door of a barber shop. "A bad-boy chop," he ordered of the barber, who swung him into a chair, hacked a bit with a razor and knife, and stepped away. Smee rose and tossed the barber a gold coin. As the barber reached eagerly for it Smee jerked it away again—a string bound it to his finger. "Have to be quicker than that, mate." Smee grinned and tossed him a copper coin instead.

Back down the walkway he went, Peter and Tink in pursuit once more. Pirates shoved and jostled Peter as they passed, a few offering curses and promises of dreadful things to come. Peter tried to ignore them, his eyes on Smee. His peg leg was killing him by now, enough so that he really did feel like growling. He was beginning to wonder if he had any idea at all what he was doing.

Smee slowed and turned in to a tavern where a player piano was hard at work and a collection of rummies sang lustily before a sagging wooden bar. The rummies were an aged and worn lot, pirates possessed of an entire inventory of glass eyes, peg legs, false teeth, wooden hands, and other replacement parts.

Their voices rose raggedly in song.

Smee sauntered up to the crowd, displayed the hook imperiously, and announced, "Drinks are on Smee, for all those who've got a knee that was once a tree!"

He tossed down some coins amid shouts of acclaim and bounced out the door again, nearly running over a harried Peter, who was hanging on the frame, exhausted from trying to keep up.

Ahead, the pier tunneled into a cluster of old ships, a hazy corridor of torchlight and smoke. Smee skipped along, the hook balanced on the pillow, and disappeared into the gloom. Peter hurried after, growling now and again when other pirates approached, losing enthusiasm for the whole business. But Jack and Maggie depended on him, so he could not turn back. He groped his way along the tunnel, his eyes watering. Ahead, he could hear pirates singing and shouting, "Hook! Hook! Hook!"

Peter pushed clear of the tunnel, free of the haze of stinging smoke, and blinked against the sunlight. Smee was just ahead, slowing at a pen tended by two rangy pirates wielding whips. Within the pen were four cowering boys in the process of having their shirts stripped from their backs. They whimpered and cried out pleadingly.

"Misters Jukes and Noodler," Smee greeted cheerfully, nodding first to the one whose muscular body was as black as ebony and then to the one whose blond hair and beard had the appearance of a rat's nest. "Top of the morning, mates!"

He skipped on, whistling once more, but Peter slowed in spite of himself, horrified at what he was seeing.

"They're just children," he whispered up to Tink.

He could hear her hiss with disdain and anger. "Hook's a scummy slaver. He makes his prisoners count his treasure for him—over and over and over again."

Suddenly there was a roar from behind Peter, and a flood of pirates surged out of the smoky tunnel, singing and chanting. Peter had no time to get clear of the rush, and he was quickly caught up and swept along. Down the wharf front the crowd flowed, past the collection of scavenged ships that formed the town's entrance, out from the huge sign that hung over the tunnel and read in bold letters GOOD FORM PIER, to the end of the dock and the gangplank leading up to the only vessel moored in the entire harbor.

But such a dark and sinister craft it was! A brigantine, fully rigged and outfitted, cannons bristling from its gun ports, its hull rakish and gleaming in the light. A skeleton with an upraised sword formed the spine of its prow, its death's-head grinning with the anticipation of its next victim's demise. A huge cannon, four times the size of any other, sat alone atop the aft deck behind the wheel, its massive barrel swung about to guard the harbor entrance, its cradle mounted on a revolving base. Below, the captain's quarters were framed by a stern crafted like a huge skull with windows forming luminous eyes and gilt the outline of its jaw, nose, and brows. The railing above was shaped like a captain's hat with serpents hissing at the corners. The hull was painted red and black with gold trim, and brass fittings gleamed in the sunlight. The pirate ship looked fast and wicked, like a cat prepared to pounce.

Atop its highest mast flew a gold shield and crossbones on a field of black with banners proclaiming GOOD FORM and JAS. On the port side of the main deck, protruding like a tongue, was the dreaded plank.

The pirates about Peter chanted wildly: "Show us the Hook! Hook! Hook! Show us the Hook! Hook! Hook!"

One thing Peter Banning was not was a coward. But he also understood that at times discretion was the better part of valor. He found himself wondering if now wasn't one of those times. Perhaps Tink had been right. Perhaps he wasn't ready for Hook.

Unfortunately, it was too late to worry about that now. The pirates were sweeping up the gangplank and onto the ship, and Peter was being swept right along with them.

Hook Confronted

Crammed port to starboard and bowsprit to mainmast aboard the brigantine *Jolly Roger,* the pirates roared out, "Hook! Hook! Hook!" Arms raised, some brandishing weapons, some bare fists. The pirate ship rocked with their cries.

Atop the quarter deck, Smee stepped forward and signaled for silence.

"Good mawning, Neverlaaaannd!" he bellowed, cheeks puffing out, belly shaking. "Tie down the mainsail, mates, 'cause here he is—the cunning kingfish, the baaad barracuda, the sleaziest sleaze of the seven seas, and a shipshape dresser to boot, a man so deep he's nearly unfathomable and so quick he's even fast asleep! I give you our very own steel-handed stingray—Cap'n James Hook!"

A pirate named Tickles pumped wildly at a concertina while cannons exploded in sheets of fire and the cheers of the pirate crew rose to new heights.

From behind Smee, the doors to the captain's cabin burst wide and out strode the infamous James Hook.

At first glance he looked very like his ship—or perhaps it was the other way around. He was sleek and narrow and wicked looking from his sharp-nosed face to his pointed toes. His captain's coat was cut from red and black cloth and trimmed in gold filigree. He wore a gold-fringed sash across one shoulder with a cutlass sheathed at its loop. Ruffled white lace hung at his neck, and the angular face above it was reminiscent of a ship's prow cutting through a sea's white froth. His black hair hung down about his shoulders in ringlets like the rigging from a mast. His captain's tricorne was broad-brimmed and tailored and looked exactly like the aft railing of his vessel save for the absence of serpents hissing at its corners. What was lacking in serpents, however, was more than made up for in Hook's face. Cruel, hard, sneering, with mustaches that coiled like vipers and eyes that could freeze a bird in flight, he was a formidable-looking figure standing there before his riotous band of brigands.

At the end of his left hand he had affixed the dreaded hook for which he was so well known, its newly sharpened hook point gleaming in the sunlight.

His sneer firmly in place as he faced the crowd, he lifted his lace-sleeved right hand condescendingly in acknowledgment of their adulation.

"See how greatly the men favor you, sir!" prompted Smee, beaming.

Hook's lip curled and out of the corner of his mouth he whispered, "The puling spawn. How I despise them."

Two hundred strong, and not a man among them could read past the second grade, only one or two could distinguish a spoon from a fork, and less than a handful could count to ten. It was disgusting.

Hook sighed. Still, they were his to command.

"Gentlemen!" he called out. "You ignorant, flogging, sorry, parasitic sacks of entrails!"

His crew cheered wildly at the praise.

Hook's claw slashed the air. "Revenge!" There was instant silence. Hook beamed. "Is mine. I have baited the hook—so to speak—with the fish's children. Peter Pan's kids will bring him to me. At long last I will be rid of that loathsome boy who cut off my hand and . . ." His voice lowered into the darkest recesses of his throat. "And threw it to the crocodile."

He choked on the words and could not go on. Smee quickly leaped into the gap.

"And who was it killed that cunnin' croc?" he demanded.

"Hook! Hook! Hook!" roared the pirates as one.

"Who stuffed 'im and quieted 'is clock for good?"

"Hook! Hook! Hook!"

"Who went 'round the world to snatch Pan's kids, all the way to England, sailing' uncharted waters and bravin' unknown perils?"

"Hook! Hook! Hook!"

The captain had recovered himself sufficiently to realize that Smee was usurping his speech. He collared his bosun roughly and shoved him aside.

"It's my show, Smee," he hissed. "Go away." He turned to his crew once more, and his gaze turned dark. "Now then—which of you doubted me?"

The raucous crowd quieted uneasily.

"That's right!" Hook snapped. "There's a doubter out there. Where is he? Who among us does not belong? Someone here does not belong."

He let his eyes flit across their terrified faces.

"A stranger amongst the loyal! He must be weeded out!"

Now there was utter silence. All the pirates stood frozen in place, not daring the twitch of an eyebrow, not the flicker of a lash. No one wanted to call attention to himself now. You could have heard a pin drop. . . .

And suddenly one did. A pirate foolish enough to attempt to wipe the sweat from his brow loosened a silver stickpin from his cap and sent it tumbling to the deck.

Ping!

Every eye turned toward the unfortunate.

Hook snarled. He started to descend the quarterdeck stairs and abruptly stopped, horrified. His gaze settled on Smee.

"Where's my carpet, Smee?"

Smee gulped. "Sorry, Cap'n. Sorry, your worship." The bosun stamped on the deck purposefully. Gears groaned and squeaked, and the stairs flipped over to reveal a red carpet tacked beneath. Hook smiled and continued down. A long finger lifted and pointed.

"You! You, sir, you!"

Every pirate tried to disappear into the ship's woodwork.

"You!" he ignored the pin offender and pointed his hook toward a ratty little pirate hanging off to one side by a cringing, fat, one-legged pirate with atrocious taste in clothes. "Yes, you!" He forced himself to ignore the other. "You bet against me bringing Pan here, didn't you, you slimy bilge rat?"

The pirate, whose name was Gutless, though Hook wouldn't have remembered if given a week of Sundays to try, cringed as the captain approached. "No, Cap'n, I swear on me mother's sweet soul. I didn't, I didn't!"

Hook reached him, smiled, bent down, and gave him a fatherly pat on one shoulder. "Tell the truth now, come on, Captain wants to hear the truth. . . ."

Gutless collapsed in Hook's arms, sobbing. "Oh, I did, I did!"

Hook's smile turned frosty. "Well, you made a boo-boo. The boo-boo box for you, then."

He shoved the other away disdainfully. Gutless crumpled to the deck, wailing. Other pirates reached down for him instantly, hauled him to his feet, and dragged him away.

Hook sauntered on, the crowd parting before him. "Don't think I didn't hear those who whispered when they thought I couldn't hear, 'He's off! Hook's finished!' "

"Or those who said, 'That limp metal no-fingers will never rise again!' " added Smee before he could think better of it.

Hook gave him a withering glance. Off to one side, the lid to a coffinlike box was thrown open and Gutless was shoved inside, still sobbing pitifully. A bag filled with snakes, spiders, and centipedes was shoved in after him. Hook was pleased to discover that when the lid slammed shut, the cries quickly diminished.

"Look around, you scavengers!" he advised sternly, gesturing toward the remnants of the hulks that formed the buildings of the waterfront. "Look around and take note of the trophies I have won for you so that you could live a pirate life in a pirate city."

"It's paradise!" one pirate cried out enthusiastically.

"Yesss, isn't it?" Hook sniffed. Such idiots. "Raise your weapons high, mates!" he shouted suddenly. Cutlasses, clubs, daggers, pistols, and blunderbusses were hoisted aloft. Hook smiled wickedly. "Proud pirates, mates one and all, prepare yourselves for a celebration! Prepare for the killing of youth, the maiming of joy, and the strangling of innocence in her fetid cradle! Peter Pan is coming soon! And when he does, I will grind his bones to dust and salt my food with the leavings. I'll hurl Pan into the blackest abyss, the deepest coldest chasm, right off the face of the earth for all time!" Hook's arms rose. "I shall have my glorious war, and I shall win it!"

He wheeled about. "Bring up the prisoners!"

A wild cry rose from the pirates as the hatch to the main hold was thrown open with a bang, and a winch began to haul a net from out of the black below. The net twirled slowly as it came into view, and there, imprisoned within, were Jack and Maggie, still dressed in their pajamas, wide-eyed and frightened as they struggled against the ropes. Jack carried his baseball glove. Maggie still wore Tootles's paper flower in her hair. Pirates jeered and jabbed playfully at the children as the net rose to eye level before Hook and stopped.

"Hi, kids," he greeted with a smirk.

Suddenly there was a commotion from behind, shouts and growls rising up as someone pushed through the crowd. Hook turned, irritated. Then his eyes went wide. That badly dressed, overweight, one-legged pirate, his eye patch knocked so far askew that it rode halfway down his nose, had thrown down his crutch and was heading straight for him!

"Jack! Maggie! Everything's all right now!" the pirate shouted. A finger pointed threateningly at Hook. "Those are my kids! I'm their father."

Hook stared. The pirate stumbled and his wooden leg dropped off. He kicked and twisted and a good leg popped into view! The cape he was wearing was twisted about, and the way he was squinting past his eye patch from beneath the cocked tricorne made him look like a bad imitation of a vampire. Hook was astonished. What sort of pirate was this?

"You there! And you!" The fellow was gesturing at an

incredulous Jukes and Noodler. "Lower my kids right now! And do it carefully." The roundish face lifted, a sappy smile puffing out the ruddy cheeks. "Daddy's here!"

Hook pushed Smee in front of him, wondering if the fellow was mad, if there was danger that he might even be rabid. Then he glanced over at the net where the kids were yelling, "Dad!" and "That's my Daddy!"

No, it couldn't be. . . .

Pirates closed about Peter Banning, who had charged to the rescue, any measure of common sense thrown to the winds, heedless of Tink's frantic protests from within the brim of his hat. Hands fastened on him, swords were thrust into his face, and he was hauled up short. He thrashed to free himself in vain, then sagged back helplessly as the full realization of what he had done settled in.

Hook stared at Peter. The peg leg and eye patch were gone. The cape was torn and the waist sash shredded. All that remained was the tricorne. And underneath, a dress shirt, waistcoat, and fine English wool slacks. Hook's eyes lit up. Could it be? He came forward, peering at his captive, closer and closer until they were eye to eye.

Hook smiled malevolently. "You? My great and worthy opponent?"

Pirates hooted and howled about him, their laughter shrill and derisive. But Hook motioned quickly for silence.

"No, no, no, watch out! He's in disguise!" He stepped back again quickly, hook and hand out to ward off any attack. "Remember the time he stole my voice? Remember all those tricks he played? Yes, he may look like a chubby degenerate, but careful, lads! Peter Pan is there, somewhere inside, and he's gong to explode out of that fleshy canister any moment! How wonderful!"

He cleared a space for himself, engaged in a few hurried knee bends to loosen up, then drew out his cutlass and began to stab and parry.

"Stand back, you scrugs! Watch out, he'll try to fly! Pop out, Pan! Come on, I'm waiting! Out, out! Ha! Watch him, now! Come on, come on! Prepare to die!"

He snatched a second cutlass from a pirate close at hand

and flipped it blade-first at his enemy. Smee ducked away as the sword flashed by and embedded itself in the mast by Peter's head. The pirates scattered, leaving Peter momentarily alone.

Peter looked befuddled. His voice was plaintive. "I can't fight you. I don't know how. I just want my kids back."

Hook stopped his fencing and straightened deliberately. "Smee!" he howled. His bosun charged up to him and was grabbed by the shirtfront. "Who is this impostor!"

"Ah, ah, ah," Smee stuttered, and began riffling hurriedly through a leather bag slung by a strap about his shoulders. "Let me see. P-P-Pan, Cap'n. Ah, here we go—adoption papers. Medical records, sworn affidavits, dental records, birth certificate, social security, business cards, all in order, sir."

"Bah!" Hook frowned like a bulldog. "Never mind all that. Check this bloated, fleshy miscreant yourself. Look for the *detail*."

Smee crossed to Peter, yanked back the cape, pulled up his dress shirt, and probed. Peter fought to keep from laughing, but Smee had found his ticklish spot. He brushed Smee away and pulled his shirt back in place.

"The scar's there, Cap'n," Smee reported dutifully. "Hypertrophic. Right where you gave it to 'im during the Tiger Lily incident. He's Pan or I've got me a dead man's dinghy for a brain."

Hook seemed to consider which was the more possible for a moment. Then his face reddened. "But it can't be! Not this pitiful, spineless, pasty-skinned worm! He's not even a shadow of Peter Pan!"

Hook sheathed his cutlass dejectedly, and his gaze dropped. "Oh, what cruel hand has fate dealt me now?" he moaned.

Peter took a deep breath and stepped forward to confront him. Hook's sad eyes raised. Their gazes locked.

Peter cleared his throat. "Mr. Hook," he offered. "As gentlemen, we have an obligation to try to clarify this misunderstanding."

"This disaster," Hook amended quickly.

Peter shrugged. "Which must be remedied nevertheless."

Hook nodded. "Expediently. I agree."

Peter drew himself up, a new confidence emboldening him. Hard-nosed bargaining—this was familiar territory. "For me the stakes can go no higher. I want my children."

Hook drew himself up as well. "And for me they can sink no lower. I want my war."

"It seems we must negotiate," said Peter.

Hook scowled. "Negotiate? Very well. I propose you fight me with all the cleverness and skill of the true Pan and win the brats back."

"Fight?"

"Pick your weapon, Pan. You can't have forgotten everything!"

Peter gave Hook a crafty smile. "So that's what you want, is it? All right."

Peter reached inside his waistcoat. Pirates leveled weapons at him from everywhere. Peter hesitated, then pulled out his checkbook, and flipped it open.

"How much, Mr. Hook?"

Hook stared at him in disbelief. Then he snatched a flintlock from another pirate, whirled, and fired. The bullet flicked the edge of the checkbook and continued on. Unfortunately a grease-stained pirate cook named Sid was next in line. Sid fell dead without a sound.

"Who was that, Smee?" demanded Hook, casting down his weapon irritably.

"Sid the cook, Cap'n," his bosun answered with a gulp.

A polite smattering of applause rose from the pirate ranks.

"Bad form!" Hook sneered, for if there was one thing he abhorred, having adopted as his own the affectations of the well-bred, it was another's impropriety of behavior.

Forward he strode, closing the distance between himself and a startled Peter in an instant's time, his scarlet-and-gold captain's coat billowing out behind him like a sail. Pirates leaped out of the way. Hook knocked the checkbook from

Peter's hand and sent it spinning off the ship and into the water. It hit with a splash and sank.

Then he grabbed Peter and slammed him up against the mainmast, the hook coming up to his exposed throat. Peter swallowed in terror. Hook's eyes were as red as fire, his mustaches dancing, his curled black hair whipping about his lean face in a frenzy.

"I escaped death by crocodile," he raged. "I waited, in good faith, and in perpetual boredom, here in this dreadful place, surrounded by cretins! Nothing to do besides chase and kill dirty little Lost Boys! But I waited! I waited for that special moment in time when I could fulfill the destiny that was due me. . . ."

Hook took a deep, steadying breath. "And now this?" he finished, barely able to form the words. "This is my reward? You?"

His sneer faltered, and his face fell. There was a sudden tear in his eye. He took the hook from Peter's throat and placed his arm about the other companionably, turning him away from the befuddled crew. "How could you do this to me—after everything we've meant to each other?"

"I just want my kids," Peter answered.

Hook sighed. "And I my hand! But there are some things in life you simply cannot have back." Then he brightened. "Tell you what. Since I am possessed of more than a modicum of good form, I shall give you the chance you never gave me. I'll make you a deal, Mr. Chairman of the Board." He turned Peter toward the mainmast. "Climb, crawl, slither if you must, up to the yardarm and touch the outstretched fingers of your beloved children and I will set them free. That's right. Free. I promise."

Peter stared up at his children, dangling in the net just below the spar. "Ah, um, well, I have a real problem with heights," he ventured.

"Have you, now?" Hook asked sympathetically.

"Save us, Daddy," Jack and Maggie cried. "Climb! Hurry, please! We want to go home!"

Peter took a deep breath. "Hang on, Princess!" he called up to Maggie. "I'm here for you, Jack! I'm coming!"

He walked to the rigging, grabbed on, and started to climb. He was only a few feet off the deck when the dizziness began. He slowed, breathing hard and sweating. Pirates began to chuckle.

"I don't think we've explored all of our options yet," he called down to Hook. "Let's work together on this, you and me. You have prime waterfront real estate crying out for development—condominiums, time-shares, office space, you name it. The sky's the limit. No building codes! Go for mineral rights while you're at it!"

Hook pointed. "Touch them, Pan. Just touch them, and all this will be a bad dream."

Jack and Maggie were pleading with him to go on. He closed his eyes and climbed another few loops. The pirates craned their necks expectantly. Then Peter opened his eyes again, and the deck rushed up to meet him. He gasped and grappled with the rigging as if hanging off a cliff, unable to go on, his terror so great that it even shut out the cries of his children.

Below, the pirates were laughing and sneering.

Hook turned to Smee. "You see? I knew he couldn't fly. He can't do anything anymore. He's a disgrace." He threw up his hands and turned away. "I cannot bring myself to soil my hook with his blood. Someone else kill them. Go on, kill them, kill them all."

Jack rose up inside the imprisoning net and began to shake the ropes wildly. Maggie collapsed in tears. "Fight, Daddy, fight," they yelled in despair. "Don't leave us!"

A whip-thin pirate scrambled up the rigging, lashed one end of a rope to a rung and the other to Peter's ankle, and shoved him off. Down Peter hurtled, screaming. But at the last possible moment he was jerked up short, bouncing and twisting, inches from certain death. A handful of pirates, in stitches over the look on his face, released him, tipped him upright, and with swords and daggers in hand began to prod him across the deck.

In the direction of the plank.

Hook glanced disconsolately over his shoulder at the proceedings. Jukes and Noodler were swinging the brats away from the hold toward the prisons on the dock. As the netting passed over Pan's head he reached up, trying in vain to brush fingertips with his children.

Touching, thought Hook.

The net swung down to the dock, and the brats were dragged out and dumped into their cells.

Truly touching.

"I am retiring," he announced to Smee, who was tagging along dutifully. "Cancel the war. Cancel my life. Pan has ruined everything. I never want to hear his name again."

He mounted the carpeted deck stairs to his cabin, so depressed he did not think he would ever smile at a Lost Boy execution again. He was almost to the door when a flash of light darted in front of him and Tinkerbell appeared.

"And what about the name Hook?" she demanded. "Is this how you want to be remembered? As a bully of your enemy's small children? As the destroyer of a fat, old Pan?"

Hook swung at her, missing, burying the point of his claw in the deck rail. In vain, he tried to yank free, cursing furiously. Tinkerbell zipped about to hover before his face, her tiny dagger drawn, the point pressed into his hawk nose.

"Give me one week, Hook, and I'll get him in shape to fight you. Then you can have your old war."

Smee charged up, a blunderbuss in hand. He leveled the barrel at Tink, inches from the captain's nose. Hook blanched.

"It's a trick, Cap'n," growled his bosun. "Lemme blow the pixie vixen straight to Davy Jones."

Tink ignored him. "You promised the war of the century, Hook!" she said, jabbing at his nose for emphasis. "Your whole life has been building to this single moment. Mortal combat—your one moment of glory—Hook versus Pan!"

"*That* is not Peter Pan!" Hook sneered, indicating a terrified Peter, who was now wobbling uncertainly on the plank.

"Seven days," Tink repeated. "A pittance of time for

you, a blink of the eye to a man of your infinite patience—an important, powerful man who can afford to wait.''

She zipped away, gone in an instant's time, leaving Hook staring down the barrel of Smee's blunderbuss.

"Smee," the captain said quietly. "Lower that, will you?" His bosun quickly complied. "Now, bring me my cigars. I need to think.''

Smee hurried off, disappearing into Hook's cabin, baggy pants flapping like sails. Hook finally freed his claw from the deck rail and stood staring at its point thoughtfully. The faerie was right, of course. He could afford to wait. Needed to, in point of fact, if it meant getting a crack at the real Pan.

As if she had read his mind, Tinkerbell flashed back into view, gossamer wings spinning threads of light. "Seven days for a battle with the true Peter Pan," she whispered. "Seven days.''

Smee rushed back through the cabin door bearing Hook's favorite cigar holder, a twin-stemmed affair. Hook accepted the holder and placed it in his mouth. Smee struck a match to one cigar while Tinkerbell flashed past with faerie magic to light the other. Hook puffed thoughtfully and looked out to sea, gazing past Peter as he was prodded slowly back along the length of the plank.

"Two days," he said quietly.

"Four," countered Tink. "The bare minimum for a decent Pan.''

"Three." Hook's eyes pinned her. "Final offer.''

She flitted to the end of his nose. "Done.''

Tiny hand extended, she shook the captain's hook guardedly. A few of the pirates gathered on the deck had been listening, and they sent up a ragged cheer. Soon the rest were joining in, ignorant of what it was they were cheering about, but happy to be yelling all the same. A few flintlocks discharged and one final cannon. The noise was deafening.

Hook unplugged his ears. "Listen, lads!" he shouted them down. They turned dutifully, even those who had been working Peter along the dreaded plank. Hook's smile could melt butter. "I have made an agreement in the interests of good sportsmanship and so on and so forth. This pitiful specimen"—he gestured disdainfully at Peter—"this degenerate pretender shall have three days to prepare himself to do battle with me, at which time he shall return here and face judgment by the blade."

"Cap'n says take up the flint and powder, men, and wave the bloody shirt!" yelled Smee. "It's going to be—"

Hook clapped a hand over his mouth. "My show, Smee." He smiled anew. "It's going to be a perfectly wonderful war, gentlemen. A war to the death between Hook and Pan."

"A war to the death!" repeated Smee through the captain's fingers.

"Or if not"—Hook sniffed with a glance toward the prisons on the docks—"Pan's rug rats perish in the most horrible fashion I can devise."

Smee bounded forward. "A toast! To the ultimate battle—Hook against Pan!"

Hook's smile threatened to rival the crocodile's. "Children admitted free, of course."

The pirates drank from flagons of ale and rum pouches, cheering lustily, pounding fists and glasses on the ship's railing. "Hook! Hook! Hook!"

The captain watched Peter inch his way back along the plank toward the safety of the deck, relief etched in his chubby features. He can't help being pitiful, it seems, Hook thought, sighing. He hoped this fat, old Pan would find a way to offer him some small challenge. It wouldn't be good form, after all, to kill him the way he was.

He strode briskly to the end of the plank to confront his enemy a final time. "Go on, whoever or whatever you are." He sneered. "Get out of my sight. Fly, why don't you? Fly your fat carcass off my ship!"

He jumped up and down on the plank furiously, sending Peter catapulting into the air.

"But I can't!" Peter Banning wailed. "I don't know how!"

Tinkerbell flitted swiftly into view. "Come on, Peter," she urged. "You've got to! Think a happy thought!"

Peter landed uncertainly on the plank again, balanced precariously above the waves. "Now?"

"Of course, now! Think of Christmas!"

A pirate hit the end of the plank a final time. Peter lost what remained of his composure and tumbled away. Down he went, Tink yelling after him, and disappeared in a splash.

"You really can't fly?" Tink cried in despair. "Then swim, Peter! You can swim, can't you?"

"Doubtful," murmured Hook, peering down.

Peter's face could be momentarily seen beneath the surface of the water, and then it was gone.

"Terrible luck," Hook sympathized with a smile.

Tinkerbell darted toward the water and away again, rushing this way and that. No sign of Peter. When it was clear that he was gone, she burst into tears and disappeared in a flash of light. Hook yawned, growing bored. The whole bargain-making business had been a waste of time. Three days or three years, it wouldn't have made a snail's ear's worth of difference.

Then abruptly, impossibly, Peter resurfaced, cradled in the arms of three shimmering mermaids, each giving him long, deep mermaid kisses, breathing air into his lungs. One after another, they kissed him, over and over again. Then they raised his head clear of the water and sped toward the entrance to the harbor, fishtails propelling them swiftly away.

Hook watched incredulously for a moment, then rolled his eyes and blew a kiss after them. "Pan, luckiest of devils. See you in Hades!"

But before he could turn away, a fourth mermaid leaped from the waters directly in front of him, a shining, graceful woman-fish, paused nose to nose with the scourge of the seven seas, the only man the infamous Barbecue had ever feared, and spat water right in his eye.

As she dived from sight, Hook wiped the water from his face with his sleeve and glowered after her. Intentionally or not, she had put out his cigars.

The Lost Boys
Found

For Peter, waterlogged and exhausted, rescue happened in a dream. He was borne on the crest of the ocean's waves for many leagues, the soft arms of the mermaids wrapped tightly about him, keeping him safe and warm. The fish-women sang to him, their voices sweet and reassuring. The stories they told were of a time and place only dimly remembered and forgotten again as soon as the words were spoken. There was a boy in the stories, a child who refused to grow up, who lived in a place where adventures were the food of life, and no day was complete without at least several. The boy was fearless; he dared anything. He lived in a world of pirates and Indians, of magical happenings, of time suspended and dreams come true. He was a boy who, Peter sensed, he had once known.

Somewhere along the way the remnants of his pirate garb disappeared and with them his immediate memory of why he had ever worn them.

His journey ended at a column of rock that lifted out of the ocean like a massive pillar, and the mermaids placed him in a giant clamshell tied to a rope that ran up through its center. The clamshell closed about Peter, and he felt himself rising, slowly, steadily, rocking gently in his cocoon. When his ascent was complete, the clamshell's lid cranked open, and he was tossed like a coin on which a wish had been made, landing with an *oomph* on a grassy bank.

His eyes fluttered open. The waters of a small, clear lagoon sparkled behind him. The clamshell was gone. The mermaids were gone. Their memory was all that remained, and he was already starting to wonder if he might not have imagined the whole thing.

Taking a deep breath, he staggered to his feet, water dripping from his hair onto his face, and from his clothing to the ground. He brushed at himself futilely, then lifted his gaze to look around.

His breath caught in his throat. He stood at the top of the rock column of his dream, hundreds of feet above the ocean, so far up that it seemed the clouds in the sky might pass close enough to brush his hand. The atoll stood just off the coast of the island to which he had been carried, surrounded by azure waters, white foam, and the glistening backs of waves. Mountain peaks rose from the island's spine, their tips white with new snow. Twin rainbows arced from a series of waterfalls into the sea. Far below and miles away, hunkered down within its protective cove, was the pirate town of James Hook. Farther still, where the sky and ocean met in a perfect horizontal line, the sun was a flare of gold and purple light. The afternoon was waning. Sunset approached.

Peter glanced skyward and was astonished to find not one, but three moons, one white, one peach, and the last pale rose. They shared the sky comfortably, as if they might actually belong.

And behind Peter, away from the lagoon and at the exact center of the atoll, stood the largest tree he had ever seen in his life—a great, gnarled, old forest denizen somehow removed to this rock, jutting toward the sky, its limbs stretched forth as if in supplication. It might have been a maple or an oak or a mix of each and still it would have to have been something more. It was like no tree that Peter had ever seen.

It was like something imagined in boyhood.

Or in a dream.

Nevertree. The wind whispered the name in his ear.

He took a step toward the tree, past a patch of rose-tipped yellow flowers that leaned over curiously to sniff at him. He jumped away in disbelief. The flowers sneezed. What is this? He took another tentative step, and another, moving away from the flowers. Flowers that sniff? That sneeze?

He was still wrestling with the concept when he stepped into a rope snare that closed about his ankles, yanked him from his feet, and hoisted him upside down high into the network of tree limbs. His pockets emptied—business and credit cards, wallet, keys, and loose change all falling to the ground below. His breath left him in a gasp, and he flailed in an effort to right himself. But the rope went taut, and he was left hanging helplessly.

I don't believe this, he announced to himself.

He hung there for a moment, trying to decide what to do. Finally, he managed after repeated attempts to jacknife upward far enough to catch hold of his own legs (he really was going to have to get into an exercise program) and from there pulled himself up until he could reach the rope that bound him. Looking vaguely like an oversized tetherball, he began working to swing himself toward a nearby branch that appeared heavy enough to offer support.

That was when he saw the clock. It was hanging from the branch he was trying to grasp, an ornate, scrolled, wood-carved affair that looked as if it had once been the top of a grandfather clock in an English manor house. The clock face was inlaid with gold and silver, and there was an attractive arrangement of flowering vines hanging down about its shell and works.

Peter snatched at the branch from which the clock hung, catching hold finally, causing it to shake violently. From inside the clock came an "Oh!"

Then the clock face swung open and out flew Tink, roused from the shell that served as her bed, her eyes darting this way and that before finally settling on Peter and growing instantly to twice their normal size.

"You're alive!" she gasped.

And everything came back to Peter in a rush, the floodgates of his memory opened in that instant's time.

"Tink! I've got to save Maggie and Jack! Get me out of this trap!"

But Tink was too busy flitting back and forth across his

cheek, pecking at him with her faerie lips, crying out joyfully, "You're alive, you're alive!"

"Yes, it was mermaids, I think. I'm not sure really. Are there mermaids here?" He didn't want to make too much of it at this point. "But my kids, Tink. What can I do? How can I fight Hook? I can't! Look at me! I'm a mess! I'm fat and out of shape, I can't fight my own shadow, let alone some pirate—"

"The Lost Boys!" she exclaimed, as if that answered everything. "This is the Nevertree, Peter! This is their home! And you'll need them if you're to do anything about Hook! All we have to do is make them believe that you're the Pan!"

Peter groaned. "But I'm not! I'm Peter Banning!"

"Ha! That's today! You don't look it yet maybe, but you're more Pan than you think! You'll deal with Hook and get your children back. I promise you will! You wait and see!"

Up she flew to where the rope snare bound his legs, produced a pair of tiny scissors, and began to snip.

Peter cast a hurried glance down—which was a long way. "Wait, I don't think—" he started to say, and then the rope parted and he fell with a long, frightened cry to land flat on his back in a bed of moss, the breath and the sense knocked from his body.

"He's back, he's back!" he heard Tink cry out sharply, and caught a fuzzy glimpse of her darting upward into the limbs of the great old tree. "Lost Boys, come out! It's the Pan! He's back!"

Peter blinked to clear his vision. From his vantage point beneath the Nevertree, looking up into a web of limbs that seemed to stretch on forever, he watched in amazement at what happened next.

As Tink flitted from branch to branch, a flash of light against the bark and leaves in the shadows of the fading afternoon, the Nevertree came alive. Branches shook, bells sounded, whistles blew, chimes rang, and doors slammed open. Boys appeared from everywhere, as quick and nimble as cats. The first had long blond hair, a vest and top hat, and carried an antler horn. He blew into it instantly, a deep, lowing call that seemed to trigger everything else. Out of the cacophony the boys appeared, a ragged bunch dressed in every form of vestment imaginable, flashes of motion and color as they filled the Nevertree and began to descend, yelling "Pan! Pan!" Down they came, on vines and ropes, on slides formed of hollow logs and bark, from nets lowered on winches, in buckets, and along ramps.

Peter shoved himself up on his elbows, astonished at their energy. Now the ground was opening up as Lost Boys emerged from underground tunnels and caves, exiting through large tufts of saw grass, stumps, and tree roots, popping up like weeds in summer heat. Ten, fifteen, twenty at least, materializing from everywhere. They were all shapes and sizes and colors, bright-eyed and eager every last one of them, hands and arms waving as they shouted out for the Pan.

A moment later they were gathered about him. Peter climbed unsteadily to his knees to face them. They backed away a step, staring, then all of them began talking at once.

"Is it him? Lemme see. That's really Pan?" some said.

"Too old and fat. He's a grown-up! He's not Pan!" declared others.

"I'm Peter Banning," he ventured.

Immediately they began shouting their names back at him, almost like challenge. Ace, the blond kid with the antler horn. Don't Ask, wearing a tie, a shirt with a round collar, and a fifties kind of blue and white plaid jacket. Latchboy, a round-cheeked little fellow with curly red hair and a winning smile. No Nap, ebony-skinned and wearing striped coveralls and a newsboy cap. Pockets, a dark, sweet-looking youth with huge brown eyes and a plaid, floppy cap and pockets sewn everywhere on his red coveralls. Too Small, who really was, possessing an uncertain smile and curly brown hair the same color as Jack's.

Like Jack's, Peter thought in despair.

And finally Thud Butt, who arrived in a barrel, bursting out of it with a *whommph* that left everyone gasping, a rotund, exuberant kid with a tam, his chubby face puffing as he emerged, clutching what appeared at first glance to be some sort of medical chart with a diagram of a human figure and arrows pointing to various parts of the body.

There were others as well, more names than Peter could remember or even hear in the clamor. He stared from face to face, from outfit to outfit. Children! All boys, the Lost Boys.

Carrying weapons, he noticed suddenly. Knives, tomahawks, slings and bows of all shapes and sizes. And rattles! Baby rattles! Each Lost Boy wore one, proudly displayed about his neck or from his belt or wherever. Peter couldn't believe it.

"Tell us a story, tell us a story!" some were shouting now, noticeably the smaller ones.

But others were beginning to ask, "What would Rufio say? What about Rufio?"

Tink flashed into view, zipping among them, saying, "Listen to me! It's him! It's really the Pan!"

Then a piercing cry sounded, like the crowing of a cock at sunrise, fierce and proud. The Lost Boys turned as one, crying out "Rufio!"

Instantly Tink flashed to Peter. "Rufio's here. He's leader now, and he'll be hard to convince. You don't know about Rufio, do you?" She pursed her lips thoughtfully.

There was a flash of movement in the limbs overhead, far out at the edges of the Nevertree. Something that resembled a sailboard, its cloth sail colored with pictures, whipped like a roller coaster down a wooden track along a ridge line backing the Nevertree, a boy mounted at the mast. In one hand he held the slim, golden sword that had once belonged to Peter Pan. As the sailboard reached a bend in the track the boy vaulted off, diving into the wind, arms outspread. Down he plummeted, holding his body arched, then at the last minute reached out to grab a trailing vine, pulled out of his dive, and dropped gracefully into the midst of the Lost Boys, arms and sword raised triumphantly.

"Rufio! Rufio!" the Lost Boys cheered.

He was bigger than the others, coffee-skinned with a broad, confident smile, black hair styled in punkish fashion and dyed with red stripes. He wore pants and shirt fringed with red and black buckskin strips and red boots. Leather bracelets were strapped to his wrist and a large knife was sheathed at his belt.

His smile remained in place as the cheers continued, then faded quickly as he turned to face Peter.

Peter was already moving, striding forward, finger pointing. He was shaking with anger. "Okay, mister, you've had your fun. Now put that thing down before you poke somebody's eye out! Don't you know how dangerous that stunt was? My God! You fell from a very high place with a sword in your hand! This is ridiculous preadolescent anarchy! Where are your parents? I want to talk to whoever's in charge!"

Most reactions we can find ways to control, no matter the situation. Only a few are so explosive that nothing short of an iron band across the mouth will prevent them from bursting forth. Such, unfortunately, was the case with Peter Banning's sense of Parental Responsibility.

Tink flashed in front of his eyes, hissing, "No, Peter, no!"

Rufio brought the sword up threateningly. "I'm in charge."

Peter drew up short. "A kid? I want to speak to a grown-up—and I mean right now!"

Rufio's frown had turned dangerous. "All grown-ups are pirates. We kill pirates."

Peter drew himself up. "Well, I'm not a pirate. It happens that I'm a lawyer!"

A howl went up from the Lost Boys. Rufio thrust his sword into the air. "Kill the lawyer!" he cried.

The chant rose from every quarter. Peter hesitated only long enough to admit to himself that quite possibly he had said the wrong thing, and then he was off and running.

"Kill the lawyer! Kill the lawyer!"

Peter fled into a tunnel and found himself on the sailboard track. He scrambled along, not caring where he was going, knowing only that he had once read *Lord of the Flies,* remembering how things had turned out there. He called desperately for Tink—perhaps she could make things right—but there was no response. The shouts and cries of the Lost Boys followed after him, spurring him on. He emerged from the tunnel on a span of track that bridged a grassy stretch close by the lagoon and a waterfall.

Thud! Thud!

He looked down to find arrows sticking out of him. Or, rather, sticking to him—knobby things that seemed to have adhered to the front of his dress shirt. One was dangling from his crotch.

"I've been shot!" he exclaimed in horror.

A ragged cheer rose from a small group of Lost Boys gathered below.

"Heart Stopper, Rib Tickler, Barf Button, and Nut-cracker!" declared Don't Ask, plaid-jacketed arm pointing to the diagram held by Thud Butt. There were names and point totals indicating a score for every hit.

Peter examined himself. "What is this stuff?" He touched the end of detached arrow experimentally. Glue! How disgusting!

A rolling sound from ahead signaled the arrival of Rufio aboard the coaster. Peter turned and raced back into the tunnel, panting for breath. Cries sounded from that direction, too. Having no choice, he ran on, back the way he had come, emerging from the tunnel to find Latchboy and No Nap running away from him.

"Help, somebody!" cried Latchboy and No Nap. "He's chasing us!"

"I'm not either!" Peter insisted between breaths. "You're chasing me!"

"No," they persisted with small-boy logic, "you're chasing us!" And they dived off the track into the grass.

Twins in tattered, old-fashioned Boy Scout uniforms rushed to intercept Peter, but now Tink appeared, flashing to intercept them, yanking up a vine, which tripped them and knocked them flat.

She buzzed in front of their faces. "He married Wendy's granddaughter! Hook kidnapped his kids! We have to get him in shape to fight!"

The twins stared at each other. "What's she talking about?" they said as one.

The coaster and Rufio caught up with Peter seconds later and bumped him off the track. He sprawled in a heap, gasping for breath. How could this be happening to him? Lost boys cheered all about. Peter dragged himself to his knees—only to discover flowers sniffing at him once again. *Sniff, sniff.* They seemed to like the glue. He slapped them away, struggled up, and began running once more.

Lost Boys charged after him in pursuit, yelling gaily. For them, it was all a game.

"Help me!" howled Peter.

"Help me!" howled the Boys.

Ace rushed to the forefront of the pack, notched an arrow in place on his bowstring, aimed, and fired. The arrow fastened onto Peter's rear, bobbing as he ran.

"Poop Shoot—five thousand!" Ace cried jubilantly, cocking back his top hat.

Don't Ask propelled Thud Butt and the point chart up beside him. "Nope. Butt Tick—two hundred."

Ace whirled about angrily. "I complain of you!"

"I double complain of you!" Don't Ask snapped back.

Tink darted between them and sent the point chart spinning. "I complain of all of you! Pan's your captain! He needs you!"

Up ahead, Rufio was aiming a slingshot at a fleeing Peter. Tink flew to stop him, grabbing his red v-tipped black hair and pulling him to the ground. "Rufio, you're the best with a sword! Teach him! We have to make him remember who he is!"

But her efforts were for naught. The Lost Boys continued in pursuit, harrying Peter through a bamboo gate that led to the Nevertree's inner sanctuary. Bursting through the graffiti-covered gate, his strength almost gone, his breath so short he was certain he was on the verge of a major heart attack, he found himself trapped and encircled by Lost Boys. Many of the Boys were on makeshift skateboards and roller skates now, darting and dodging about him, zipping up and down banked walls, yelling and whooping and jumping about. Someone with a basketball dribbled past. Someone leaped on a trampoline, vaulting over his head. Vines swung down with Lost Boys attached. Peter ran this way and that, but there was no escape.

Finally, he turned back to the entrance he had come through—only to find Rufio standing atop the bamboo gate, waiting. Down the leader of the Lost Boys leaped, his sword drawn and held high. Peter faltered, stumbled and gave it up.

Rufio came to a skidding halt before him and tapped the sword playfully on his shoulder. "You're dead, jollymon."

Peter blinked. "What the heck?

Now Ace swung down as well, clutching a vine. He released his grip as he landed, brought up his war club, and tapped Peter a second time.

"Bangerang!" he yelled.

Rufio grabbed an astonished Peter and shoved him into the fence. Peter tried to climb, completely confused now, beginning to think he was in a madhouse. He grappled unsuccessfully with the bamboo and ended up sliding down again, trapped as the Lost Boys closed about, war clubs thumping, feet stamping, voices taunting and howling in victory.

Rufio jerked Peter back to his feet contemptuously. "Look, if you're the Pan, prove it. Let's see you fly!"

There was a whisper of "fly, fly," which grew quickly to a shout. "Fly! Fly! Fly!" they all cried, and waited expectantly.

Peter stared back helplessly.

"Can you fight, then?" demanded Rufio.

The Lost Boys drew their swords and knives and pointed them at Peter. Ace shoved a broadsword into Peter's hands. Peter stood holding it, a blank look on his face, until Rufio knocked it away.

"Last question, Pops," declared Rufio. "Can you crow?"

Peter took a deep breath and let out a sound that closely resembled a chicken's cluck. Rufio plugged his ears in disgust. Lost Boys groaned and jeered.

Tink reappeared, confronting them all. "Silly asses! I could have told you he can't do any of those things! He can't even play simple games! He's forgotten how! What matters is that Hook's got his kids, and I've got three days to get him ready to fight the captain! He needs everyone's help!"

From somewhere among the sea of Lost Boy faces came a low, astonished voice. "Peter Pan's got kids?"

"A family, responsibilities, and a few extra pounds," Tink advised solemnly. "But he's still our Pan."

Rufio growled something unintelligible, backed the Lost Boys away from the fence, and drew a line in the earth with his sword. He crossed the line to stand alone and pointed at Peter.

"He can't fly, fight, or crow—so any of you says this ain't the Pan, cross over to me!"

Peter immediately started across the line, but Tink grabbed him by his suspenders and yanked him back. "You're embarrassing me!" she snapped.

The Lost Boys looked from Rufio to Peter and back again and then crossed the line one by one until only Pockets was left, peering out at Peter from under his floppy hat. He approached hesitantly, reached up to tug on Peter's shirt, and kept doing so until Peter bent down so that they were face-to-face. Solemnly, Pockets stared into Peter's crumpled, worn visage, then methodically began to smooth out the wrinkles and lines, to push back the sagging cheeks and chin, to knead and prod the flesh of Peter's face. Suddenly he stopped, hands held carefully in place, and a huge smile appeared.

"Oh, there you are, Peder," he announced.

Several of the Lost Boys pushed forward, peering at the rearranged features intently.

"Is it him?" they whispered to one another. "Is it the Pan? Peter, is it you?"

"Mfftt, mmrrwft," said Peter, his mouth distorted.

"But Peter, you've grown up!" complained Latchboy. "You promised never to grow old!"

"His nose got real big, didn't it?" observed Don't Ask.

"Welcome back to Neverland, Pan the Man," said Too Small.

There was hope in each face, and it spread quickly to the faces of those still standing with Rufio on the other side of the line. They began to edge forward.

Rufio alone refused to be swayed, anger flaring in his dark eyes. "Don't listen to that gnat-brained faerie and that sag-bellied grown-up. I got Pan's sword. I'm the Pan now. You think this guy's gonna take it away from me?"

Ace, No Nap, Thud Butt, and Latchboy crossed back to Rufio.

"Wait," said Pockets. "If Tink bleeves, mebbe he iz."

The four Lost Boys crossed back to Peter.

"You gonna follow this drooler against Capytan Hook?"

Everyone crossed back to Rufio this time, save for Pockets, Thud Butt, and Too Small.

"Whads he doin' here if he's nod Peder Pan, huh?" asked Pockets solemnly. "He don't look habby here. Who are dose kidz Hook's got? Gib him a chancz."

Peter straightened, alone with his three supporters. "Those *are* my children, and Hook is going to kill them unless I do something to stop it. Help me, please!"

Pockets stared up at him. "You said the p-word," he whispered with a frown.

Shadows were closing fast about the courtyard now, laying down their nighttime patterns through the branches of the Nevertree. The sun was almost gone, sunk so far into the ocean's waters that it was little more than a glaze of orange frosting melting rapidly away. Tink flew overhead in the silence, lighting lanterns to chase the dark. The Lost Boys and Peter watched wordlessly.

When she was finished, she settled comfortably on Peter's shoulder. "When Peter Pan's away," she said solemnly, "don't you always ask the same question: What would Peter do?"

The eyes of the Lost Boys went wide. "Yeah, what would Peter do?" they repeated the words. "Let's do what Peter would do!" Frowns and chin rubbing. "What *would* Peter do?"

"I know, I know!" Ace exclaimed excitedly. "He'd get the Lost Boys back!"

"But aren't you the Lost Boys?" Peter asked.

"Oh, yeah," agreed Don't Ask, frowning. Then he brightened. "But not all. Hook's got lots of us. He snags us when we're not looking. Then he shoots us out of cannons."

"And chains us to rocks and lets the tide roll over our heads," Latchboy added.

"Or makes us walk the plank!" declared Ace.

"The little ones have to *crawl*!" whispered Too Small. He glanced cautiously at Rufio. "We're afraid to rescue them without the Pan." His voice got very quiet. "Even Rufio."

Rufio spat. "Survival of the fittest. Hook gets the slow ones. Slow legs, slow minds. We're better off without 'em."

Peter glanced around, seeing for the first time since they had begun chasing him the children hidden beneath the garish outfits and dirt, seeing the uncertainty mirrored in their eyes, doubts of who they were and of how to stay that way. Whispers passed from mouth to mouth in the darkness.

They're all I've got, he realized helplessly. Kids. But like it or not, I need them if I want to save Jack and Maggie.

He stepped away from the bamboo fence cautiously. "Look, I got off on the wrong foot with you. I admit that." He took a deep breath. "Things are turned a little upside down here, but I'm getting used to it now. And I can tell you this—I'll do whatever it takes to save my kids. If I have to eat crow, I'll eat crow."

Thud Butt tugged at his sleeve. "You don't have to eat crow, Peter," he said. "You just have to crow crow."

"Okay, fine. I'll crow crow. I'll do anything I have to do. If I have to fight, I'll fight. If I have to fly, I'll fly. . . ." He trailed off, reconsidering. "Or I could run real fast," he muttered. "I could at least do that."

Pockets grinned up at him. "Yup! Peder would say that! Yes, he would! Yes, he would!"

Peter grinned back.

Rufio sneered, threw up his hands, and walked away.

The rest of the Lost Boys shuffled after him, muttering uncertainly among themselves. Finally only Pockets remained.

"C'mon, Peder," he said quietly, and beckoned.

Chastened and bone weary, Peter followed. It was clear he had convinced nobody.

The Ultimate Revenge

The sun disappeared finally, dropping beneath the horizon, sinking into the ocean's vast waters, and the dusk faded to a summer night's darkness—warm, soft, and filled with pungent smells and intriguing sounds. The darkness was a blanket of hidden life that buzzed and flitted and crept about, a world of mystery and adventure that small boys searched for eagerly in their dreams.

Aboard the *Jolly Roger*, Captain Hook was thinking about one small boy in particular—or, rather, one small boy who had grown up.

"How could he do this to me?" he muttered to himself disconsolately.

He was seated in his cabin at the dinner table. All about him lay the ill-gotten gains of his many conquests—gold, silver, and jewels in all shapes and sizes; furniture stolen from kings and queens of first-rate nations; tapestries and paintings from the private collections of greedy men from six (or was it seven?) continents; hand-crafted weapons used by gentlemen to murder one another; bolts of silks and English wool from garment districts and boutiques; brass instruments of navigation, some of them rumored to have belonged to Columbus; and leather-bound books by the world's foremost authors—Sir James Barrie was one of his favorites.

At the back of the room sat a three-dimensional map of Neverland, complete down to the last detail, including replicas of his ship and the pirate town, of the Indian village, of the Mermaid lagoon, and even of the Nevertree, the whole of it floating in a pool of real water.

But Hook had no eye this night for any of it. He sat staring blankly at the lavish, steaming dinner Smee had just set before him. Roast warthog, Indian-skin corn, tender new potatoes, pirate jelly sprinkled with fish eggs, and good-form crumb cake—all of them his favorites. Smee stood close at hand, awaiting approval, the hopeful smile pasted across his chubby face threatening to falter with the passing of each second.

Finally Hook bent to sniff at the food, took fork in hand, prepared to take a bite, and then stopped. He placed the fork back on the plate.

"How can I eat!" he lamented. "Smee, do you know what it's like to look forward to something so badly that you can taste it? Do you have any idea what it's like to anticipate an event with all your heart and soul?"

Smee thought he might, but he wasn't sure what sort of answer the captain was looking for. Experience had taught him that with Hook if you didn't know the correct answer, it was best not to speak.

Hook was still staring at the table. "The day before yesterday I couldn't sleep, so great was my anticipation. I wished to sleep, of course—that would have made the next day come quicker. Yesterday, I could only think of how long it would be until today. And today? Today I was knotted into knots, all jumbled up inside. The sheer, unbearable anticipation, Smee! Pan's arrival and the commencement of my glorious war!"

A smile crossed his features and his brown eyes lit up with delight. For an instant the wrinkles of despair departed and he was the old Hook, cunning and ruthless.

Then the brightness departed, and the frustration returned. Gloom built upon his brow until it was a thunderhead. Up he rose with a roar, and his claw raked the wooden surface of the table before him in fury.

"I'm so disappointed! I hate being disappointed! I hate Neverland! I hate everything!" His voice rose to a scream. "But most of all I hate Peter Pan!"

He wheeled from the table and yanked a gold-inlaid, diamond-studded dueling pistol from his sash.

"Not again," groaned Smee.

"My life is over!" Hook declaimed dramatically. "I'm not going to have my war! Pan stole it! My lovely, glorious war! I could smell the cannons and taste the steel! Now it's gone! My war is gone!"

He put the barrel of the pistol to his heart and cocked the hammer.

"Cap'n, stop that," scolded Smee, hands waving.

Hook straightened, rising to his full height. "There will be no stopping me this time, Smee. Farewell!"

His jaw jutted forth and his finger tightened about the trigger. His eyes squinched shut, but he managed to peek surreptitiously out of the corners. Seeing Smee hesitate, he screamed, "Smeeee!"

Smee lunged, jammed his finger between the cap and hammer as the trigger released, and yelled in pain. Hook hissed in response, pried the offending finger loose, and jammed the barrel of the pistol into Smee's nose. Smee grabbed the gun with both hands, trying to turn the barrel away. Around and around they danced, grappling with the pistol and each other.

"I want to die!" howled Hook. "There's no more adventure in Neverland! I've been cursed with a fat Pan! Death is all that remains for me!"

"Cap'n, that's not the answer, Cap'n," Smee huffed into the pistol barrel.

They careened into the dinner table and toppled onto it. The table held them for only an instant, then collapsed, wood splinters flying everywhere. Hook's pistol discharged with a deafening roar. Smee, fortunately, had moved the barrel off his nose. The pistol ball whistled past his ear, struck the replica of the *Jolly Roger* at anchor, and sank her on the spot. Hook and Smee stared in shock as the tiny ship disappeared in a cloud of bubbles. They faced each other, still locked together in a tangle of arms and legs, panting from their struggle.

"Even this," whispered Hook, "isn't as much fun as it used to be."

He disengaged himself, rose, brushed away the crumbs

and smoothed the wrinkles from his coat, straightened his mustaches, righted his chair, seated himself, and began the painstaking process of reloading the pistol.

Smee rolled back his eyes, exhaled wearily, and followed his captain up from the floor. There was crumb cake in his beard and jam on the end of his nose. When the reloading process was complete, Smee reached over quickly—trying not to appear too anxious—and extracted the weapon from the captain's hand. Patting the other solicitously, he placed the pistol in the drawer of the Queen Anne bureau and locked it safely away.

"There now, Cap'n," he said soothingly. "Things will look better in the mawnin'. Let's get you off to sleep. Smee will tuck you in. That's a good cap'n. You know you look a Marley poop without your proper rest."

Hook looked up gratefully, the weariness apparent in his eyes. Smee moved to a large wooden crank set in the wall and began to turn. Slowly Hook's bed lowered out of the ceiling, settling in place finally over the map of Neverland.

Smee crossed back again. "Now, I ask you," he posited. "What kind of world would it be without Captain Hook? Aye?"

He led Hook across the room like a small child and sat him down on the edge of the bed.

"Good form, Smee," Hook announced softly, something vaguely akin to gratitude in his eyes. "What would the world be like without Captain Hook?"

And overcome by a sudden rush of emotions, he clasped Smee to him, hugging him as he would a long-lost friend— had he any.

Smee disengaged himself carefully, one eye on Hook's claw. "Cap'n, methinks you need a little mischief to take yer mind off this Pan business."

Nose to nose, they stared at each other. Smee reached up to lift off Hook's tricorne, then bent down to pull off his boots. Hook lost almost a foot of height in the bargain.

"First thing tomorrow mawnin' let's you and me go shoot some Lost Boys out of Long Tom. That should do the trick."

Long Tom was the monstrous cannon mounted on the aft deck. It was Hook's favorite weapon. Hook thought it over for a moment, then shook is head dejectedly.

"We can always kill Lost Boys," he whined. "I don't want to kill Lost Boys. I want to kill Pan!"

Smee worked the buttons loose on the captain's coat and slipped the garment from his shoulders. Within was a framework of padding designed to make the captain appear twice his real size, brawny and tough. Bereft of it as he was now, sitting hunched over on the bed, he looked very small indeed.

"Don't torture yourself, Cap'n," Smee went on, oblivious of what he had seen countless times before. "It doesn't do a skewer's worth of good. Besides, you can't let the men see you this way, now, can you?" He paused in his endeavors. "Lookit the bright side, Cap'n. You still get to deep-six his ruddy curtain climbers."

Hook shook his ebony locks, so that they swished like snakes. "Oh, Smee, terribly bad form. Terribly bad. To kill the defenseless children of a defenseless foe? I should think you would know better."

Smee shrugged, bent close, and began pulling off Hook's bushy eyebrows.

"Gently, gently," Hook admonished.

"Quickly," Smee replied, and yanked them free. "Better a sharp stab than a lingrin' pain, you always say."

Hook grimaced. "Don't quote me, Smee." He rubbed the nearly hairless patches of skin that remained. "Oh, I wish I could devise the most lingering of pains for Peter Pan!"

Smee considered the prospect as he lifted Hook's wig from his head. Hook was almost bald beneath. Sitting there bereft of his hat, hair, eyebrows, padded coat, and boots, he had the look of a frail, wizened Lost Boy. Smee gathered up the captain's discarded clothing and carried it behind the dressing screen at the far end of the room.

Suddenly he stopped dead, his shadow behind the screen straightening. "Sir! Lightnin' just struck me brains! Cap'n, you could make the little buggers like—no, mo'rn like—

you could make 'em love you! Love you like, like . . .''
Here, words failed him.

Hook buried his head in his hands, dejected anew. "No, no, Smee. No little children love me."

He peeked through his fingers at the screen concealing Smee, reached surreptitiously beneath the pillow on his bed, and removed a small key. Slipping the key into the bureau lock, he turned it, pulled open the drawer, and removed his pistol. Hand on the butt, hammer cocked once more, he placed the barrel to his heart.

Behind the screen, Smee was eyeing Hook's boots. With a cautious glance over his shoulder, he slipped them on. "Cap'n, that's the point! The ultimate revenge, doncha see! Pan's kids in love with Cap'n Hook! The perfect payback!"

Hook looked up slowly, thinking. His forehead furrowed, adding ten years to his apparent age. The pistol lowered. Just maybe . . .

Smee, busy behind the screen trying on the captain's coat, turned to admire himself in the mirror. "Can you imagine the look on Pan's face when he returns and finds 'is kids standing beside you!" Smee pirouetted rakishly, the captain's coat flaring. "The two of them ready to fight for the sleaziest sleaze of the seven seas? For Cap'n James Hook? Oh, I tell you, Cap'n, it would be beautiful, it would!"

A light came into Hook's tired eyes. "I like it,' he whispered. "It has a certain symmetry."

"And you'd make a fine father, too, I might add," encouraged Smee, fitting Hook's wig on his head.

"Me?"

"Oh, yes, Cap'n, if I do say so meself."

"Really?" Hook considered the idea. "I do know a little about neglect."

"A very fine father," said Smee, setting Hook's tricorne in place.

Hook leaped to his feet, suddenly animated, and clapped his hands together in delight. "Oh Smee, what a fine idea I've just had! I will not only destroy Pan, but I shall have his own children—except they'll be my children, by the bones of Barbecue—lead the battle against him! I shall be so loved, Smee! James Hook, family man!'' He took a deep breath. ''James Hook, father!''

Smee eyed himself in the mirror, then picked up the cigar holder with its twin stems and placed it in his mouth, puffing contentedly. '' 'Tis the wickedest, prettiest plan I've ever 'eard,'' he declared with a smile.

The object of all this villainy was miles away, curled in a ball in the crook of a limb not too high up in the branches of the Nevertree, cold and hungry and discouraged. All around him the Lost Boys were sleeping, each of them sheltered in the tree house that had been built for him when he had come to Neverland. There was no house for Peter, of course; he had arrived too late to have one built, and besides he wasn't a Lost Boy. He wasn't anything much at all, he thought dismally. He was odd man out in this ridiculous world.

Overhead, Neverland's moons hung like giant Japanese lanterns against the night sky, crowding so close that they seemed in danger of falling into the ocean, their brilliant light hiding the stars beyond. Peter stared at the moons and wondered what had become of Moira and home. He wondered if he would ever see either again.

A light flashed out of the darkness and Tink settled beside him. He looked up at her, lost and lonely and frightened. In a bizarre and unsettling world, she had become the most familiar thing. She saw what was mirrored in his eyes and gave him an encouraging smile.

''Believe your eyes, Peter,'' she whispered. ''Believe in faeries and Lost Boys and three suns and six moons. It will be all right, if you do.'' She bent close. ''Search inside yourself for one, pure, innocent thought and hold on to it. Because what used to make you happy will make you fly. Will you try, Peter?''

Peter stared at her, trying to comprehend. Finally, he said, ''If all this is real, was the rest of my life a dream?''

She shrugged. Faeries do not engage in philosophical discussions, it's said. ''What used to make you happy will make you fly,'' she repeated, preferring practical advice.

Peter nodded wearily and closed his eyes. "Okay, Tink. I'll try."

Tinkerbell waited as his breathing slowed. When sleep claimed him, she came forward cautiously, leaned upward from where she stood on his chest, and stole a kiss from his lips. Then she turned about and crawled inside his shirt, a tiny glow working its way about. Finally she found a comfortable spot close to the collar and settled in. Peter had begun to snore. She joined him, her own snores little more than tiny breaths. Her light pulsed with each one, fading gradually as she, too, fell asleep.

Nearby, sitting cross-legged at the entrance to his own house, Rufio watched the tiny light wink out. A scowl lined his smooth features. He didn't like this imitation Pan, this fat, old grown-up trying to steal what was his. Jealousy wormed its way through him. He intended to be rid of this intruder as quickly as possible.

He pulled the Pan sword close against him, and his eyes were as bright as fire in the dark.

One by one the lights of the Nevertree went out, extinguished by the faeries who kept night watch as they flitted down through the branches in search of dewdrops to drink and ladybugs to ride and tiny rainbow crystals to treasure. The lights disappeared in their wake, leaving only the moons of white and peach and pale rose to color the dark. Neverland drifted away into children's dreams—to the belief that kept it timeless, to the promise that kept it young.

Why Parents
Hate
Their Children

It was a rejuvenated Captain Hook who had Jack and Maggie brought to his cabin the following morning. Gone was the gloom that had beset him the evening prior, gone the despair and disconsolation. A smile wreathed his angular face, as broad and inviting as a crocodile's (though neither Hook nor any self-respecting crocodile would have appreciated the comparison, I am sure). He was dressed in full regalia—boots shined, coat brushed, wig curled, tricorne set carefully in place. He wore new lace at his throat and sleeves, and his hook gleamed wickedly. The room was restored to its former elegance as well, the furniture righted, the remnants of dinner cleared away, the shattered dining table and the blasted replica of the *Jolly Roger* replaced, and the few pictures knocked askew straightened or rehung.

Hook was pleased. It had taken Smee hours to accomplish all this, but it had been worth it.

The captain was at his craftiest this day. There was an inevitability about his plan that gave him an unshakable confidence as he stood waiting at the door, hands clasped behind his back, a benevolent look fixed upon his countenance. Pan's children turned against him—it was delicious. Pan's children made to love Captain Hook—it was charming. Best of all, it was devious.

Hook's smile broadened even further as Smee ushered the children in. A flush of expectation colored his bony cheeks.

"Good morning, children!" he greeted effusively, and tried not to brandish the hook. "Sit down, right over there."

116

Smee propelled the little dears across the room—Hook could not help noticing their undisguised interest in the map of Neverland—to the chairs and desks that had been set up for them facing Hook's own gilt-edged walnut desk. Maggie's chin was barely above her desktop. Jack was already squirming. Neither looked the least bit comfortable with the situation.

Hook moved over to stand in front of a chalkboard that had been unearthed from one of his warehouses. It was two-sided and revolved on pins. The side facing the children was blank.

"Do you know why you're here, children?" he asked solicitously.

They shook their heads.

"You are here to attend school," he announced.

"What sort of school?" Maggie asked suspiciously.

Hook drew himself up. "The school of life, my dear," he replied grandly. Then he cocked his hook admonishingly. "Henceforth, if you wish to speak, you will raise your hand."

"You're not a teacher!" Maggie declared defiantly.

Smee struck the edge of the desk with the flat of a ruler and Maggie jumped a foot. Hook smiled benignly. "Order, now. You don't want me to have to put you on detention, do you? Detention can be most unpleasant."

He reached back to the chalkboard, gave it a sharp spin, and then caught it with the reverse side facing forward.

Jack and Maggie stared. The chalkboard read:

WHY PARENTS HATE THEIR CHILDREN

Hook turned back again. "Now pay attention, class. We have a lot to cover in today's lesson. Which is: Why Parents Hate Their Children."

As he turned back to the board Maggie leaned over to Jack and whispered, "Parents don't hate their children!"

Out of the corner of his eye Hook watched the boy. Jack seemed less certain of this than his sister. He whispered

something back. Hook couldn't hear what it was, but he
didn't need to, judging by Maggie's reaction.

"They don't!" she insisted angrily. She seemed to search
her memory for proof, then exclaimed hurriedly, "Doesn't
Mommy read us a story every night?"

Hook turned slowly, still smiling, and pointed to Maggie.

"You, the cute little urchin in the front row. Won't you
share your thoughts with the whole class?"

He waved his hand expansively as if there were others
besides the two, all waiting to hear what Maggie had to say.
The little girl was white-faced, but her jaw stuck out
determinedly.

"I said Mommy reads to us every night because she loves
us very much!" she declared loudly.

Hook feigned astonishment. "Loves you?" He repeated
the words as if they lacked validity. He glanced knowingly
at his bosun. "That's the l-word, isn't it, Smee?"

Smee shook his head reprovingly. Hook came forward to
stand before the children, then scraped his hook slowly,
deliberately down the middle of the desktop.

"Love? No, I think not. She reads to you to stupefy you,
to lull you to sleep so that she can sit down for three measly
minutes—alone—without you and your mindless, inex-
haustible, unstoppable, repetitive, nagging demands!"
Hook cocked his head and began to mimic, " 'He took my
toy! She hid my bear! Give me my cookie! I want to potty!
I want to stay up!' I want, I want, I want—me, me, me,
mine, mine, mine! Now, now, now!" His voice lowered.
"Mommy and Daddy have to listen to it all day long and
they *hate* it! They tell you stories to SHUT YOU UP!"

Maggie's lip was trembling. "That's not true." Her
voice lowered. "You're a liar!"

Hook backed away instantly, hand and hook clasped to
his heart. "Me? Lie? Never!" His smile was bright and
hard. "The truth is *way* too much fun, my dear."

He assumed a look of tragic resignation. "Before you
were born, they would stay up all night long just to watch
the sunrise. Then they would sleep until noon. They did

silly things for no reason. They laughed very loud. They
played all sorts of games and sang all sorts of songs. None
of which they do now, do they?''

He paused. ''Before you were born''—he sighed
longingly—''they were so much happier.'' He glanced
quickly at Smee. ''Am I right?''

''Happy as flappin' flounders in the deep blue sea,
Cap'n,'' Smee agreed.

Both children shuddered with recognition of the possibil-
ity that it was true. Hook was exceedingly pleased.

''Can't you see what you've done to them?'' he demanded, a pleading look on his face. ''You've given them
responsibility! You've made Mommy and Daddy grow up!
How could they possibly love you for that?''

A knock on the door brought them all about. Hook
muttered something unintelligible, and the pirate Tickles
stuck his head through hurriedly.

''Cap'n?'' he ventured hesitantly.

''Yes, what is it, Pickles?'' Smee rushed forward to
whisper hurriedly in his ear. ''Very well!'' stormed Hook.
''What is it, *Tickles*?''

The pirate cringed. ''Cap'n, it's time to give the order for
the firing squad!''

Hook brushed him back with a casual wave. Sauntering
over to the door, he opened it wide and bellowed, ''FIRE!''

Flintlocks crashed from somewhere outside and then
there was silence. Jack sat rigid in his chair. Maggie sat
with her eyes closed.

Tickles tried sneaking back through the door without
being seen and came right up against Hook. Belly to belly,
they faced each other.

Hook sniffed. His nose wrinkled in distaste. ''It's a bath
for you tonight, Tickles,'' he hissed, and booted the pirate
back the way he had come.

Hook closed the door without having ever once looked
through it and returned to stand in front of the chalkboard.

''Time for the dreaded pop quiz,'' he announced.

He spun the board once more and this time when it

stopped, he wrote the words "I LOVE YOU." He turned to face the children, waiting until Smee had completed handing out blank sheets of paper. This was really going quite well, he thought delightedly.

"Are we ready, now?" he asked. "All right. What do your parents really mean when they say, 'I love you'?"

Maggie raised her hand excitedly, forgetting momentarily that she had decided she didn't like any of this and wasn't going to play the game. "I know! I know!" She took a deep breath. "They mean we make them really, really, really happy all the time!"

Hook shook his head. "Really, really, really wrong! Sorry, you flunk." He turned to Smee. "Give her an F."

Smee took a quill with red ink and marked a huge F on Maggie's blank sheet of paper.

"Hand me Pan's dossier, Smee," ordered Hook, ignoring the stricken look on her face.

Maggie's face crumpled. "He gave me an F. I never got an F before on anything!"

"Stop complaining," muttered Jack.

Hook was paging through a thick folder that Smee had handed him, shaking his head. "What do we have here? Broken promise after broken promise. What sort of father is he, Jack?" He watched Jack's eyes snap up. "Your father went to little *Maggot's* school play, didn't he? But did he go to your baseball game? No, of course not. He missed the most important event in your young life, didn't he?"

Maggie surged to her feet, screaming. "This isn't a real school! You're not a real teacher! You can't give me an F! You let us go home!"

She charged around the desk and threw herself on Hook, tugging and pulling at his coat.

"Maggie, stop it!" cried Jack, appalled. "Let go of him! He'll just lock you up again! What are you doing?"

"Smee!" Hook shouted, trying unsuccessfully to hold Maggie at arm's length. "Get this little . . ." Words failed him. "Just take her outside for recess, Smee. Let her play with the keelhaul ropes or the gaff hooks or something. Shoo, shoo."

Smee pulled Maggie off the captain, kicking and screaming. "Mustn't depress the cap'n," he advised.

"He loved my school play!" Maggie howled as she was hauled through the cabin door, punching at Smee. "I was terrific! Don't listen to him, Jack! He hates Mommy and Daddy! He wants us to hate them, too! He wants us to forget about them! You've got to always remember, Jack, because Neverland makes you forget! Don't do it! Don't . . ."

And then the cabin door slammed shut and there was absolute silence.

Hook and Jack faced each other wordlessly. Hook smiled. Time to turn up the charm a notch now that the girl was gone. A disruptive influence if ever there was one and of nowhere near as much use as the boy. There was a look in the boy's eyes that Hook recognized.

He bent close. "Well, Jack?"

Jack shifted in his seat. "How did you know about the game?" he muttered.

Hook smiled mysteriously. "I have a very good spyglass." He moved over to Jack's side so that they were both facing the chalkboard. "WHY PARENTS HATE THEIR CHILDREN" faced back at them.

"He's missed every important moment in your life for years, hasn't he, Jack?" Hook said softly, cajolingly. "He's got an excuse for everything, but the fact remains, he's never there. Your sister is too young to realize the truth, but you're not. If he really loved you, wouldn't he be there for you when it counted?"

The room was so quiet Hook could hear the boy breathing. His face was lowered into his chest, his lank brown hair shadowing his elfin features.

Hook placed a hand on his shoulder. "They tell us they love us, Jack, but the proof is in the pudding. Do they show it as well? Are they there when they should be?" He paused, sighed. "It's all so clear, really, when you think it through."

There was a barely perceptible nod. "Jack, Jack." Hook seized on it. "I think you and I have a lot in common." The boy's head lifted, astonishment in his eyes. "Wait, now—

don't be too quick to judge. Hear me out. You look like a
boy with pluck in him. Tell me—is it true what I see in your
eyes?''

He lifted Jack out of his seat and steered him across the
room to a large, iron-bound chest. He turned Jack about,
stepped back in a swagger, cocked his head, and slurred,
''Didst y'ever wish to be a pirate, me hearty?''

Jack's eyes were wide now, but no longer simply with
astonishment. There was longing there as well, a need to be
accepted, a hunger to belong.

''No,'' he whispered, ''just a baseball player.''

''Ah, baseball!'' breathed Hook.

Reaching down dramatically, he flipped back the lid of
the chest. Inside were thousands of baseball cards.

Jack gasped. ''I never saw so many cards!'' he whispered.

Hook bent close. ''Take a few, why don't you.'' He
waited as Jack filled both hands. ''You see, Jack, you can
be anything you want on my team. It's all up to you.''

And he put his arm about the boy and gave him a
possessive pirate squeeze.

Think Happy
Thoughts

That same morning found Peter Banning becoming reac-
quainted with his body. It was not a pleasant experience.
Too many places sagged, pouched, jiggled, and otherwise
stuck out in some inappropriate or embarrassing manner.
Too many parts simply didn't work. For countless months
he had been telling himself that he needed to get in shape,
that he had to start exercising. And now the moment of truth
had finally arrived.

It was all Tink's doing. "If you want to get your kids
back," she had announced, rousting him from his tree
branch at sunrise with Pockets, Latchboy, Too Small, No
Nap, Ace, Don't Ask, and Thud Butt looking on, "you
have to be ready for Hook. You can't face him looking like
this. We have to get the old Pan back."

The old Pan. As if there really was such a thing. As if *he*
were it. But she kept insisting, and the small group of Lost
Boys who wanted to believe it was possible kept insisting
right along with her—all of them peering down at him
rather like they might at something odd spied on a zoo
outing.

So up he got and off he went to exercise—fat, old Peter
Banning, attorney-at-law and sometime developer, strayed
from the real world into this imaginary one, out on a
when-you-wish-upon-a-star kind of expedition that a faerie
and a bunch of little boys were convinced would result in
the discovery of his own personal fountain of youth.

It was midmorning, and he had been at it for more than
three hours already. *Lord have mercy!*

Down the pathway into spring he jogged once more,

grateful to be past winter, looking forward to summer. His breath came in gasps, his feet were on fire, his muscles ached, and his whole body puffed and shook and generally refused to respond in any positive way to the torture he was putting it through. Tink jogged on his shoulder, going nowhere, enjoying it nevertheless. His entourage of Lost Boys ran circles around him, darting here and there, urging him on, singing and dancing and calling out enthusiastically, covering three times the ground and possessed of at least twice the energy.

Oh, to be twelve again—just for the morning!

He trudged elephantlike through the wildflowers, their scent pungent and sweet in the warming air, spring in full bloom now where it dipped down the rise beneath the limbs of the Nevertree and approached the lagoon. Around and around the tree he had gone, in and out of the four seasons. Real seasons, not pretend. Summer, fall, winter, spring. At first he hadn't been able to believe it—an entire year's seasons grouped around a single tree, never mind how big the tree might be. It wasn't environmentally possible. It wasn't rationally conceivable. And yet, nevertheless, there it was. It took him a dozen times or so of trooping about the tree and passing through each to accept that they were there—a dozen times of sloshing through winter's snows, tripping through spring's flowers, dancing through summer's grasses, and sprinting (well, almost) through fall's colors. But in the end he had accepted what was happening because, after all, it wasn't any crazier than anything else he had encountered, and now was hardly the time to start being choosy.

Sweat dripped off his forehead and ran down into his face. He licked his lips. The temperature warmed as he left spring, passed the lagoon, and started up into summer.

He would give anything for a cold beer!

"Gotta train! In the rain! Gotta run! In the sun! In the snow! Ten below!"

"Shape up! Lose weight! Get thin! Gotta win!"

"Pick 'em up! Move 'em down! Pick 'em on up! Off the ground!"

His little band of followers shouted slogans from all around, pushing him from behind, pulling him from ahead, leading him from season to season, from ache to ache. The remainder of the Lost Boys, Rufio at their head, were gathered in clusters about the Nevertree, watching. Mostly, they were laughing—rolling on the ground in hysterics, yelling very unkind (however true) remarks about Peter's body every time he passed them.

"Hey, jollymon, catch a bus!" shouted Rufio, bringing laughter from all quarters.

"Must be more than one of you in there!" roared another.

Peter kept on, ignoring them as best he could, conscious of the fact that he looked ridiculous, continuing only because he didn't know what else to do. If there was even the slightest chance that Tink was right, that this was the way to get Jack and Maggie free of Captain Hook . . .

He closed his eyes momentarily against what he was feeling, then staggered on toward fall and its slippery carpet of leaves where he always fell at least once, then winter and its curious penguins, and back again into spring, and on and on and on.

When he was finally allowed to stop running, he was somewhere between spring and summer and total exhaustion. Allowing no rest, Tink directed him briskly to the makeshift exercise equipment that the Lost Boys had constructed. Peter's old clothing was in tatters by now—his dress shirt and the remnants of his tux. The waistcoat had disappeared entirely. His shoes were scuffed and dusty.

Tink started him first on a bar attached to a rope, counterbalanced by Lost Boys sitting in a basket. Too Small and Latchboy started, the lightest of the group, and then heavier boys took their place. When that wasn't enough, they added rocks. Peter succeeded in pulling the bar down by dint of excess weight alone and not because of muscle tone. He gave it up after a dozen tries.

From there he was moved to the leg-lift machine, where a rope tied to a bar and affixed to his ankles ran to a cluster of what the Lost Boys claimed was poison ivy suspended over his face. Failure to keep the legs up resulted in the obvious. Peter grunted and strained, his stomach muscles turned to water, and his face was bathed in sweat. He would have dropped the poison ivy into his face in the end if Thud Butt hadn't grabbed the rope a moment before his collapse.

Peter rolled away, gasping. He looked up at his entourage forlornly. "I know I'm in lousy shape. I know I'm old and fat. I know I'm going on forty. I accept all that. I accept my mortality. How is all this going to help me get my kids back?"

Pockets bent down as if to study a specimen on a slide, floppy hat dipping over one eye. "The only way ta be uh kid is ta look like uh kid," he answered solemnly.

Then they hauled Peter to his feet again and steered him to a huge tree stump over which he was unceremoniously draped. Most of what remained of his clothes was stripped off. Surrounded by Lost Boys, he had another flash of the horrors of *Lord of the Flies*, but it turned out they had something much worse in mind. Crowding close, they began to pummel him with fists and hands in a sort of haphazard massage, kneading and rubbing his flabby flesh and rubber-band muscles, bringing out from within every last smidgen of pain he had spent the morning building up and trying to forget. Finished with one side, they flipped him over and began on the other, singing and calling out as they worked. Peter was certain he was going to die. Secretly, he began to wish for it.

This will never work, he told himself dismally. Never.

Rufio walked up and gave his stomach a double twist with his knuckles. "Ain't missed too many meals lately, 'ey, Mr. Pretend Pan?" he jeered.

The massage ended and the Lost Boys raised him up, somewhat the way you would a limp noodle, and took a look at their handiwork.

"Gettin' there," ventured Thud Butt, hands on hips. His bluff, chubby face broke into a toothy smile.

"Still doesn't look right." Don't Ask frowned.

Pockets, Latchboy, Ace, and No Nap crowded close.

Then Too Small wormed into view, reached out, and pulled a tuft of Peter's chest hair. The Lost Boys stared at each other. Amusement twinkled in their eyes. No Nap scratched himself like a gorilla, bringing peals of laughter from the others.

Within moments a steaming bowl of soap lather was brought forward by Don't Ask. Ace followed, top hat cocked back, a very large, very sharp knife in his hand. Peter's eyes went wide. He backed off the stump and tried to run, but the boys tackled him and wrestled him to the ground. With arms and legs securely pinned, Peter decided that twisting his torso against the knife blade was counter-productive, and so he lay quite still as Ace carefully shaved the hair from his body, front and back, then worked his way down both legs and arms as well, until Peter had been scraped pretty well clean.

Clad only in his shorts now, he stood staring down at his smooth, pink-skinned body in disbelief. All that hair had covered a whole lot of flesh, he decided. There seemed to be a lot more of him now.

The Lost Boys stood around, eyeing him critically, a few nodding their approval. Rufio reappeared and stood watching without comment. Tink darted this way and that, appraising him from all angles.

Suddenly Pockets began whispering to the other Lost Boys. Peter knew from experience now what that meant and began looking for a way through their ranks. But once again he was overpowered as they descended on him with war paint decorating him with stripes and squiggles and strange faces in the wildest colors, making him look as much as possible like them, to disguise the last vestiges of who and what he had been when he had come to them, trying to find the Pan hidden somewhere within.

When they were done, they stepped back once again. For a moment, no one spoke. Then Pockets said quietly, "Godda see ib you can still fly, Peder."

Singing and dancing anew, they paraded him through the clearing and up through spring and along the edges of winter to a cliff. A giant sling sat just back from its edge. The sling was made of wood and ropes and had a leather pouch into which Peter was summarily plopped.

"Wait, no, this isn't going to work!" Peter protested, wide-eyed with fear.

Pockets and Ace walked to the edge of the cliff and peered down. Below, standing next to a giant mud puddle, was a Lost Boy holding a cutout of Peter. Blond hair pushed carefully back beneath his hat, Ace raised his spyglass and called out a distance to Pockets, who marked it down on a small chalkboard. A hurried discussion ensued with several others and an agreement was reached. Ace lifted his hand to signal.

Peter heard the sound of a crank being turned and felt his pouch begin to draw back through the heavy framework of the sling. The band of the catapult slowly tightened.

Ratchets caught and slipped. *Click! Click! Click!*

Peter couldn't speak. He could barely breathe. He was paralyzed with fright. They weren't really going to do this, were they? Not really? This was ridiculous! This was incredibly dangerous!

Tink appeared beside him, walking along in time to the clicking of the ratchets, eyeing him critically. "All you need is one happy thought, Peter. Just one, and it will make you fly."

Peter swallowed. "Get me out of here, Tink!"

"One happy thought," she persisted.

"Not being in this slingshot would make me very happy! Ecstatic, in fact!"

Below, where the cutout had been measured, a gathering of Lost Boys were raising a huge net. They think they're in a circus, thought Peter in horror.

"Think, Peter," urged Tink, still following his progress backward in the pouch. "Try."

Peter thought, desperate now. "Wait! I have one!"

Tink bounced excitedly. "I knew you could do it! What is it?"

"Last February, the market shot up two hundred points!"

Tink stared. "What market? What are you talking about?"

Peter's head bobbed, frantic. "No, you're right—I was underinvested. Wait, let me think. Got it! This one will fly!" He cringed at his choice of words. "It's the perks!"

Tinkerbell tossed her head. "Are they wonderful, rich, round cakes with lots of frosting?"

Peter laughed tonelessly. "I'm talking about a five-line phone in a super-stretch limo, last-minute tickets to any sporting event, to any theater I name, corporate jets with precleared flight plans and priority landing. . . ."

Tink held up her hands to shut him off. "This can't be the right direction, Peter. Look, maybe this will help. I'll say some things. You see what comes to mind. Close your eyes and picture it."

Peter was happy to close his eyes. "Okay, I'm ready. Hurry!"

Tink flitted close. "Puppies."

Peter frowned. "They try to commit suicide under your feet."

"Cotton candy."

"Disgusting, cavity-inducing pink goo that gets all over your hands."

"Snow."

"Awful—turns to slush and ruins the finish of your car." Peter's voice was a wail. "I'm not happy!"

Tink flared. "Are you happy in spring?"

Peter's lips compressed. "Taxes."

"Summer?"

"Mosquitoes."

"How about swimming?"

"Chlorine."

"Play-Doh?"

Peter hesitated. "What's that?"

"Christmas?"

"Gifts, bills, credit cards. I'm not happy!"

"Swings or slides?"

"Fact of life. Happens all the time if you play the market. You've just got to learn to live with it."

"M&Ms?" Tink was growing desperate.

"Melts on your couch, not in your hand."

Tink exploded. "Peter, nothing makes you happy!"

Peter's whole face was crumpled tight in concentration. "No, now that's simply not true. Just let me think, let me think. One minute. How much time do I have left?"

"None," whispered Rufio in his ear.

Peter's eyes shot open. Rufio towered over him, legs spread, arms folded as he balanced on the end of the sling frame. Almost as if by magic, the Pan sword appeared, slicing down through the taut rope. The sling released, catapulting Peter skyward. Arms and legs flailing madly, his voice raised in a howl of disbelief and terror, Peter tried desperately to fly. Down below, Lost Boys shouted and leaped about, some holding up placards that spelled out words like HORSIES, CANDIE, BUGS, and PENNIES. None of them meant anything to Peter. He seemed to sail overhead for a very long time, the eyes of the boys below tracking his progress hopefully. Tink watched with them, peeking out from between the slits of the fingers she had clasped over her eyes, wings and heart beating madly.

Just one happy thought!

But it was not to be this day. Down plummeted Peter, tumbling into the safety net in a frightened heap, the air whooshing from his lungs, his body bouncing like a balloon in the wind. Tink flew to his side, followed by the small entourage of Lost Boys who were still in his camp.

The rest turned doubtfully to Rufio.

Rufio lifted his sword. "I'm more man than Pan—and twicet the boy! Now, who is wi' me?"

They charged from where they stood to join him, crying out, "Rufio, Rufio, Rufio!" He raised the sword high to signal victory, leading them away from the cliff. In seconds they were gone, headed back to the Nevertree.

Peter sat up, dazed. Tink and the seven Lost Boys stared down at him disconsolately.

"There was the Proctor and Gamble deal," he announced hesitantly. "That made me happy."

No one seemed impressed.

Bangerang,
Peter!

Peter was last to the dinner table that night, so bone weary he could barely manage to hold his head up. Everything hurt from his hair to his toes. Bruised, battered, and bandaged, he was a certifiable wreck. Tink and the little band of Lost Boy followers had kept him going the entire day, from one exercise to the next, over and over and over again.

Except for the sling routine—they hadn't bothered to try that on him again.

Not that it mattered. Nor that anything they did mattered. Because nothing they did was going to work—of that Peter was certain. They could run him, pummel him, and sling him hither and yon until the cows came home and it wouldn't change things. He was still fat, old Peter Banning and *not*—he couldn't bring himself to say the name—who they wanted him to be. Worse, none of this was getting him any closer to rescuing Jack and Maggie.

So as he trudged from the jogging track and exercise machines to the long table set back close beneath the branches of the Nevertree within the shadow of summer and hailing distance of spring, he found himself confronted with the fact that he was on the verge of failing his kids once more. Not being there for baseball games or piano recitals was one thing. Not being there to save Jack and Maggie from Hook was something else again. It would be the culmination of a long line of disappointments he had given them—only this one was likely to prove fatal.

He wiped away the tears that sprang to his eyes, not wanting anyone to see, and moved to take a seat. Despite

131

his distress, he was hungry. No, make that starved. He'd had nothing to eat all day, kept busy by Tink and the Lost Boys trying to find the boy in himself. Which was long since gone, of course. Which was dead and buried. He shoved the thought away. At any rate he needed to eat. However slim his chances of helping his kids might be in any case, they were nonexistent if he didn't eat.

The table was crowded from end to end, with Rufio and his pack occupying most of it. Peter's bunch was gathered in a small section at the opposite center. A space had been left for him, and he settled into it gratefully, sandwiched between Pockets and Ace. Tink was seated at the center of the table in a place of her own.

Rufio sat directly across from Peter. He smiled disdainfully as Peter sat down, mischief dancing in his eyes. Peter ignored him.

I have to eat. I have to build up strength.

He took a deep breath.

I can't stop trying.

A handful of Lost Boys appeared, bearing steaming dishes from clay ovens fired red-hot. Peter inhaled the aromas and sighed. Whatever it was, it smelled wonderful!

Ace passed him a dish, and he set it down in front of himself, brushing away the steam to see what was on it.

The dish was empty.

Peter stared blankly, then lifted his gaze to look down the table. Everyone was eating ravenously, scooping food into their mouths, chewing in delight. Except that they were eating nothing. All the dishes were empty.

"Mmmm! All my fav'rite Neverfood!" declared Pockets next to him, his mouth full of nothing. "Yams, mammee apples, banana splash, wash id down with a calabash of poe-poe. Then Neverchicken and . . . Hey, Tink! Led go!"

Tink was tugging at one end of nothing while Pockets tugged at the other. Peter blinked. Across the table, Rufio was watching intently.

"Drink your poe-poe, Peter," invited Ace, and poured

nothing from a pitcher into Peter's empty mug. Don't Ask and Thud Butt clinked mugs and drank air.

Peter sat there without moving for an instant longer, then threw up his hands. "I don't get it!" he exclaimed. "Where's the food?"

Tink glanced up. "If you can't imagine yourself as Peter Pan, you'll never be Peter Pan."

"What's that got to do with . . . this!"

She gave him a stern look. "If you don't eat, you won't grow."

Peter was as steamed as the dishes. "Eat what? There's nothing here to eat!"

"That's the point," said Tink. "Peter, have you forgotten how to pretend as well? That's how we eat."

Rufio laughed. "He can't! He doesn't get it!" Then he jeered, "Eat your heart out, you crinkled, wrinkled bag of fat!"

And he tossed his empty dish across the table and hit Peter directly in the chest. Peter jerked away, the blow sharp and stinging. He was stunned.

"My God, you are a badly raised child," he managed.

Lost Boys all about repeated the words "badly raised child," laughing and jeering as they did, mocking Peter.

Rufio straightened. "Slug-eating worm," he taunted.

Tink leaped up, hands on hips, sunrise eyes fiery. "Come on, Peter! You can do better than that!"

Rufio laughed. "Yeah, mon—show me your fast ball. C'mon, dustbrain. You pouchy, old, sag-bottomed, puke-pot!"

"Bangerang, Rufio! Bangerang!" shouted the Lost Boys. Even Peter's group joined in.

Peter had had enough. He pointed at Rufio and shook his finger. "You are an extremely poor role model for these children."

The Lost Boys whistled and used their hands to mimic the crashing of airplanes.

"All right!" snapped Peter, not wanting to back off. "You . . . you are a third-rate person!"

"Hemorrhoidal sucknavel!" Rufio sneered. He looked cocky and self-assured sitting there, his eyes laughing.

"Fourth-rate person!" charged Peter.

More whistles and crashes sounded, and the entire table began to jeer.

Rufio leaned forward. "Boil-dripping, beef-fart sniffing bubblebutt!"

"Bangerang, Rufio!" screamed the Lost Boys in glee.

"You are a scatologically fixated, psychotic, prepubescent child!" shouted Peter.

Boos sounded from every quarter accompanied by less polite indications of disdain. More whistles. More crashes. Peter knew he was losing this contest as well.

"Fungus factory!" taunted Rufio.

"Bangerang, Rufio! Bangerang!"

"Slug-slimed sack of rat guts and cat vomit!"

The cheers were deafening. Lost Boys were leaping up and down in their seats, hands clapping.

"Cheesy, scab-picked, pimple-scoured, finger bandage!"

Fake moans and retching sounds rose from the assemblage, the Lost Boys now become connoisseurs of revulsion, loving every dreadful image Rufio's words conjured in their minds. Rufio beamed.

"Week-old, double maggot burger with everything on it and flies on the side!"

Peter surged to his feet, his hands braced on the edge of the table, his face flushed dark red. He had lost his composure completely. Everyone scrambled to get out of the way. Even Rufio jerked back uncertainly.

Peter's teeth were clenched. "Arbitrageur!" he howled.

Everyone stared. Glances were hurriedly exchanged.

"What's that?" demanded Rufio finally.

Peter recognized an opening when he saw it. He smiled, disdaining to answer. "Dentist!" he hissed.

Lost Boys everywhere gasped in recognition of that one, recoiling as if struck. Rufio flinched, then quickly straightened.

"Nose hairs infested with lice and ticks!" he tried.

"Substitute chemistry teacher!" Peter retaliated.

"Slug-eating worm!"

Too Small leaped up. "Repeat! Repeat! Rufio repeated. He loses points!"

All the Lost Boys began to shout at once. "C'mon, Rufio!" cried his supporters. "Hit 'im back! Don't let 'im get to you!"

Rufio made a last run. "Lizard lips! In yo' face, camel-cake . . ."

"French tutor!" Peter cut him off. "Assistant Dean of Students! Parole officer! Accountant! Theatrical agent of animal acts! Prison—"

"Lying, crying, spying, prying, ultrapig!" screamed Rufio.

Peter laughed. "Easy for you to say—you lewd, rude, crude bag of prechewed food!"

That brought the Lost Boys to their feet with a howl. "Bangerang, Peter!" they cried out. "Peter's Bangerang!"

Now it was Rufio's turn to be stunned. The smug look had disappeared from his face. There was genuine shock mirrored there—and hurt.

"You . . . you man!" he howled. "You stupid, stupid man!"

Peter had him. He took a deep breath. "You tight-brained, three-button, gold-card, alligator-belted crock of shishkababble-toothed, liberal left-wing corporate lawyer, eating his boogers . . . like a paramecium suffering from Pan envy!"

There was dead silence. Peter's gaze stayed locked on Rufio.

"What's a par-a-meeze-e-um?" asked Too Small softly.

"A one-celled organism with no brain," Peter answered triumphantly.

Shouts of glee rose from the Lost Boys. Mugs thumped down on the tabletop, feet stamped the ground, and everyone went absolutely bonkers.

"Banning! Banning! Banning! Bangerang Banning!" they all roared, including Rufio's followers.

Peter grinned, caught up in the moment. Without thinking, he reached down to his plate and scooped up a handful of nothing.

"While I'm at it, Rufio," he hissed, drawing the other's downcast eye, "something else just occurred to me. Go suck a dead dog's nose!"

And he hurled the handful of nothing into Rufio's face. Cheers and shouts rose anew from among the Lost Boys. The nothing struck, and green and orange globs of vegetables dripped suddenly from Rufio's dark face. Peter stared at him momentarily, then glanced down at his empty hand. *How about that?* His smile was reborn in that instant, alive with the wonder of discovering something he had thought impossible.

Across the table, Rufio reached down to a nearby plate, came up with a fistful of nothing, and hurled it back at Peter. It struck him squarely in the face as well—hot steamy dressing, thick rich gravy, and candied yams. It ran down into his mouth, and he licked it away, his smile even broader. It was real! It tasted wonderful!

When he looked down again, the entire table was laden with food, all of the empty platters piled high. Stunned, delighted, an unimagined sense of joy taking hold, Peter seated himself and began to eat ravenously.

Too Small's round face was beaming as he clapped his hands. "You're doing it! You're doing it!"

Peter looked up, genuinely puzzled. "Doing what?"

"Having fun with uz, Peder," Pockets answered softly.

All the Lost Boys crowded to him with a cheer—Ace, No Nap, Don't Ask, Thud Butt, Latchboy, Too Small, and Pockets in the vanguard, hands raised to exchange high-fives. Cries of "Pan the Man" lifted. Peter ate, and never had food tasted so good. Across from him, a Lost Boy smiled and showed him a mouthful of food. Peter grinned and showed him a mouthful back.

Tink flew from the table into the limbs of the Nevertree and down again, crying to anyone who would listen, "I knew he could, I knew he could!"

A Lost Boy belched as he finished eating. Another mimicked him. And another. Peter reared back and gave a gigantic belch that sent them all into gales of laughter, a few so overcome with merriment that they tumbled from their seats to the ground. Peter laughed harder than any of them. He had forgotten who he was or why he was there. He had forgotten his aches and pains. He was too busy having fun to worry about any of it. He grabbed a turkey leg and pretended to make off with it. Lost Boys grappled playfully to stop him. Peter sprang up as if to hurdle the table, turkey leg held high.

As he did, a sullen Rufio, nursing his anger in silence until now, finally lost control. Seeing this "Pretend Pan" playing and cavorting as if he were one of them was just too much to stomach. With a howl of rage, he snatched up two coconuts and threw them with all his strength at Peter's head.

What followed was to be a blur in Peter's mind ever after. Someone yelled in warning, Peter whirled, dropped the turkey leg, and caught a sword thrown by Ace all in one motion. He spun—gracefully, easily, as if he had been doing such things all his life. The sword became a natural extension of his hand, its blade whipping through the air, cleaving both coconuts apart in a single stroke so that the halves fell neatly at his feet.

A gasp came from the throats of the Lost Boys followed by silence. Everyone, Rufio included, stared at Peter in undisguised awe. Peter stood for an instant without moving, sword in hand, balanced on the balls of his feet, uncertain even then what it was he had done or how he had done it. Then he let the sword drop, and he slowly sat down again to finish his meal.

Tinkerbell was hovering in the air above them all, her face alive with joy. "What times," she whispered to herself. "What great games."

There were tears in her eyes.

Magic Hour

The sunset colored the western skies scarlet as day faded and night approached, and the waters of Hook's pirate harbor were turned to blood. At anchor, the *Jolly Roger* rocked in slow cadence to the lapping of the waves against her dark hull. The waterfront was quiet now, the day's work finished, the pirates gone to the alehouses and taverns and less reputable dens for an evening's fun. The ramshackle hulls of the cannibalized ships formed stark skeletons in the gloom, bones jutting out, faces blanched and peeling paint.

Jack, wearing a tricorne hat that was a smaller version of Captain Hook's, stared down from atop his perch on the muzzle end of Long Tom, a knight astride his charger, the master of all he surveyed. The redoubtable captain rode the breech, hands in place on the barrel as Smee steadied him against a possible fall. Like children on a seesaw, boy and man faced each other watching the moons of Neverland grow large in the sky.

Jack waved his hand impulsively, and his smile was dazzling.

What a wonderful, exciting day it had been!

School in Hook's cabin hadn't lasted much longer than the discovery of the chest of baseball cards. From there, Hook and Smee steered Jack out on deck and down the gangway to the docks, where lines of pirates were practicing with cutlasses. Back and forth the pirates surged, the blades of their weapons glistening in the sunlight. With barely a pause Hook led his bosun and Jack right through the center of it all, seemingly oblivious to any danger from the sharp edges. Down through the scything iron he strolled, as bold as you please, Jack and Smee following with heads ducked and eyes wide.

Exiting safely at the far end of the deadly gamut, Hook paused, excused himself to Jack, snatched a cutlass from Smee, parted the final pair of fighters, and engaged one in combat.

"Parry and thrust. Parry and thrust." He forced the hapless pirate back. "Lean right, and . . ."

Ugh! He ran the pirate through, swift as thought.

"Odds bodkins, did you see that, Smee?" Hook sniffed as the pirate collapsed at his feet. "He bent his knee!"

Smee shook his finger at the fellow. "You have to concentrate!" he had admonished.

"Tense your abductor muscles and the movement follows!" Hook added.

Jack thought he saw the pirate nod dutifully just before he died. At least Smee seemed to find some reason for giving him a reassuring pat on the back.

"To breakfast!" Hook announced.

Voiceless, stunned, yet titillated as well, Jack followed Hook and Smee through the gates heralding GOOD FORM PIER, down the wharf front, and into the town. All about, the pirates swarmed, colorful and bold in their jaunty outfits, calling out and laughing gaily. It reminded the boy of a carnival, with some new attraction, some wonderful event, waiting around every corner. There were jugglers, tattooed men, fire breathers, and exotic women of a sort he had never seen before. A stuffed-animal vendor caught their attention, and Smee grabbed up a toothy crocodile and pretended to chase Hook with it until the captain gave him a look that would have melted ice.

At last they turned into a door with a sign that read:

TAVERNE
BREAKFAST NOW BEING SERVED
BOTTOMLESS CUP OF COLA

Inside, there were pirates lounging in chairs and on stools, some smoking, some cleaning knives, a few reading tattered copies of newspapers labeled *Pirate Today* and *The Daily Pirate*. Tables were occupied by pirates eating from plates heaped with cream puffs, pies, cakes, and sweets of all sorts accompanied by tall mugs of cola. A table was reserved for Hook, and he and Jack shared a monstrous banana split to which Smee kept adding spoonfuls of whipped cream. Jack advised Hook beforehand, rather embarrassed to have to do so, that he was not allowed to have sweets before breakfast. But the captain simply laughed and announced that in his town sweets *were* breakfast.

From there they went on to the square and a mock horse race with Hook riding Tickles, Jack riding Smee, and a gaggle of other pirates riding each other, all charging around the crocodile tower, yelling wildly. Though Hook urged Tickles on rather insistently with his claw, Jack emerged the winner. Jack thought there was a chance that the captain might have let him win, but he was having too much fun to care.

Then there was the imaginary boat ride in the raging thunderstorm, with Hook, Smee, and Jack sitting tight in a lifeboat rocked wildly by a corps of pirates who hoisted them aloft while other pirates and pirate town denizens clashed swords to make lightning and thunder and shook sheets and towels to make wind. Buckets of water sloshed perilously close, as if the sea were really down there, threatening to capsize the boat and send them all to Davy Jones. How real it seemed!

Finally there was the pirate drill with Jack in command and Hook looking on, beaming his approval, as the boy marched an increasingly irritated gang of pirates about the decks of the *Jolly Roger* until they were on the verge of mutiny.

Boy, oh, boy—what a day!

But now it was coming to a close. The memories danced through his mind, and Jack could only grin and wonder what lay ahead. Tomorrow would bring new adventures, Hook had promised. Just wait, little man. Just wait.

His reverie was interrupted as a small, anxious voice called his name.

"Jack! Jack!"

He stared down at the wharf, where the barred window of a basement prison framed a little girl's dirt-streaked face.

"What do you think you're doing? Why are you playing games with him? Look at me, Jack! You think you're funny, but you're not! You wouldn't be acting this way if Mommy and Daddy were here!"

Jack was silent. Hook slid down from Long Tom and walked to Jack's end, his smile little more than a twitch of his lips.

He reached up and put an arm about the boy. "Do you know who she is, Jack?" he asked softly.

Jack shrugged. "Sure."

"It's me, Jack!" Maggie shouted insistently.

"She's so loud," whispered Hook, sounding sad. He paused. "What's her name again?"

Jack frowned. "Ah . . ." His mind was suddenly blank.

Hook's smile broadened appreciably. Things were working out better than he had expected.

"I'm Maggie, your sister, you idiot!" she screamed. "When I get out of here, I'm gonna break every model you own! I'm going to mess up your room so bad you won't recognize it!" She sobbed. "It's me! Don't you remember anything? What about Mommy and Daddy? What about them? Jack, it's me!"

Maggie watched in despair as Hook lifted Jack off Long Tom and with his arm about her brother's shoulders led him from view. Jack barely remembered her. He had forgotten her name completely.

She sagged against the bars, her lower lip quivering. She really, really, really wanted Mommy and Daddy!

"Mommy," she said softly.

A tiny voice behind her whispered, "What's a mommy?"

She turned to find one of the littlest captive Lost Boys staring up at her intently. The others were huddled in the dark behind him, all of them dirty and ragged and unkempt, their eyes wide and their faces upturned. From dawn until dusk they had been kept busy by the pirates counting Hook's treasure, chained to chests of it, made to count in cadence the same baubles over and over, sorting, polishing, and then putting them back again. Pirates with whips had urged them on. Pirates with buckets had brought them dreadful food to eat and dirty water to drink. Maggie had hated every minute of it. It almost made her wish she had stayed in Hook's school.

The slave kids were all looking at her expectantly. "Doesn't anyone remember his mother?" she asked incredulously.

They glanced at each other and shook their heads no.

Maggie climbed down from the box she had been standing on to face them. "What's wrong with everyone here?" she demanded.

"What's a mommy?" the first kid repeated tonelessly.

Maggie frowned thoughtfully. Her eyes glanced down at her favorite nightdress, violet hearts on a cream field. Jack had been wearing a pirate hat. Stupid old Jack.

"Mommies," she repeated. She walked to where another little boy was resting on the floor, whimpering from a bad dream. She lifted his head, fluffed his pillow, and lay him back down again. The whimpering stopped.

"Mommies make sure you always sleep on the cool side of your pillow," she said quietly. She sat down, facing the anxious faces. One by one they crowded close. She thought suddenly of Granny Wendy and her stories of Peter Pan. "They're the ones," she intoned gravely, "who put all your thoughts in order while you sleep so that when you wake up, all the good ones are right on top where you can find them."

Blank stares greeted her pronouncement. "You don't know what I'm talking about, do you?" Heads shook. She thought some more. "Mommies are great," she declared, taking another approach. "They feed you, kiss you, give you baths, and drive you to piano lessons. They play with you when you're lonely. They take care of you when you're sick. They paint, draw, color, hug, kiss, and make everything better when you hurt. And they tuck you into your bed every night."

More blank looks. Except—there! One little boy seemed on the verge of remembering. And there! Another was scratching his head.

Maggie leaned forward. "They give you Band-Aids when you cut yourself, they bake you cookies on rainy afternoons, and they sing you songs, and—"

"Wait!" a Lost Boy exclaimed. "I remember! They're not songs—they're . . . lullabies!"

"Right!" exclaimed Maggie.

"Sing us one!" called out the others. "Sing us a lullaby!"

Maggie grinned. "All right."

She smoothed out her wrinkled nightgown, tossed back her strawberry-blond hair, and softly began to sing.

Hunched over the railing of the aft deck, facing out toward the harbor mouth where the mix of colors from Neverland's moons formed wondrous patterns on the ocean's surface, Hook, Smee, and Jack lifted their heads as one at the sound of Maggie's voice. For a long time no one spoke, caught up in the enchantment of her singing, lost in their private thoughts.

Then Jack whispered, so low he could barely be heard, "My . . . my mother sings that song."

Instantly Hook was alert, a scowl chasing the momentary rapture from his angular features. His hook lifted and his eyes fixed on Smee. *Do something!* he mouthed in fury.

Smee straightened and clapped a hand on Jack's shoulder. "C'mon, me lad!" he bellowed as if calling hogs. "Let's have another go at Long Tom!"

He steered Jack to the cannon, mounted him in place, raced to the other end, climbed aboard, and began whooping and hollering as if he had never had so much fun in his entire life.

Hook walked across to the opposite railing and stared downward at the docks. In a shaft of moonlight, he could see Maggie Banning seated on the floor of his prison.

Far distant, walking alone along a limb of the Nevertree where he could watch the last of the sun's color spread away into the water and the moonglow take its place, Peter Banning came to an uncertain stop. Below, silhouetted against the dark backdrop of the island's cliffs by a shimmer of twinkling lights, sat Hook's pirate town and the *Jolly Roger*. The air was so clear that he could see the movement of tiny figures on the wharf and streets amid the jumbled ship hulls. It was so still that he could hear their footsteps.

But what he heard now, suddenly, improbably, was the sound of someone singing a soft, sweet lullaby.

I know that song, he thought in surprise.

He had finished his meal in something of a fog. Lost Boys crowded about, all of them talking a mile a minute, asking this, asking that, anxious to be close to him. He had smiled at them, nodded cheerfully, and given pithy answers to their questions—all the while trying to figure out what had happened with that sword and those coconuts. For a moment there, for just a moment, he had been . . . transformed. It was a ridiculous thing to say, but it was the only description that fit. He shouldn't have been able to do that—to split those coconuts—not even if they had been lying on the table, let alone flying through the air. It was such an incredible piece of luck, such a fluke.

And yet, for just a moment . . .

He had watched Tink's flash of light as she darted down in front of a glum Rufio. "Did you see?" he had heard her ask. "He's in there, Rufio. Help me get him out. Teach him to fight so he can stand up to Hook. Look in his eyes—he's there!" And she had yanked on his gold earring for emphasis.

But Rufio had simply swatted at her in response and growled, "Tink, you Neverbug! Let go!" so that she had flown indignantly away.

I know that song.

He stared transfixed at the lights of the pirate town, straining to hear the words. As he did so Thud Butt appeared beside him. For a moment neither spoke, listening together to the sound of the music.

"I was thinking, Peter," said Thud Butt when a little time had passed. His round face lifted and his dark eyes gleamed. "When you were like us, there was a Lost Boy named Tootles. Do you remember Tootles?"

Peter nodded wordlessly.

Thud Butt reached up and removed a bag from around his neck. "Hold out your hands, Peter."

Peter did, and Thud Butt emptied the contents of the bag into his cupped palms. Peter stared down. He was holding a handful of marbles.

"These are his happy thoughts," said Thud Butt solemnly. "He lost them a long time ago. I kept them, but they don't work for me." He smiled. "Maybe they'll work for you."

The smile was sad and hopeful all at once. He handed Peter the bag. Peter dumped the marbles back into it, tucked it inside his shirt, and reached over to give Thud Butt a hug.

Thud Butt hugged him back, saying, "My happy thought is my mum, Peter. I can't remember her, though. Do you remember your mum?"

Peter broke away gently and shook his head no.

Thud Butt started to speak, but Peter silenced him with a finger to his lips. "Wait. Listen."

Maggie's lullaby wafted on the night air, rising up like the scent of flowers carried on the wind.

Thud Butt's chubby face beamed in the moonlight. "It sounds like Wendy, Peter," he said softly. "She was our mother once." He paused and glanced over hesitantly. "Do you think she's ever coming back?"

In the pirate prison of the Lost Boys, everyone was drifting off to sleep. Maggie sang more softly now, lower, watching eyes close and heads nod and breathing slow to a whisper. She finished the lullaby but continued to hum the tune, staring off into the darkened corners, thinking of home.

A slight rustle at the barred window caused her to shift her gaze. There sat Captain Hook, cross-legged before the sill, eyes glittering in the moonlight, angular face lowered into shadow, the silhouette of his wig and tricorne unmistakable against the brightened sky.

Maggie quit humming, hesitated a second, then gently moved the heads nestled in her lap. She rose and crossed to stand before him. Hook's eyes had a distant, dreamy look, and his hands were clasped childlike before him.

"Who puts you to sleep, Captain Hook?" Maggie asked quietly.

Hook's smile curled like the ends of his mustaches. "Child, I alone hold the pirates of Neverland together. No one puts Captain James Hook to sleep. I put myself to sleep."

Maggie's clear blue eyes fixed him. "Well, then, that's why you're so sad. You have no mother."

Hook seemed taken aback. For a moment it appeared he was about to protest, that he was about to deny the fact, that somewhere in the dim recesses of his memory lay the fragments of a time when Maggie's assertion had not been true.

But then he just shrugged. "No. I'm sad because I have no war."

Maggie shook her head slowly. "All day long, giving orders, being in charge, making people do things. No one takes care of you. A mother would take care of you. You need a mother very badly. Very, very badly."

Hook stared at her, his face thoughtful. His eyes wandered to the children she had sung to sleep, and for just an instant his face softened.

Then the iron crept back and the softness disappeared. He rose wordlessly and stalked away.

The Tick Tock Museum

Tick. Tick. Tick. Tick.

The sound was pervasive, insistent, and terrifying. Even in his sleep, Hook could not escape it. It followed after him relentlessly. It invaded his dreams, a ghost out of his past wearing a face that was all too familiar.

Tick. Tick. Tick. Tick.

The crocodile slithered from the depths of Davy Jones's locker, crawling from the netherworld to which Hook had dispatched it, seeking its revenge in the form of a further taste, of a bigger bite. His hand had not been enough to satisfy it. His hand had only given it a craving for more of him. Up the side of the Jolly Roger *the crocodile crawled, jaws opening and closing eagerly, eyes bright. Hook tried to run from it, of course. He tried to flee. But he found that he couldn't move. His boots were nailed to the deck. When he tried to escape them, he found that his socks were glued inside. Wrenching and groaning in terror, he fought to break free, prepared to rip the skin from the soles of his feet if need be.*

Laughter assailed him in his misery. Nearby stood Peter Pan, head thrown back in merriment, a hammer and nails in one hand, a pot of glue in the other.

Tick. Tick. Tick. Tick.

Hook lay curled in a ball in his bed, his blankets hauled up about his chin, the side of his face twitching in time to the ticking sound so that his mustaches and eyebrows jumped like the inner workings of the clock that pursued him.

Tick. Tick. Tick. Tick.

Finally he awoke, and a bloodshot eye flicked open abruptly, one brow still twitching above, one mustache below. The eye stared wildly at nothing, mirroring both terror and rage. Hook flung off his covers and leaped from his bed, nightshirt billowing about him like sailcloth. His claw gleamed wickedly in the early-morning light as he glanced about frantically, trying to locate the hideous sound. He looked right and left. He looked high and low. He rose on tiptoes to scan the top of the bureau. He dropped to his knees and peered under the bed. He rushed to the latticed windows aft and peered down to the waterline and up to the railing.

Nothing!

Flushed with anger, his eyes gone to slits, he charged through the cabin door and out onto the quarterdeck.

Tick. Tick. Tick. Tick.

He wheeled about, following the sound up the side stairs to the aft deck and Long Tom, his entire body twitching rhythmically now.

It couldn't be back, could it? Not after he'd finally done it in? Not after he'd stuffed and mounted it in the square?

Hook's eyes scanned the empty deck wildly, then settled at last on the hammock where Jack Banning lay asleep.

Slowly, cautiously, Hook approached, hearing the ticking grow louder with every step. He stopped when he reached the boy, shaking as if he were caught naked in a blizzard. His claw stretched out in tiny jerks, closer to the boy, closer, and then deep into his pocket.

When it reappeared, the pocket watch Peter Banning had given to his son was snagged on its tip.

Tick. Tick. Tick. Tick.

The steady, monotonous, horrid sound built inside Hook's head. The second hand jerked and stopped, jerked and stopped. Hook held the watch up between his finger and thumb, regarding it as he might a poisonous snake. His entire body was shaking and his eyes had gone as red as fire. Hook's face changed from something merely frightening to something hideous. He moved forward as if in a trance, and his shadow fell over the sleeping Jack. Slowly, deliberately, he raised the hook.

In that instant Jack awoke. His eyes opened, still heavy with sleep, and through the yawn that squinched his eyes almost shut, he saw the terrible, menacing form that towered over him. His eyes snapped open, caught sight of Hook's face and claw, and went shut again instantly. Cowering beneath his covers, he cringed, expecting . . .

"No, Cap'n! Keep yer powder dry, sir!" Smee's hand deftly closed over the watch, muffling the ticking sound to near silence. "Cap'n," he pleaded hurriedly, "the lit'le imp di'n know any better."

Hook's eyes shifted abruptly and settled on his bosun, causing the other to shrink back in spite of himself. Then the madness faded, and the anger died away. Hook straightened, nodding. His smile was gruesome.

"Yes, Smee, quite right. Penalize our guest for the accidental importation of contraband? Bad form!"

The smile wavered through gritted teeth as he extracted the watch from Smee's uncertain hand. "Only one place for this, Jack, lad," he announced to the boy, whose eyes were still as big as saucers. "To the museum at once!"

He hauled Jack out of the hammock with a thunderous laugh, clasping an arm about the boy so that the wig curls danced on his nose and made him sneeze. They threw on their pirate clothes and off they went, Hook hand in hand with Jack and Smee trailing. Down the gangplank and onto the wharf, down the wharf and through the tunnel, out of the tunnel and onto the pier, along the pier and through the pirate town and crowds of anxiously fawning pirates until at last Hook turned them into a cavernous, dark old hulk that seemed entirely deserted of traffic. As they entered they passed from the clamor of a circus midway into a churchlike silence.

But this was no church. It was a monstrous room filled with clocks of all sizes and shapes. Some were old and some new. Some were large and some small. Some were stately grandfathers and some upstart alarms. Some were for the wrist and some for the pocket. They were made of wood with gold and silver inlaid and of plastic and metal with bright patterns. Some bore the faces of sun and moon, others of mice and men. They hung from the walls and they lay on tables. They stood alone like sentries and they crouched on metal bands like insects. They were everywhere you looked, hundreds of them, perhaps thousands. Jack stared about in wonder at the incredible array.

Then all at once he realized that something was wrong. It took him a moment to realize what it was.

None of the clocks worked.

Hook lifted his arm and swept the room possessively. "My own, personal, wonderful museum. Jack! Isn't it grand! A bounty of broken clocks! Once, each tick-talked, and now—no more. Now all is well. Listen, lad."

Jack looked about doubtfully. "I don't hear anything."

"Exactly! That's just the point!" Hook was euphoric. He charged across the room to a particularly garish old clock with a mix of emeralds and fishes carved into its wood surface. "This was Barbecue's very own bedside clock. Quite the terror of the seven seas was Barbecue. Almost as feared as myself!" Hook's grin was enormous. "I smashed his clock right after I keelhauled him!"

Aside, to Smee, he added, "But a very polite man, Barbecue, right to the very end."

Smee grinned back. "Aye, Cap'n. A right salty old scag for a devil's cut! And his ship made such a pretty bonfire against the water's blue."

The two erupted in laughter, hanging on each other for support. Jack, recovered now from his earlier fright, found himself intrigued anew by this latest wonder. He picked up Barbecue's clock to examine it. As he did so the broken hands clicked suddenly, sharply against each other.

Hook sprang back instantly, disengaging himself from Smee, whirling about wildly, the terror returned to his eyes. "What's that? Smee, what do I hear? No! A ticking! A ticking, Smee!"

Smee had hold of him instantly. "Cap'n, no, there's no

ticking here, nothing left to tick, by my bones, all's plainly pulverized. . . ."

But Hook was having none of it. He snatched Barbecue's clock from Jack's hands and smashed it anew. He pounded it with his claw and threw it on the floor. Jack stared in amazement, mouth open.

"Very well!" declared Hook, stepping back, tricorne and wig askew. Primly he straightened them. "This is for the ticking that might have been!" He began jumping up and down on the broken pieces. "And this is for dinner being late last night!"

He stopped suddenly and glanced over at Jack, a sly glint coming into his cold eyes. "Care to join me, my boy?" he asked, and casually tossed Jack his pocket watch. "Go on. You know what to do."

Jack stared at him for a moment, and the fire in Hook's eyes seemed to transfer to his own. He held the watch up, regarded it somberly for just a moment, then dashed it to the floor.

"This is 'cause I always have to be home for dinner!" he cried exuberantly, joining in the game. "If I'm hungry or not!"

Hook laughed merrily and tossed the boy another clock. Jack threw it to the floor and jumped on its face. Hook tossed him another and another. Jack threw them all down, smashing each one anew.

"Come on, Jack!" Hook encouraged. "That's the lad! Now break a window! Break a window!"

Hook snatched up a clock and hurled it at the closest window, shattering the glass. Without thinking, Jack followed suit, smashing another. Together they threw clocks at windows, at other clocks, and at anything else they could find, reveling in the sound of breaking glass and collapsing works. Smee leaped up and down behind them, urging them on gleefully.

"This is for brushing my teeth!" raged Jack, his hair and eyes wild, his face sweating. "And for combing my hair! And washing my hands! And making less noise! And not talking so much! And for being told to grow up!"

"And for having a fat, old Pan for a Daddy!" howled Hook, hauling down a whole armful of clocks and scattering them every which way.

"Who wouldn't save us!" Jack cried in sudden despair. "Who wouldn't save us!"

"Who wouldn't even try!" hissed Hook, almost in his ear.

Jack dropped to his knees in tears amid the wreckage of the clocks, crying bitterly. "He wouldn't save us. He wouldn't even try. Daddy didn't even . . . try."

He was sobbing so hard he couldn't speak. Hook glanced at Smee, and they shared a conspiratorial wink and grin. Then quickly Hook knelt at Jack's side, his arm resting comfortingly about the boy's shoulder.

"Oh, well, Jack," he said, his voice smooth as syrup. "He may yet try, you know. He will, in fact, I think, try." He waited for the tear-streaked face to lift and the damp eyes to meet his own. He wore a mask of sad understanding for the boy. "The question is, lad, when that time comes, do you want to be saved? Do you want to go back to . . . more disappointment? Do you want to go back with . . . him?"

Hook shook his head quickly. "No, don't answer now. No, no, no. Now's the time for other things. Now's the time for being whatever you want, be it pirate or . . ."

A twinkle came into his dark eye. Jack hesitated. "Or what?" he asked curiously.

Hook's smile was dazzling. One arm came out from where it had been hidden behind his back. Wedged in the crook of his claw was Jack's baseball.

He held it out to the boy. Jack's eyes went wide, and he reached eagerly to accept it.

"So tell me, Jack," Hook asked softly. "Have I ever made a promise I haven't kept?"

The click of Hook's teeth was like the closing of a trap.

Hook Throws
a Curve

While the nefarious Hook was coming to grips, so to speak, with the ghosts of his past, Peter Banning was in the process of confronting some hard truths about his present. Foremost among these was the continuing and growing belief of the Lost Boys that he was—well, you know who—when he wasn't.

"En garde," hissed Rufio.

He stood toe to toe with Peter in a clearing at the base of the Nevertree, a wary look in his dark eyes. Both wielded swords with varying degrees of confidence. Rufio looked as if he had been born clasping his. Peter looked as if he wasn't sure which end was pointed.

"Take it easy on me," he pleaded. He was already breathing heavily. "I'm just a beginner, remember."

"Yeah, sure," Rufio growled. "I saw de coconuts. I am watching you, ugly mon."

He went into a crouch, dark limbs crooking smoothly, black eyes intense, red feathery spikes like streaks of fire through his black hair. Peter tried to imitate him without success. This was a bad idea, he thought. This was a terrible idea. As usual, it was Tink's idea. It wasn't enough that he run and jump and be slung about; it was also necessary that he learn to sword-fight. Sword-fight, for heaven's sake! What did he know about sword fighting? He could barely manage to slice a roast at Sunday dinner!

Rufio circled to his left, feinting. Peter circled with him, not knowing what else to do. Rufio can teach you, Tink had insisted. Rufio's the best. He can show you all the tricks. He can help you remember.

Sure, but when all was said and done, would he be alive to say thanks?

Gathered all about, the Lost Boys cheered, some for Peter, most for Rufio. Last night was last night and quickly forgotten. Rufio was still the boss.

Tink flashed down out of the cooling shadows to land on the tip of Peter's sword. "Remember what I told you," she admonished. "Back straight, shoulders relaxed. Step in there to meet him, don't be afraid. Take care of him the way you took care of those coconuts."

Peter shot her an irritated glance. "I told you, I don't know how I did that! It was a reflex!"

Rufio's sword kissed his own with a click.

"Lik dis, mon," the other said, smiling. "*Uno, dos, tres . . .*"

And his blade flashed inside Peter's like a striking snake. Peter heard a shredding of cloth and felt a draft. When he looked down, he found his pants in a heap about his ankles. Cries of disapproval went up from the Lost Boys.

"I complain of you!" they shouted as one.

Rufio ignored them. He lifted the Pan sword, threw back his head, and crowed.

"Ya can't fly, ya can't fight, and mon, you rally can't crow!"

Pockets shoved forward, floppy hat bobbing. "Thad's nod fair. He hasn't dun nuttin' to make himself proud. How cud he crow?"

The Lost Boys shouted in agreement, coming to Peter's defense. Rufio eyed them sourly for a moment, then smiled wickedly.

"So tell me, then. Wot coul' de fat mon do?"

Pockets's small face tightened. "Lods of tings," he insisted enthusiastically. "He cud swallow fire!" Peter's hands came up to his throat in horror. "He cud write a letter or draw a picture! He cud play Lost Boys and Indians!" The dark eyes went wide. "I know! He cud go into town and steal Hook's hook!"

Peter's gasp of dismay was drowned out by the howls of approval that erupted from the Lost Boys. They surged forward excitedly, crowding about, clapping him on the back, trying to slap hands with him, all the while yelling, "Steal Hook's hook! Steal Hook's hook!"

Standing apart from the others, certain that his fondest wish was about to be fulfilled, Rufio grinned like the proverbial cat.

Another dumb idea, thought Peter bleakly. The dumbest yet.

Nevertheless, here he was, going along with it as if he believed it nothing of the sort. It was as if he had lost all sense of proportion in his life, as if he would do anything that anyone suggested simply because he didn't seem to have any ideas of his own. Removal from the real world to Neverland had stripped him of his ability to think and act like a rational person. How else could he explain sneaking into the pirate town to steal Hook's hook, all for the purpose of impressing a bunch of raggedy, dirty-faced Lost Boys so that they would believe he was someone he wasn't and help him save his kids from a lunatic?

Of course, there was more to it than that, but Peter Banning was in no position to reason it through. He was an adult cast back into a children's world, where dreams were real and adventures the order of the day. Peter had spent too much time immersed in rules of law and legalese, none of which makes much sense to the average person and most of which is written by people who skipped through their childhood as quickly as they could so that they could be adults. Peter was not one of these, but he had spent sufficient time among them to begin to think as they did, and he had forgotten all about being a little boy. Making money and closing deals had replaced building sandbox castles and riding merry-go-rounds. Winning lawsuits had supplanted watching Fourth of July fireworks. Playing board games had assumed a completely different context. Peter had been too long without any real understanding of what makes life worth living, and he was struggling badly to survive the lessons that would give that understanding back to him.

So all he could think about on what would turn out to be the most important morning of his life as a grown-up was how foolish he was to let a bunch of children manipulate him.

The four pirates lurched down the town's rotting board-walk, three of surprising height, the fourth shorter but meaner looking. They wore tricornes, greatcoats, sashes, and boots. An eye patch and scraggly beard hid most of one's face, and a bandanna and scars hid most of another's. The shortest of the four had a face so twisted and lined that no pirate cared to give it more than a passing glance before hurrying on. An arsenal of weapons was strapped about each one, cutlasses and flintlocks tucked in belts, daggers and dirks poking out from everywhere.

As they passed a candy store the three larger pirates swung about abruptly, and a familiar face peered out from between the folds of one coat just above the belt.

"Sugarplums!" breathed Thud Butt before a hand shoved his face back inside again.

For the pirates were not pirates at all, of course, but Peter and his Lost Boy followers. Thud Butt and Pockets made up one pirate, Ace and No Nap another, Latchboy and Don't Ask a third, and Peter the fourth. Too Small, who really was, had been left home. Tink rode in the brim of Peter's tricorne, issuing directions.

"This way!" she would insist. "No, that! Slow down! Stop! Over there, away from that floozy! Watch your step! Growl! Growl!"

Peter had no trouble growling. If an opportunity had presented itself, he probably would have been happy to bite as well.

They had slipped down along the beachfront and into the town through the back alleyways, dressed in their disguises, appearing big and tough enough that no one wanted anything to do with them. They had searched for some sign of Hook and quickly discovered that everyone was gravi-tating toward Pirate Square and the crocodile clock.

Now, approaching along the walkway, swaying and weaving like drunkards as they tried to keep upright on one another's shoulders, they could hear cheers and shouts. Ahead, dozens of pirates encircled the square. On reaching the back of the crowd, Peter mounted a barrel and peered curiously over the sea of heads.

He could scarcely believe his eyes. Pirate Square had been transformed into a baseball field!

Gone was the debris of countless nights of pirate revelry. Gone the pushcarts and jewelry stands. Gone the pickpockets and sleight-of-hand artists (or at least they were keeping out of sight). Everything and everyone had been pushed back to make space for the field. Neat white lines had been painted to indicate base paths and a batter's box. Fluffy satin pillows that fairly dripped with jewels had been set out as bases. Bleachers had been erected in the outfield, back between the ship hulks of the buildings, and even the crocodile tower was in use as a scoreboard.

But most amazing of all were the players—a whole team of pirates, every one of them dressed in a turn-of-the-century baseball uniform with PIRATES lettered boldly across the front. They wore gloves and caps. A few wore spikes, although most had chosen to stay with boots. Some even carried pistols and daggers stuck in their belts.

Smee was on the mound—a rather narrow, oblong rise with a tombstone stuck at its back end—warming up with Jukes as catcher. Far out in the centermost section of the bleachers sat Hook, a buxom tavern wench at his side.

As Peter and the Lost Boys stared wide-eyed at the scene a gnarled little pirate streaked onto the field, snatched up the jeweled pillow that was serving as second base, and bolted for the crowd.

"Look out!" cried Smee from the mound. "He's stealing second!"

A bulky pirate acting as plate umpire took a step forward, pulled out a blunderbuss, and shot the thief dead in his tracks. Second base was retrieved and returned to its proper place.

"Play ball!" growled the umpire.

Peter and the Lost Boys were already making their way out to the bleachers. When they reached them, they aban-

doned their disguises and crept under the iron stanchions
and wooden planking, keeping carefully back in the shadows and out of sight. When they had reached a position
almost directly beneath Hook, they lifted their heads and
peeked out.

Jack Banning was stepping up to the plate. He wore the
same old-time uniform as the pirates and carried a peg leg
as a bat. He was flushed with excitement, his smile huge
with anticipation. He swung the peg leg confidently, eagerly.

Peter started to his feet and might have leaped right out
onto the field and gone for his son, except that Hook
suddenly shouted, "Jack, Jack lad, this is the ultimate
makeup game. It makes up for all the games *Daddy* missed.
Old Hook would never miss your game."

Peter flinched at the sneering way Hook referred to
"Daddy."

Jack paused at the edge of the batter's box and waved
brightly in acknowledgment. "This one's for you, Captain!"

"Tear the leather right off 'er!" Hook shouted back,
laughing gaily. "Rip that bauble, son!"

Peter sagged back in disbelief. There was no disguising
the camaraderie that existed between his son and Hook.
There was no hiding from what he had seen in his son's
face—the joy, the excitement, the anticipation. Jack was
having fun. Jack and Hook together.

Hook led a sudden cheer as pirates seated in the bleachers
to one side began to flip cards that flashed crude drawings of
first Hook's face and then Jack's.

"Jack! Jack! Jack's our man! If he can't do it, no one
can!"

The cards flipped again, and a huge message read: RUN
HOME JACK! Jack, standing at home plate with the peg leg
gripped tightly in both hands, stared at the message in
confusion, a hint of doubt creeping into his eyes. Smee
paused, turned, saw the sign, dropped the ball with a gasp,
and raced out to the stands, yelling and waving his hands.

Moments and a few bruised heads later, the order of the cards had been reversed to read: HOME RUN JACK!

Smee stood poised on the pitching mound, eyeing Jack steadily. He held Jack's own autographed baseball, working it around in his fingers. Jack stepped into the batter's box and then out again. He scratched his head and adjusted his cap. On the field, all the pirates scratched their heads and adjusted their caps. Jack spat. The pirates spat. Jack tugged at his belt and the pirates tugged at theirs.

Jack stepped back into the batter's box, peg leg cocked. Smee straightened, ready for the first pitch.

"Hold on, Smee!" Hook yelled to his bosun. "I need a glove!"

He turned to the woman beside him, who gingerly unscrewed the captain's claw and replaced it with a glove. Hook beamed. The tavern wench placed the hook on the bleacher seat next to the captain.

And inches from Peter's face.

The eyes of the Lost Boys went wide. Never had there been such a glorious opportunity as this! They had come looking for a way to steal Hook's hook, and the hook had practically been presented to them on a platter! *Take it, Peter!* they mouthed, gesturing wildly, jumping up and down in excitement. *Take it! Take it!*

But Peter wasn't listening. He barely noticed the hook in front of him. His attention was focused entirely on his son, standing in the batter's box with his peg leg cocked and his face flushed and smiling.

Smee threw a ball, high and wide. Jack barely gave it a look. Smee threw a second ball, low and away. Jack was not tempted. He was all business now, all concentration.

Smee reared back and released.

It was a wicked, sweeping curveball.

No, Peter thought in incongruous dismay. *He can't hit a curve ball!*

Jack tensed, the peg leg came back an inch or two, and he swung.

Crack! He caught his prized baseball squarely on the fat

part of the peg leg and sent it winging skyward. It continued to rise, sailing up and away, out of the ballpark, out of Pirate Square, out of the town itself, and completely out of sight. Never had a baseball been hit so far.

Hook jumped up, his eyes shining. "Did you see that!" he cried out. "Did you see it! Oh, my Jack! You hit the curveball. You did it! Jack, my son!"

Down the stands he bounded, flinging his glove into the air, calling out wildly. Jack was trotting around the bases, leaping and hooting every few steps, shaking every pirate's hand he passed. Hook caught up with him at home plate, lifted him up, and swung him around, both of them smiling and laughing ecstatically. Pirates appeared with a huge barrel marked "CrocAde" above a picture of a grinning crocodile and dumped the contents all over Jack. The entire town cheered wildly.

Hook hoisted Jack onto his shoulders, spun him about, and led the entire procession of players and fans back through the town in celebration.

Beneath the stands, Peter watched in shock, a single, terrible thought running through his head: *He's having so much fun. I've never seen him have this much fun.*

He turned then and stumbled away, forgetting everything that had brought him there, everything that he had come to do. The Lost Boys stared after him in astonishment. What was the matter with him? What was he doing?

Finally, seeing that he indeed had no intention of returning, that he really had lost all interest in finding something to crow about, they exchanged looks of disgust and disappointment and followed after.

A Welcome-Home Party

Peter wasn't quite sure how he made it back to camp. A good eye and a clear memory would certainly have helped had he possessed either, but since he lacked both, it was most probably luck that saw him safely through. He ran the entire way, and the Lost Boys never did catch up to him. He believed he'd left Tink behind as well, for he neither saw nor heard from her during his flight. Pursued by demons he recognized all too well, he charged down the winding island trails with blind disregard for his safety, heedless of the heights he scaled and the drops he descended, consumed by bitterness and despair. Everywhere he turned, in shadowed woodland niches, in the mirrored surface of a pond, in the clouds that sailed peacefully overhead, he saw Jack with Hook.

I've lost him, was all he could think. *I've lost him.*

He couldn't bear to consider what had become of Maggie, what Hook might have made of her. It was a parent's worst nightmare—his children stolen away by a terrible influence, a bad habit, lured to a life that was doomed to end badly. Peter railed against himself furiously, laying on blame in thick layers, salt on his wounds. He knew he had failed, that Hook had won, that he had lost his fight for Jack and Maggie. How awful to realize the truth, to see clearly for the first time that things might easily have been different. A little more time spent with his children, a little more attention paid to them, a little extra effort to be there when they needed it, and none of this would be happening. Jack and Maggie were with Hook because Peter had chosen too many times not to be with them.

It was irrational thinking, of course. But then Peter Banning was in an exceedingly irrational state, a parent stripped bare of the armor of Parental Responsibility, an adult bereft of childhood memories, an authority figure only marginally in command of himself.

He crossed the rope bridge from the island to the atoll where the Nevertree stood straight and tall against the blue waters of the ocean, and he raged anew at fate and circumstance, at missed chances and poor choices, at heaven and earth and Hook. He did not fully know where he was as he stumbled on, grasping now in belated hope at the promises Tink had made him, at the wishful looks in the Lost Boys' eyes, at the dreams of rescue that seemed to have eluded him forever. He lurched about in a fog, muttering words of power that had gone empty and flat, now spreading his arms as if they were wings and jumping up and down in a vain effort to fly, now crouching to thrust and parry with an imaginary sword. Back and forth, left and right, hither and yon he staggered, descending into a madness that shut him away within himself as surely as barred doors and latched windows close an empty house. Tears blurred his eyes and ran down his cheeks, and the bitter taste in his mouth choked him until he could barely breathe.

And then, suddenly . . .

WHAP!

Something hard smacked him squarely on the top of his head. Down he went in a heap, his arms and legs outstretched, his body limp. He lay without moving for a time, stunned and frightened, drifting on the edges of consciousness, curling up within himself and hiding away from the pain of the world.

When he finally opened his eyes again, he found himself sprawled at the edge of the Nevertree pool. He took several deep breaths to clear his head, then struggled to his knees and bent over to splash water on his face. He remained kneeling when he had finished, watching the waters clear before him. As they did, the face of a boy appeared. The boy was perhaps fourteen and had wild, blond hair and mischief in his eyes. The boy, Peter thought, seemed familiar.

For though he wasn't, he looked very much like Jack.

Jack! Jack! Jack!

In the distance somewhere, the pirates were chanting his son's name, over and over.

He reached down and touched the reflection in the pool, tracing the lines of the boy's face. The water rippled slightly with the movement, and the image changed.

Peter caught his breath. The face had become his own.

Jack! Jack! Jack!

He caught sight of something beneath the image, something round and solid that rested at the bottom of the pool. He reached down into the waters and carefully extracted it. He held it wonderingly in his hand. It was Jack's autographed baseball, the one his son had hit out of Pirate Square.

Understanding flooded through him. It was the baseball, falling at last out of the sky, that had struck him.

Jack's baseball.

Come somehow to him.

It was a small thing, really—a meaningless circumstance, some would argue. But Peter Banning held that ball aloft as if it were a trophy, and something primal came alive in him, something so feral he could neither understand nor contain it. He reared back and screamed. But the scream did not come out a scream at all, but a crow as wild and challenging as any given forth by Rufio.

Peter surged to his feet, galvanized by the sound, backing away from the pond in a crouch until he was up against the trunk of the Nevertree. A voice whispered. *Here! Here!* He whirled around, searching for the speaker. A shadow thrown against the shaggy old tree was poised to flee. Peter moved and the shadow moved.

Then he saw that the shadow was his own.

He stared down again at Jack's baseball, and as he did so he saw out of the corner of his eye his shadow move, gesturing to him, beckoning anxiously. The voice whispered again. *Here!*

Peter glanced up hurriedly and the shadow froze. Peter traced the shadow's legs downward to its feet, finding them attached to his own. He lifted his leg and so did his shadow. All well and good.

He rubbed his head where the baseball had struck and took a step closer. This time his shadow did not follow, but actually charged ahead, waving him anxiously on, calling out to him to hurry. *Come on, Peter, come on!* He went obediently, not bothering to question that such a thing could be, wondering only where it would lead. The shadow pointed downward to a gnarled hole. Peter pushed back a tangle of vines and grasses that half masked the wood and bent close. What he saw was the outline of a face, revealed by just the right slant of the sun's bright light, the image etched clearly in the worn bark, eyes and nose and a mouth that stretched open as if it were . . .

Crowing.

And there was more. There were names carved in the bole's flat surface, names out of time and memory, names from a past he had thought lost to him forever.

TOOTLES.   CURLY.   SLIGHTLY.   NIBS.
JOHN.   MICHAEL.

Forgotten for so long, Peter realized as he traced the carvings with his finger, feeling the familiar roughness against his skin. Forgotten in the loss of childhood. Forgotten in growing up.

"Tootles," he whispered. "Wendy . . ."

And then the knothole opened before him, a door to something that lay within. Peter hesitated just an instant, then began to crawl through. There was a hollow space beyond. It was dark and the fit was tight, but he kept at it, knowing somehow that the rest of what had been lost to him, the rest of who he was, was waiting inside.

Halfway through, he became wedged like a cork in a bottle. He braced his hands against the sides of the opening and pushed. Abruptly he popped through, tumbling head-first into the darkness to land on his hands and knees.

Behind him, the knothole closed. Peter reached out blindly, groping without success for something solid to grasp.

Then a light appeared, approaching out of the darkness, growing steadily brighter. Abruptly Tinkerbell appeared, tiny and radiant as she hung in the air before him, no longer dressed in her faerie garb, but in a flowing gown of lace and satin, of ribbons and silk, of colors that shimmered like sunsets and sunrises and rainbows after thunderstorms.

"I've been waiting, Peter," she said.

Peter stared.

"Well, why don't you say something?"

He swallowed. "You look . . . nice, Tink."

"Nice?"

"Beautiful."

She blushed then, bowed in the faerie way, and straightened, smoothing back the gown's ruffles.

"Do you like it?" she asked him, and pirouetted slowly one full turn.

He grinned like an awkward boy and nodded. "Very much." He came forward a step and bent close. "What's the occasion, Tink?"

She grinned back. "You are. You've come home, you silly ass."

Peter rubbed the bump on his head tentatively, confused. "Home?" he repeated doubtfully.

She began to brighten, to extend her glow in steady waves, lighting up the darkness that lay all about, chasing back the shadows to the farthest corners until all was revealed.

Peter looked around wonderingly. He stood in an underground room that had been hollowed out beneath the trunk and within the roots of the Nevertree. There was a huge fireplace at one end, blackened and cold, and the ruins of a rocking chair and a great cradle bed lay piled at the other. A flat section of the tree humped out of the earth at the center of the room and might once have served as a table. Everything had been charred by a devastating fire, and where once the floor must have been swept clean and smooth, there were clusters of mushrooms at every turn.

I know this place! Peter thought excitedly.

"What happened here?" he asked Tink, bending and touching as he examined the wreckage.

"Hook happened," she answered.

"Hook?"

"Yes, Peter. Hook burned it when you didn't come back."

A light came into Peter's eyes as he rummaged through a pile of debris shoved into a far corner. Gently, almost reverently, he began picking up bits and pieces of what had once been the wooden walls and thatched roof of a child's playhouse.

His hands shook. "Wendy," he breathed. "This is where . . . This is Wendy's house. Tootles and Nibs built it for her. There were make-believe roses for decorations and John's hat for a chimney."

He gasped in shock. "Tink, I remember!"

He whirled about. "This is the home underground!" He rushed over to the remains of the rocking chair. "Wendy used to sit and tell us stories in that chair—except it wasn't here, it was over there! We'd come back from adventures, and she would be darning our socks. She slept here. Tink, Tink, your apartment was here as well—right here! And little Michael's basket bed was here! And John slept here!"

He was charging about now, pointing to first one spot and then another, the words flooding out of him. Tinkerbell watched breathlessly, rapture shining on her face, adoration mirrored in her eyes.

Peter stopped, catching sight of something else amid the wreckage. He knelt, brushed back the ashes and silt, and held up a worn, half-burned, one-eyed teddy bear.

"Taddy. My Taddy," he whispered. His eyes lifted, and he seemed to look somewhere far away. "Taddy used to keep me company in my pram. My mother . . ." He swallowed. "I remember my mother. . . ."

Tink darted forward, her light flashing as she came. She hovered at his ear. "What about your mother, Peter? What do you remember? Tell me!"

Peter was clasping Taddy to his chest now, his head shaking slowly. "I remember her . . . my mother . . . and my father . . . looking down at me, talking about how I would grow up and go to the finest schools. . . ."

The words triggered old, forgotten memories, and they came to life once more, bright and vivid.

He lay in his pram, just a baby, tucked beneath his blue blankets, staring upward at the sky, at the clouds that floated, at the birds that soared.

"*. . . you can be sure, very fine schools indeed.*" *He could hear his mother speaking, her voice insistent.* "*First Whitehall, then Oxford. Of course, after graduation he will prepare for a judgeship, then perhaps a term in parliament. . . .*"

"It was only what all grown-ups want for their children," Tink advised solemnly, her soft voice like a bell in his ear.

"Yes, but it frightened me so," said Peter. "I didn't want to grow up . . . and someday die."

The baby thrashed wildly in his pram and the brakes came loose. Down the walkway it went, gathering speed, rolling toward a pond. Peter's mother gave chase, frantic to catch up. At the edge of the pond, the pram suddenly stopped, safe.

But the inside of the pram was empty. The baby was gone.

It was night then. Rain tumbled down from the clouded sky. Thunder rolled and lightning flashed. On an island at the center of the pond lay the baby, soaked to the skin and crying dismally. A tiny light appeared and transformed into Tinkerbell. She stood looking down at him, then picked up a leaf to shield his face from the rain. Cooing and whispering, she calmed him. The baby murmured, and she replied. Then she threw a sprinkling of pixie dust over him, took hold of his tiny hand, and away they flew into the night.

"I brought you here to Neverland," whispered Tink.

Then Peter was three, flying back again to Kensington Gardens, night all about, moon and stars distant and pale. He flew to a third-story window and tried to open it. But the window was locked. The boy stared at it in confusion.

Despair filled his eyes as he saw that inside his mother slept with her arms wrapped close about another child.

"She had forgotten me," Peter said softly. "She had found . . . someone else."

Then he was twelve, flying boldly through the nursery window at 14 Kensington Gardens at a dozen years past the turn of the century. The Darling house was dark and still and the nursery bare of the furniture it held now, save for a few of the toys, which looked newer and brighter. He'd found other windows to visit since his own had been locked. He'd chased his foolish, stubborn shadow in and out of this one a few times, and finally it had been caught by Nana and then shut away by Mrs. Darling in a bureau drawer. He came looking for it, found it, and was unable to reattach it. They wrestled in the dark. He tried to stick it on with soap and, when that failed, burst into tears, waking the sleeping girl. . . .

"Boy, why are you crying?" *she asked him.*

They bowed to each other and he asked her back, "What's your name?"

"Wendy Angela Moira Darling. What's yours?"

"Peter Pan."

Peter's eyes were wide and staring and his breathing was rapid. How many times had he come back for her after that? Always in the spring, to return her to Neverland for cleaning, to take her away once again. . . .

He saw her aging, growing up while he did not, leaving her childhood while he remained oblivious and unchanged. Thirteen, fifteen, seventeen . . .

And then one day he forgot to come for her and did not come again for many years. When at last he did, when finally he remembered, he found her kneeling in the nursery by the fire, her face in shadows, the room transformed once more. . . .

"Hullo, Wendy," *he greeted.*

"Hullo, Peter," *she replied. A pause.* "You know I cannot come with you. I have forgotten how to fly. I grew up a long time ago."

"No, no! You promised you wouldn't!"

But she had, of course, despite her promise, because in the world outside of Neverland you always grew up. So Peter became friends with her daughter, Jane, and for many years they went together to Neverland.

But Jane grew up as well, and one day Peter came to the Darling nursery to discover that Wendy was a grandmother and Jane's daughter now slept in her bed. Peter, ever adventurous, skipped onto the bedpost to view the sleeping child and found himself face-to-face with Moira. Something in the way the smile on her lips hid their kisses enchanted Peter and made him reluctant to leave. Every time he tried to go, he was forced to turn back again. A dozen times he ran to the window and started to fly away, Tink beckoning from without, anxious to go on to other windows, to blow out the stars in other skies. But each time he hesitated and went back for another look.

Then Wendy appeared, slipping through the door of the nursery, racing to stay his passage for a single moment, so anxious was she to see him. But Peter needed no staying this night, drawn by what he saw in Moira's face, caught in a net that even he could not escape.

"I shall give her a kiss," he offered finally.

But Wendy dashed to stop him. "No, Peter. No buttons and no thimbles for her. Moira is my granddaughter, and I cannot bear to see her dear heart broken when she finds she cannot keep you—as I once found I could not."

She cried then, overcome with a vision of what might have been. Peter sat next to the sleeping Moira, twirling a thimble between his fingertips. But at the last minute he changed his mind for reasons that would be forever unclear. Captivated by the girl, he bent to kiss her on the lips as he had seen others kiss, and as his lips touched hers the thimble dropped away.

He failed to see the sudden closing of the latticed windows—as if a breeze had sprung up. He failed to hear the click of their lock. He failed to see the look of horror on Tink's face as she peered through the glass from without. . . .

"I thought I had been shut away from you forever," she whispered, remembering with him.

Then Peter was in school, dressed in a jacket and tie and polished shoes, his hair cut and combed, everything neat and proper and in place. He sat at a desk among other schoolchildren, staring out the open window into a fall afternoon thick with colored leaves and musty smells. A teacher walked to him, smiled, and said, "Peter? Where did you go?"

She closed the window, startling him, so that he replied, "I don't remember. . . ."

The memories faded. Peter stood staring into space, Tink hovering now at his nose, a splash of light against the gloom.

"Oh, Peter," she said, and her voice was small and troubled. "I can see why it is so hard for you to find a happy thought. You carry so many sad ones."

Peter did not answer, stunned at the truths his memory had unearthed. He was who they said he was. He was who they believed him to be. Tink and the Lost Boys—they were right.

He was Peter Pan.

He groaned as his eyes scanned the wreckage of his boyhood, the devastation of what he had once held so dear. But the hard truth was that all of his lives were in ruins, both in this world and the other. He had made them so; he had given up all his happy thoughts a long time ago. He had let them slip away.

Almost without thinking, he tossed Taddy into the air in front of him. Taddy rose, and the tumbling motion slowed almost to nothing. Peter watched his teddy bear freeze against the gloom, and his gaze fixed on the single remaining eye as it stared down at him. Slowly his hands reached up.

"Wait," he whispered. "I'll catch you, Taddy. I'll catch you."

The fuzzy old bear fell toward him, but as his hands closed about its stuffed body, it was not Taddy he held, but Jack—bright-eyed and smiling at four years of age.

"Jack! Jack!" he called out to his son.

"Fly me, Daddy, fly me!" another, familiar voice cried.

"Maggie! Baby!"

He caught his daughter in his arms, holding them both close, twirling them about wildly. They laughed and shouted with glee. Moira appeared and joined their circle, her arms coming about his waist, the soft scent of her skin filling him up. He kissed and hugged them, and they kissed and hugged him back.

"Yes!" he cried happily. "My family—Jack, Maggie, Moira, I love you so much! I love being with you, having you close. Oh, I'm so lucky! Yes, Tink! Tink, this is my family, my wonderful, incredible family. They're back! They're . . ."

His eyes snapped wide—for they had been closed on his vision—and he stared about in confusion. He was fifteen feet above the floor, hanging in midair. A surge of panic swept through him. He flailed at nothing and began to drop.

"No, Peter!" Tink howled, pushing up from beneath to keep him in place. "That's your happy thought! Don't lose it!"

He continued to fall, frantically trying to regain control of himself, shouting, "How? What?"

"It's yours forever!" Tink squealed. "Hold that thought!"

Peter's eyes squinched, his body tensed, and he brought back the image of Jack, Maggie, Moira, and himself twirling about and laughing merrily, of the warmth and depth of feeling his family gave to him, of the love they shared. . . .

He felt himself slow and then stop. His eyes opened. He felt himself begin to rise again.

"Yes!" breathed Tink, suddenly eye to eye with him. "Yes, Peter Pan!"

"I've done it!" Peter whispered, still rising, flooded with emotions he could not begin to describe. "Look at me! Look at me, Tink!"

He twisted about sharply and caromed off a wall. Down he dipped and then up again. The grown-up within him faded like a ghost at dawn and the sleeping child came awake. All the trappings of all the years he had struggled to find what he had lost vanished. Twisting and tumbling about, he embraced anew the dreams that had belonged to Peter Pan.

"Tink, I can fly!" he shouted. "I can really fly!"

"Then follow me and all will be well!" Tinkerbell cried in glee. "I love you!"

And up through the hollowed trunk of the Nevertree they flew.

Pixie Dust

Oh, it was a glorious moment for Peter as he soared upward through the Nevertree, his earthbound restraints shed, his identity recovered, and his boyhood found anew.

With Tinkerbell leading the way, he spiraled through the gloom, gaining speed and confidence as he went, his exhilaration welling up inside until he thought he must burst. Out through a split in the giant trunk they exploded, faerie and boy, twisting this way and that, darting among the ancient limbs like fireflies at night. Down and around they sped, whipping through leafy boughs, spinning like tops and whirling like pinwheels. Tree houses flashed by in snippets of wood and colored cloth. Birds scattered with wild cries.

Oh, look! Peter Pan is back!

He cannoned out the top of the Nevertree and rose toward the clouds beyond, laughing in delight. He was transformed, become the essence of the spirit that lives within us, that wondrous spark of childhood we all too frequently manage to leave behind in growing. It flared within him like a fire fanned, and suddenly he could contain himself no longer.

Back arched, neck stretched forth, head thrown back, he began to crow.

"Yes, Peter, yes!" he heard Tink shout. "Oh, welcome home, Peter Pan!"

Together they flew into the clouds, there to mimic each other's attempts at foolishness, to do swan dives and belly flops, to fly upside down and backward, to race against shadows and sunbeams, to play at tag and hide-and-seek. When they had exhausted themselves, when the initial thrill of flying together once again had diminished just enough, they lay back upon a cloud to float in the breeze.

There, for the first time, Peter looked down at himself and was startled by what he saw. He was no longer a fat, old Peter Banning. He was a younger, lighter version. Pounds had somehow been shed, muscles had somehow reemerged. He was sleek and hard and younger looking by years. He threw his head back and laughed at the impossibility of it all—at the wonder of what he had become.

"Oh, the cleverness of me!" he exclaimed, the boldness of the little boy easing past the grown man's restraint.

Then he leaped back to his feet and dived through the clouds toward Neverland's green jewel. Down he went, faster and faster, a mischievous gleam in his eye. Tink caught up with him, as reckless and willing as he, saw that gleam, and knew instinctively what he was about.

Where are they? he asked himself, scanning the pillar of rock and the Nevertree that sat atop it. *Where are the Lost Boys?*

He found them gathered at summer where it faded into autumn, bunched in a tight circle about Rufio. A stick traced patterns in the earth as Rufio outlined a plan of attack against Hook and the pirates. Heads arched forward in concentration as his stick moved.

Peter came in like a tornado, spinning over their heads, autumn's leaves cascading downward in his wake. Pockets, at the back edge of the crowd, was the first to look up, floppy cap knocked askew. His eyes went wide as he saw Peter, and he tumbled over onto his back.

"Id's hib!" he gasped, pulling at the clothing of those closest. "Id's really hib!"

Peter laughed and spun back again, Tink at his heels. Down he flew a second time, whooping in triumph. Other Lost Boys were looking now, turning to stare, then jumping to their feet. Latchboy and Too Small were screaming in delight, arms waving and gesturing. Rufio, distracted finally from the description of his battle plan, rose to confront the cause of the interruption.

Peter swooped low across the sea of heads, snatched a

Lost Boy's dagger from its sheath, and with a single pass severed Rufio's belt. Down went Rufio's pants to lie in a tangle about his feet. Lost Boys everywhere cheered and shouted, trying to follow Peter's flight. Peter came back a final time, skimmed the surface of the pond with his hands, and sent a spray of water cascading directly into Rufio's astonished face.

Landing finally in their midst, Peter found himself the delighted recipient of high-fives, backslaps, and congratulations of every form. Pan was back! Peter Pan had returned! They were all with him now, and in that instant they would have followed him anywhere.

Rufio realized the truth of things, and his face fell. All but forgotten by the others, he tugged up his pants and charged up a rope ladder into the Nevertree. He disappeared inside his house and emerged again brandishing the Pan sword. Back he came, climbing down a knotted rope, his eyes wild and hot, the blade of the Pan sword glittering in the bright sunlight.

Peter, with Too Small on his shoulders, Pockets in his arms, and adoring Lost Boys all about, didn't see him coming. It was not until Rufio had reached the ground and given forth a piercing crow that everyone turned to discover him bounding toward Peter with the Pan sword held high.

All of the Lost Boys scattered, terrified. Peter dropped Pockets and swung Too Small away.

"Defend yourself, Peter Pan!" shouted Ace as he ducked from view.

But it was too late for that. Rufio was already on top of Peter, who crouched to fly.

Then, astonishingly, Rufio dropped to his knees, tears streaking his coffee-colored face, his red-streaked hair in wild disarray, a look of agony and awe reflected in his eyes.

"You are him," he acknowledged, breathing hard. "You are the Pan." He held out the sword to Peter, hilt forward. "It's yours. Take it, jollymon. You can fight, you can fly, you can . . ."

Words failed him. He swallowed hard. There was disappointment and a trace of resentment reflected in his face, but admiration as well. Peter accepted the sword, stepped away, and drew a line in the earth. Peter and the Lost Boys stood on one side of the line. Rufio stood alone on the other.

Rufio rose to his feet and crossed. The boy that had been and the man that would be faced each other with faint smiles and embraced.

All around them, the Lost Boys cheered.

That night there was a huge celebration in honor of Peter Pan. The Lost Boys painted themselves in their wildest colors, dressed in their finest garb, ate all of their favorite foods until they were full to bursting, and then danced Indian dances before bonfires that lit the darkened skies for miles. Whooping and leaping about, they ringed the fires, lifting their arms and brandishing their weapons fiercely, singing songs in languages both imagined and real. Peter was the center of attention, called upon repeatedly to do flying stunts. He willingly complied, giving exhibitions of barrel rolls, loop the loops, corkscrews, and spins and sweeps so daring that he clipped the ends of branches and the tips of grass. Each new stunt demanded another, and the more daring that one the greater the cry to top it with the next. Peter laughed and joked and played games with one and all, the joy and wonder of his boyhood coming back to him as he did so, the bits and pieces of who and what he had been recalling themselves in a dazzling kaleidoscope of memories.

To think that he had ever given it up! To think that anything could ever have persuaded him to abandon it!

So great was his enthusiasm at rediscovering the boy, so intense his happiness at being shed of the man, that he was lost for a time in the living of the moment, and the larger picture of his life and loved ones became obscured.

Then finally, toward morning, the moons of Neverland gone westward to their rest and the stars grown faint in a gradual brightening of the eastern sky, it occurred to Peter that Tink was missing. She had been with him for a time, celebrating with the rest, but at some point in the festivities she had disappeared entirely.

Peter flew up into the Nevertree, calling her name, thinking that perhaps she had decided to play hide-and-seek with him. He soared to the top of the ancient tree and swooped down again without finding her. He flew 'round about and saw nothing.

At last he arrived at the little vine-covered clock that was her house. He called for her as he flashed by, but there was no response. Below, the Lost Boys danced on, their cries rising up into the deep silence of the Nevertree's limbs. Peter landed on a tree branch, bent down so that he was eye level with Tink's house, and peered inside.

Tinkerbell sat with her back to him, her head lowered into her hands, her shoulders quaking. Peter frowned in confusion, aware suddenly that she was crying.

"Tink? Tink, is that you?" he asked anxiously.

There was no answer. The room was cluttered with strange things. A man's open wallet served as a dressing screen, a spool of thread as a stool, keys as clothes hangers, and loose coins and a few red Life Savers as decorations. A driver's license hung on the wall like a family portrait.

Most of it belonged to Peter, of course, but the little boy he had become failed to recognize them.

"Tink?" he repeated, more insistent this time. "What's wrong? Are you hurt?"

The crying stopped. "No. I just got some pixie dust in my eye, that's all."

"I shall get it out for you," he offered, drawing his dagger.

Tink shook her head, still turned away.

"Are you sad, Tink?" he asked.

"No. Please go away."

Peter brightened. "Need a firefly? Or a bit of dewy webbing? I know. You're sick! You need a thermometer. A thermometer will make you all better."

"No, it's not about that."

Peter wasn't listening. "That's how Nibs got the Wendy-girl better after Tootles shot her down, no thanks to you. Nibs put the thermometer in her mouth and she got all better. Don't you remember?"

Tink quit crying and nodded. "Remember how you spoke in Hook's voice and saved that great ugly Tiger Lily and made peace with the Indians?"

"Oh, sure I do." Peter drew himself up. "Ahoy, you lubbers!" he said in his wondrous imitation of Hook's voice. "Set her free! Yes, cut her bonds and let her go! At once, d'ye hear, or I'll plunge my Hook in you!" He laughed merrily. "We had the best adventures, didn't we, Tink?"

Tink's tousled head lifted. Without turning, she asked hesitantly, "Peter, do you remember your last adventure? The one to . . . to rescue your kids?"

Peter blinked in confusion, then mimicked, "Peter Pan's got kids?"

Tink went very still. "Answer me this: Why are you in Neverland?"

He laughed anew. "That's easy. To be a Lost Boy and never grow up. To fight pirates and blow out stars. Ask me another question. C'mon, I like this game."

"Oh, Peter," she whispered.

She rose to face him.

Then her light began to blaze, flaring so brightly that Peter was forced to back away from the door of the clock house, squinting his eyes protectively. As he did so, his shadow suddenly darted away on its own, startled by what it saw. Tink's clock house suddenly began to break apart. Peter gasped, and his eyes opened wide. The light grew bigger, taller, more radiant before him—as if a piece of the sun had come down from the sky.

And all at once there was Tinkerbell, no longer tiny but grown as large as he was, the remains of her house sitting precariously on her head and shoulders.

Her smile was wondrous. "It is the only wish I ever made for myself," she said.

Peter stared. She was so . . . large. She wore a lacy gown, long and flowing in the gentle night breeze. Her eyes sparkled and her hair shimmered as if it had been sprinkled with tiny stars. She was only standing there, but she was doing things to Peter inside that he didn't understand.

He tried to speak, but she brought a finger up to his mouth quickly to silence him.

Then she stepped up to him, her arms came about his waist, and her face pushed close to his own.

Peter, a boy now to all intents and purposes, gave her a puzzled look. "What are you doing?"

Tink put her nose against his. "I'm going to give you a kiss."

Peter grinned and squeezed one hand up between them to receive it. For in his boyhood, thimbles and buttons had always been kisses, and it was one of these that he expected to receive now.

But Tink closed one of her hands over his own, pressed herself against him, put her lips on his, and gave him a real kiss.

Then she stepped back again. "Oh, Peter. I couldn't feel this way about you if you didn't love me, too. You do, don't you? It's too big a feeling to feel all by myself, you know. It's the biggest feeling I've ever had. And this is the first time I've been big enough to let it come out."

She bent forward to kiss him again. Peter held himself motionless, liking the feeling that the kiss produced even if he was unsure why, wanting to share her biggest feeling because it was, in some way, his own. But as her lips brushed his he caught sight of the flower she was wearing in her hair.

It reminded him of another.

It reminded him of . . .

"Maggie," he whispered and pulled back. "Jack. Moira."

There was a shifting within him of time and place, of memories and dreams, and the boy and man readjusted their positions, the boy giving back something of what he had taken, the man accepting what was offered without feeling the need to ask for more.

"Please!" Tink begged, trying to bring him close again. "Please, Peter," she whispered. "Don't spoil it."

But she was too late now. The spell was broken. It was there in Peter's eyes, in the look on his face, in the way the wrinkles tightened at the corners of his mouth.

"Tink," he whispered back, keeping his hands on her arms so that they would not lose contact. "You are, you have always been, a part of my life. That will never change. But my children, Jack and Maggie, are part of *me*. My family, Tink. I can't forget them."

He looked out through the branches toward the lights of the pirate harbor and the *Jolly Roger*. "My kids are on that ship. I have to save them."

He turned back to her. There were definitely tears in her eyes now, and no number of pixie dust excuses could disguise them. Slowly, she nodded. For a moment her gaze remained fixed on him. Neither moved, as if each had been frozen to a statue.

Then Tink broke away. "What are you looking at? Go on—save them, Peter."

Peter tried to speak, but her hand whipped up sharply and flung pixie dust in his face. He sneezed and backed away.

"Go on!" she cried. "Fly, Peter Pan! Fly!"

And away he soared, swift as thought, rising up against the coming dawn like a bird, the memory of Tink's kiss already fading from his mind. It was Jack and Maggie who occupied his thoughts now. The three days were up. Hook would be waiting.

He didn't look back. If he had, he would have seen that Tink, almost hidden in the dappled shadows of the Never-tree, was growing small again.

Bad Form!

Resplendent in his scarlet and gold brocade captain's coat, his claw polished and shining in the early-morning sunlight, James Hook stood on the quarterdeck of the *Jolly Roger* and thought what a lucky man he was.

A smile creased his angular features as he gazed out over the sea of pirate faces staring up at him from the main deck below. Faithful, loyal dogs, these. Smee stood at one hand, his bespectacled face beaming. Jack stood at the other, a miniature version of his new mentor, dressed like Hook from tricorne to boots. It was the third day of the captain's wait for the reappearance of Peter Pan—the new, improved version, he hoped, but any version would do. Hook gave his mustaches a friendly twist. The final day, the day on which his lovely, wonderful war would at last commence, the day on which Peter Pan would meet his well-deserved end.

He danced up on his toes like a ballerina. Ah, he could smell the powder of the fired cannons and hear the ripping of the shot.

But first things first.

"Smee, the box, if you please," he ordered.

His bosun promptly produced a flat wooden box, which he opened to Jack, revealing a velvet-lined interior containing row after row of golden earrings. Jack stared down at them wordlessly.

Hook bent close. "There's so many choices, Jack. Which one will you choose? Which one, Jack?"

Jack hesitated a moment, thinking. Then he reached down abruptly with one gloved hand and snagged a 'hook' earring just like the one worn by the captain.

"Ah, good form, Jack!" Hook declared, beaming. "Excellent choice. You know, it's a very special time when a pirate receives his first earring." He glanced down at the crew. "Right, lads?"

"Aye, Cap'n," they cried as one, and many a rough face creased in contentment. What cattle.

Hook turned back to Jack. "Now, Jack, I'm going to ask you to *mooove* your head to the side—just a little bit—"

He turned Jack's head to expose the boy's ear. "There," he advised with a smile. He brought the point of his hook up to the exposed lobe. "Now brace yourself, Jack, because this is really going to hurt."

He laughed. Jack squinched his eyes shut.

A crowing sound brought Hook up short. All eyes lifted to the mainsail where a shadow had been cast by the sun's brilliant light against the canvas.

It was the shadow of Peter Pan.

A sword sliced neatly through the sail, and the outline of Pan fell away to the deck. The toughened pirate crew flinched.

Smee's eyes went wide as he crouched behind Hook. "Cap'n! It's a ghost!" he gasped.

But Hook gave a smile that was all iron and grit. "I think not, Smee. I think the doodle-doo has returned."

"Who is it, Captain?" asked Jack, frowning.

A figure leaped from behind the canvas and slid down the sunbeam as if skating on ice to land squarely on the image he had cast.

And there was Peter Pan, a sword in his hand, a smile on his lips, youth and joy mirrored in his face. Forest green from head to foot with boots, leggings and tunic belted and scalloped like the leaves of the Nevertree itself, he looked the very incarnation of the Pan of old. Pirates backed away from him hurriedly, tripping over one another's peg legs and cutlasses in their efforts to get clear. Hook's smile broadened in blissful contentment. Smee cowered further in Hook's shadow. Jack stared.

Peter gathered himself, flipped high into the air, and

came down directly in front of the quarterdeck stairs leading up to Hook.

For an instant everyone held a collective breath.

Then the captain stepped forward. "Peter Pan," he greeted, and his voice became a snake's hiss of expectation. 'Tis true, time does fly. And so do you, I see. Good form. Tell me—how ever did you manage to fit into those smashing tights?"

His pirates gave a laugh and a rousing cheer at their captain's wit. As Peter placed one foot upon the stairs that led to his adversary, Hook stamped on the deck above and the stairs flipped over, hiding away the red carpet. Hook's smile broadened.

Peter flushed, but continued his climb until he stood on the quarterdeck, facing the captain. "Hand over my children, James Hook, and you and your men may go free."

Hook's laugh was a bark of derision. "Really? How kind of you!" He feigned a thoughtful look. "Tell you what. Why not ask the little dears what *they* want? Start with this one, why don't you? Jack? Someone to see you, son."

An unctuous mix of deference and consideration showed in his sharp face as he ushered Jack forward to stand in front of him. He did not miss the fact that some of the cockiness left Pan's eyes as he saw what had been done to his son. He took note of the shock that replaced it.

"Jack—are you all right?" Peter asked quickly. "Did he hurt you? Where's Maggie? I promised I would be here for you, and I am. You'll never lose me again. Jack, I love you."

Jack did not respond. There was no recognition in his eyes. He might as well have been Hook's son for all that he seemed to remember being anyone else. He eyed Peter for an instant longer, then stepped back defiantly.

" 'Promise,' did you say?" Hook sneered. "Hah! A cheap word for you, Peter. And did I hear you use the 'l word'? By Barbecue's bones, that's real cheek!"

Peter ignored him. He reached out to Jack. "Jack, take my hand. We're going home."

Jack shook his head stubbornly. "I am home."

Hook jeered. His narrowed gaze fixed on Peter. "You see, Peter, he is my son now. He loves me. And, unlike you, I am prepared to fight dearly for him."

He pushed Jack behind him and lifted his claw menacingly. "I've waited a long time to shake your hand with this!" he hissed. "Prepare to meet your doom!"

Peter crouched guardedly, his sword lifting. Then Hook signalled to the men of his pirate crew and an eager rumble of expectation arose. Peter hesitated only a moment, then flipped back down the quarterdeck stairs and whirled to meet the attack.

Instantly the pirates were on him, cutlasses and daggers drawn, blades flashing wickedly. Peter stood his ground, fending off slash and hack, thrust and cut, as agile and quick as a cat. Noodler and Bill Jukes were in the lead, but Peter turned them aside as if they were cut out of cardboard, and they tumbled back into their fellows.

From the quarterdeck, Hook watched, taking time to unsheathe his sword and practice a quick series of thrusts and parries. Jack, forgotten momentarily, watched the battle with an uncertain frown.

There was something familiar about Peter Pan.

"Don't I know him, Captain?" he asked cautiously.

"You've never seen him before in your life," Hook sneered, concentrating on his form.

The pirate attack was tightening about Peter, the sea of weapons coming closer and closer. Jukes and Noodler had regained their feet and were encouraging their fellows. Peter waited until they were almost on top of him, then launched himself skyward, flying up to the yardarm, where he shouted down to Jack.

"Jack! Jack, listen to me! You won't believe this, but I found my happy thought! It took three days, Jack, but when I finally did it, up I went! You know what my happy thought was, Jack? It was you!"

Hook was livid. Whirling away, he rushed to the deck railing and slashed the rope that bound the cargo net—which hung poised directly over Peter Pan.

Instinctively Jack cried out in warning, not stopping to think what he was saying. "Dad! Look out!"

Too late. The heavy cargo net collapsed on Peter, dragging him off the yardarm and down to the deck. Pirates descended on him with a yell, weapons flashing. Peter struggled to his feet, straightened with the Pan sword held high, and gave forth a battle crow.

Jack's jaw dropped. "That *is* my Dad!" he whispered to himself in disbelief. "It really is!"

Suddenly there were answering crows from all about and the Lost Boys appeared. They came from everywhere at once, yelling and sounding their battle cries. War paint streaked their faces, and they wore armor to shield their bodies—helmets formed of hollowed-out gourds, vests and knee and arm pads of bamboo sticks laced together with leather thongs, shoulder pads of shells and wood, and brightly colored feathers and ribbons hanging everywhere. Rufio led the first wave of Lost Boys, catapulting from a springboard onto the ship's rigging. The Lost Boys' skiff, the *Dark Avenger,* seemed to appear out of nowhere to swing in next to the *Jolly Roger.* A boarding party clambered up the side. Ace and a handful more launched themselves from cranes and ship spars that jutted from the wharf. Others swung down on ropes and crawled over the railing from the waters below.

Hook stared in disbelief. It seemed to be raining Lost Boys. He snatched Smee by the shirt front. "Call out the militia! We'll need every last man!"

Smee charged up the stairs to the aft deck and began ringing a brass bell. "Oh, dear, oh, dear! What about Smee?" he muttered, his enthusiasm for Hook's war noticeably diminished.

The Lost Boys and pirates engaged in battle, Rufio and his band swinging down out of the rigging with war clubs in hand to clash with sharp-edged steel. Peter had freed himself from the cargo net and joined them. The main deck turned instantly into a battleground.

Hook charged to the quarterdeck railing, his eyes bright. "By Billy Bones's blood, I love a good war! The perfect start to a perfect day!'' He wheeled back to Jack. "It'll be your first taste of blood, eh, son?''

Jack's small face went pale. *First taste of blood?* He was beginning to think that being a pirate wasn't so wonderful after all.

A small band of Lost Boys rushed up the stairs of the quarterdeck, war clubs waving. But Hook met them at the top and tumbled them down again like dominoes.

A new cry rose as Thud Butt appeared on the wharf front with the remainder of the Lost Boys. He charged up the gangplank, bowling over pirates as he went, knocking several into the drink.

Amidships, Peter and Rufio had rallied a skirmish line of Lost Boys to face a pirate charge forming below the quarterdeck. Thud Butt and Ace hurried to join them. Crossbows, longbows, blowguns, and slingshots released, sending a hail of hard, knobby, glue-tipped missiles into the pirates. Pistols and cutlasses went flying.

The pirate charge dissolved in a cacophony of yowls and screeches.

"Re-form your ranks, you bilge rats!'' shrilled Hook in fury. "Remember the fires that forged you!''

The pirates, of course, had no idea what he was talking about, but hastened to obey anyway. It was doubtful that they knew what they were getting into, having learned nothing from their previous skirmishes with the Lost Boys. But they were nothing if not persistent, and so on they came, giving forth bloodcurdling cries amid clashes of steel.

At Peter's direction the Lost Boys formed two lines, the front kneeling, the back standing.

"Steady, boys,'' he soothed. "Let's show them the white light we're made from.''

The pirates came on, howling. The Pan sword lifted.

"Front row—dazzle!'' Peter cried.

Up rose a line of mirrors, catching the rising sun's brilliant light and sending it squarely back into the eyes of the attacking pirates. They squinted hopelessly, blinded by the glare. Pirates crashed into one another and tumbled down.

Then Ace appeared at the forefront of the Lost Boys

holding a fearsome-looking cannon on which had been mounted a cage filled with squawking chickens. Ace swung the muzzle about, directing it at the pirates. Eggs shot out of the muzzle, splattering into the pirates, knocking them back. As fast as the chickens could lay, the eggs were fired. Yolks spat from the weapon in yellow streams. Eggshells ejected with a clatter. Faster lay the chickens and faster came the eggs.

And now the worst. Ace stepped back and the Lost Boy line re-formed. Bamboo tubes were lifted to shoulders, hand pumps were engaged, and streams of marbles caromed into the pirates and onto the deck. Feet skidded and pirates went down in a pile, arms and legs flailing.

More pirates appeared suddenly from the darkness of the tunnel, summoned by Smee's bell. They charged into the light, weapons drawn, shouting fiercely. But the Lost Boys were waiting. Two lines faced them. The front knelt with shoulder-braced Cataspluts drawn back. As the back dropped rotten tomatoes in place, the Cataspluts released. Once, twice, a third time. Pirates tumbled back, blinded and choking. Pirates slipped and slid into tangled heaps. When one misguided bunch attempted a frontal assault on the gangway, Thud Butt wrapped himself into a ball and the Lost Boys rolled him down the ramp, scattering the pirates like tenpins.

Rufio and a handful of Lost Boys had pried open the grating of the main hatch. As fast as pirates were captured, they were bundled up and rolled into the hold, cursing all the way. Bruised, egg-soaked, and tomato-splattered, Hook's crew was fast disappearing from view. Those who weren't shoved through the hatchways spilled down the gangplank onto the docks. Everywhere, the battle was being lost.

On the quarterdeck, Hook watched with a mix of despair and rage. Nothing was going as he had intended. "Smee," he wailed, "do something intelligent!"

Smee, not hesitating a moment, bolted into the captain's cabin. Hook glared. Very hard to get good help these days, he thought darkly.

He started for the quarterdeck stairs, determined that

someone should pay for this injustice, and came face-to-face with Rufio.

"Hook!" the leader of the Lost Boys hissed.

Hook smiled and beckoned him on.

But then Peter was between them, having flown up from the main deck, the Pan sword cocked. "No, Rufio," he declared. "Hook's mine."

And the redoubtable captain might well have been, except that in the next instant Peter heard a familiar voice cry out from the docks below. "Jack! Jack! Help!"

"Maggie!" Peter cried out in recognition and off he flew again.

Down on the docks, the jailer whom Hook had entrusted with looking after Maggie and the slave kids had come to the conclusion that things weren't going the captain's way. Since his fearless leader was otherwise occupied at the moment and the path out of town seemed unobstructed, he decided now was a good time to think about saving himself.

But not without a little something to see to his future needs, of course.

He slipped the iron key he wore about his neck into the lock and released it, pushing open the door. A fierce scowl greeted the anxious faces of the slave kids clustered before him, sending the pack of them scurrying.

"Jack! Jack!" one little girl called wildly from the window.

"Slag off, ye little sodder!"he growled at her. "I'll be just long enough to claim my fair share and then—"

He stopped in his tracks. Another slave kid was in the process of throwing a rope braided from old curtains out the window. "Here! Where do you think you're going? Get away from that window!"

The slave kid raced for safety and the front room emptied as the bunch of them fled into the recesses of the back. Only the girl was left, still yelling for help. He snatched her up and dragged her away.

Peter flew in just behind him, landing in a skid, coming face-to-face with a second pirate who appeared at the same instant through another door. The second pirate gave Peter a single glance and dove back the way he had come.

Peter charged ahead into the second room. The jailer dropped Maggie like a sack of hot coals and whirled about.

Maggie's eyes went wide. "Daddy?"

Peter was after the jailer instantly, chasing him about a monstrous globe, giving it a spin as he passed. "Small world, isn't it?" he observed, tickling the fellow's breast bone with the tip of his sword.

The frantic jailer flattened himself protectively against a Greek statue, but Peter was behind him almost before he could think. A shove toppled the statue and pinned the hapless pirate to the floor.

Maggie wheeled into Peter's arms.

"Daddy!" she cried gleefully.

He picked her up and swung her about joyfully, then hugged her to him. "I love you so much," he whispered.

"I love you, too," she murmured back.

"I'll never lose you again."

"Stamp me, mailman."

He kissed her on the forehead as Latchboy and half a dozen other Lost Boys rushed into the room.

Peter waved in greeting. "This is my daughter, Maggie," he announced, setting her down again.

"Hi," Maggie greeted.

"Hi," the Lost Boys greeted back, looking doubtful.

Peter was already moving toward the door. "You'll be safe with them until I get back, Maggie," he called over his shoulder. "I have to get Jack. Boys, guard her with your lives."

He gave them a hurried salute and rose into the air.

Latchboy and the others barely saw him leave, their eyes fixed on Maggie. Finally Latchboy whispered, "Are you really a girl?"

The Lost Boys were sweeping the decks of the *Jolly Roger* clean of the few pirates who remained, battening down the main hatch on those who had been captured, and chasing the rest down the gangplank and over the sides. Even Tickles was gone, relieved of his concertina and harried from the ship by Don't Ask. Thud Butt, tired of rolling down rampways, had secured his beloved Four-Way Stop. Working his way into the midst of one pirate melee after another with the bizarre weapon, he had fixed its sight, pulled its trigger, and released a foul-smelling liquid from its four directional tubes into the faces of bewildered pirates, leaving them stunned and gasping for air.

Inside Hook's cabin, Smee was busily gathering up the captain's most valuable treasures and stuffing them into his pants.

"What about Smee?" he said over and over. "It's time for Smee. Yes, it is."

A knot of pirates and Lost Boys burst through the cabin door, fighting as they came, tumbling the furniture and furnishings every which way. Smee shrank from them, hiding behind a Red Cross flag he had confiscated. When a pair of pirates came too close with their weapons, he dropped the flag over their heads, stealing a gold earring from one while doing so.

"Pretty, pretty," he murmured, testing the gold with his teeth as he moved toward the door, his pants and carry bag brimming with loot.

On reaching the far wall he paused at a statue of Hook, twisted the captain's nose, and popped open a peephole.

Can't be too careful, he thought.

Cautiously, he peered out.

Hook stood at the forefront of the quarterdeck, squared off once more with Rufio, his eyes red and dangerous. Jack was behind him, secured between Jukes and Noodler.

"Rufio, Rufio," Hook whispered, drawing the other on.

Rufio advanced, sword drawn, feinting as he came. "Looky, looky, I got Hooky," he whispered back.

Hook sneered. "Sadly, you have no future as a poet."

Peter was flying for all he was worth to reach them, but this time he was too slow. Hook and Rufio engaged, locking swords, fighting across the quarterdeck, lunge and parry, slash and block. Rufio lost his sword once, then got it back. Hook rang the ship's bell with a sweeping blow. It was an even battle between man and boy, pirate and youth, until the wily captain hooked away Rufio's sword with his claw and plunged his own blade deep into the other's body.

Rufio fell to the deck with a gasp just as Peter reached him. Peter knelt in disbelief, cradling the red-streaked head in his lap.

Jack freed himself from Jukes and Noodler and rushed forward to stand at Peter's shoulder. Rufio's eyes fixed on him. "Know . . . what I wish?" he whispered. His eyes shifted to Peter. "That I had . . . a dad like you."

And then, because even in Neverland things do not always end well, he died.

There was a momentary hush as Jack stared down at the fallen Rufio. He felt as if his stomach had been turned to stone. For despite being outwardly a replica of Hook, Jack was decidedly something else inside, where it matters. The thrill and excitement of being a pirate had long since disappeared. The anger and disappointment of being Peter Banning's son had evaporated. His dad had kept his promise this time; he had come for Jack and Maggie. And Jack's memory was stirred by the keeping of that promise—his memory of home and family, of quiet evenings playing board games at the kitchen table, of being read to and reading back in turn, of words of encouragement and wisdom offered when life got a little tough, of all the things that were good and true about his parents.

He turned to face Hook, and tears sprang to his eyes. His real dad would never kill anyone.

"He was only a boy like me, Captain," he said, his lower lip quivering. Then his jaw tightened with new determination. "Bad form, Captain James Hook!" he declared. "Bad form!"

Hook looked stricken.

Peter rose. He was starting toward Hook, the Pan sword lifting, when Jack called out. "Dad!"

Peter turned. Jack was shaking his head slowly.

"Just take me home, Dad. I just want to go home."

"But . . . but you *are* home!" Hook sputtered.

Peter stared at his son for a long moment, then bent to lift him in his arms. Jack removed his tricorne and tossed it at Hook disdainfully. Carrying his son, Peter Banning started to walk away.

Hook stared in disbelief. "Wait! Where are you going?" he demanded, his face crestfallen.

"Home," answered Peter quietly.

He rose from the ship and flew down to the wharf where the pirates were in full retreat and the Lost Boys in complete command. Shouts and cheers heralded his coming, and the Lost Boys thronged about him as he settled down with Jack at the bottom of the gangway. Maggie rushed out to greet him as well, and he clasped both children in his arms, smothering them with hugs and kisses. Jack squirmed free long enough to take off the Hook coat and fling it aside.

"Bangerang!" yelled the Lost Boys from all about. "Victory banquet! Victory banquet!"

Then Latchboy asked, "Where's Rufio?"

"Yeah, where's Rufio?" the others echoed.

"He's dead, isn't he?" Ace said quietly.

"Is Rufio dead forever?" Too Small whispered.

Peter tried to answer, but no words would come. Then abruptly Hook shouted down to him from the deck of the *Jolly Roger*.

"Peter!"

Peter refused to look. He took Maggie in his arms and, with Jack and the Lost Boys crowding close, started to walk away.

"Peter!"

Hook was shrieking at him now, incensed beyond reason. He charged toward the quarterdeck stairs. "Peter, come back and fight me! You hear me. Where are you going? I haven't finished with you, Peter Pan! Is this the best you can offer? I am shocked and dismayed! Bad form!"

Maggie glanced back over Peter's shoulder. "You need a mommy very, very badly!" she yelled back at Hook.

The captain reached the quarterdeck stairs just as Smee emerged from his cabin, pants stuffed with Hook's treasure, a bulging bag slung over one shoulder. He was slinking toward the ship's lifeboat when Hook spotted him.

"Smee!" he howled.

Smee froze, eyes squinched shut.

"Stairs!" Hook bellowed.

Smee's eyes popped open again, a hint of relief showing in his crinkled features. He stamped the decking and the quarterdeck stairs flipped from bare wood to red carpeting. Hook started down without a word.

Smee tried a reassuring smile. "I was just . . . moving yer personals, Cap'n. Out of harm's way and all . . ."

Hook went past him as if he wasn't there, headed for the gangway. "You can't escape me, Peter!" he howled. His face was as scarlet as his coat. "I'll always be your worst nightmare come true! You'll never be rid of me! I vow to you, everywhere you look there will be daggers with notes bearing JAS. Hook! I'll hang them on the doors of your children's children's children's bedrooms for all eternity!" He kicked at the decking. "Do you hear me?"

Peter stopped then, turned, set Maggie down beside him, and walked back to the gangway. He stood looking up at the enraged Hook.

"What do you want, James Hook?" he asked softly.

Hook's face twisted. "I want you, Peter."

Peter recognized the truth then. Revenge against Peter Pan was all that mattered to Captain Hook. He was for the captain an obsession that would not pass until one or the other of them was dead. Hook meant what he said. There would be no peace for Peter or his family until this business was finished once and for all. Peter sighed. "You got me, old man."

On the main deck, Hook had discarded his captain's coat and ripped open his sash. He held his sword balanced and ready in his good hand. His claw gleamed wickedly.

Ace and Don't Ask started forward, their own weapons drawn, but Peter motioned them back.

"Put up your swords, boys," he ordered, and his eyes were grim. "It's Hook or me, this time."

Crocodile Clock

James Hook strode down the gangway of the *Jolly Roger*, sword in hand, his eyes bright and anxious. He grinned wolfishly. "Prepare to die, Peter Pan. It's the only adventure you have left."

They rushed each other and met in a clash of steel. At first Hook had the upper hand, driving Peter back across the wharf as Jack and Maggie and the Lost Boys scattered before them. Then Peter regained control, growing stronger with each exchange. Hook reversed field, drawing Peter after him into the tunnel.

"I remember you being a lot bigger," Peter offered, parrying a wicked slash to his head.

Hook grunted. "To a ten-year-old, I'm huge."

Peter grinned. "Good form, James."

"Don't patronize me, Peter."

They fought their way through the tunnel's darkness and out the other side. Pirates and Lost Boys ran to get out of their way, then followed in their wake like flood waters churning down a dry riverbed. They battled toward a pub entrance, where Peter snatched a tablecloth off a clothesline and taunted Hook as a matador might an enraged bull.

To one side, Jack discarded his Hook vest. Hook sneered.

"Rippingly good comeback, Peter," he offered between thrusts at the tablecloth. "Three days! Imagine. Share your secret with old Hook? Diet? Exercise? A woman? The right woman can do wonders for a man, restore his youth in moments."

They surged back and forth for a minute in front of the

pub. Then the tablecloth seemed to fly up and when it came down again Peter was gone.

Hook stared about in bewilderment. Then he stalked into the pub. Onlookers crowded up to the windows and doors and peered inside.

Peter was leaning on the bar, calmly quaffing a glass of ale. Hook hesitated, then stepped up to join him. As they drank, the captain experienced a rare moment of doubt.

Perhaps I was a bit hasty in issuing that last challenge, he thought.

His mouth tightened into a thin line. It wasn't that he was afraid of Peter Pan. Not he, not James Hook, the man who had been Blackbeard's bosun. It was just that he was befuddled by him. No matter how thorough or careful his plans, Pan always escaped him. How could anyone be so lucky? It was ridiculous. Time after time Hook trapped him, and each time he found a way to get free. It was really very tiring.

Hook sighed. And where was his trusty pirate crew? He couldn't count on a one, by Billy Bones's blood! Chaos had claimed them all. The rats sensed the ship sinking, so to speak, and were looking for a way off. Even Smee had deserted him. He tried to take comfort in the fact that at least he had his long-anticipated war. He tried to ignore the fact that he was losing it.

He took a swipe at Peter, who ducked away. Down the bar they battled, slash and parry, cut and thrust, pausing every so often to take a drink. When their glasses were empty at last, they set them on the counter and backed out once again into the street.

Down the length of Hook's pirate town they fought, twisting and turning from side to side, each seeking to gain an advantage. They reached the barber shop and Peter leaped over Hook and hung just out of reach in the air above him.

Hook glared up at his nemesis, breathing hard. "You've come to Neverland once too often, Peter."

Peter laughed. "Where have I heard *that* before?"

Hook stomped furiously. "Stop hovering! Come down where I can reach you!"

Peter landed in a crouch, the Pan sword extended. Hook surged to the attack once more. Toe-to-toe they battled, sword-to-sword, hissing and grunting with the effort of their struggle.

As they reached the blacksmith's Peter switched hands, tossing the Pan sword from right to left and back again, barely losing a beat as he blunted Hook's attacks.

"Confound you!" Hook raged.

And then suddenly Peter's guard slipped just enough and Hook was through, bulling ahead wildly, too close to strike, but possessed of enough momentum to twist Peter about and force him backward against the grindstone table. Hissing with satisfaction, Hook pinned Peter fast and began to force his head downward toward the spinning stone.

"You're so cocky, aren't you?" Hook sneered. His hook brushed the stone and sparks flew. "But, you know, you're not really Peter Pan. You know that, don't you? You're Peter Banning! Yes! Peter Banning, remember?"

A hint of doubt crept into Peter's eyes.

"You're Peter Banning," Hook went on hurriedly. "And this, Mr. Banning, is all a dream. It's not real. It's just your imagination. It has to be, mmm? Doesn't rational thought say it must? And aren't you a man of rational thought? It must be that you're simply asleep!"

Peter's face was inches from the grindstone.

"When you wake up," Hook continued with a sneer, "you will be fat, old Peter Banning, a cold, selfish man who runs and hides from his wife and children at every opportunity, who's obsessed with success and money! You have lied to everyone, haven't you? Yourself, especially. And now you would pretend to be Peter Pan? Shame on you!"

Peter's strength was fading rapidly now, his fighting power flown away with the last of his happy thoughts, the reality of who and what he had been recalled by Hook's words. Was he really any different now? Wasn't he just playing at being Peter Pan?

"You are a disgrace!" Hook taunted.

The Pan sword fell from Peter's hand. At the entrance to the shop, the Lost Boys stared at one another helplessly.

Then Jack leaped forward to crouch next to his father, just out of Hook's reach, his elfin face creased with sudden determination.

"I believe in you, Dad," he cried out. "You *are* the Pan."

"I believe in you, too, Daddy," Maggie repeated at his elbow.

And then the Lost Boys took up the refrain, speaking it with such conviction that it could not be ignored. Peter glanced past Hook and saw the belief mirrored in their eyes. Ace, Latchboy, Pockets, Thud Butt, Too Small, No Nap, Don't Ask, and all the others, saying it over and over again.

I believe in you! You are the Pan!

And suddenly he was again—for the strength of belief in their voices had transferred itself to him and become his own.

He surged back to his feet, throwing Hook off and tumbling him to the floor. Hook's sword fell from his hand and a look of shock twisted his angular face. As he tried to retrieve his fallen weapon, Peter snatched up the Pan sword and blocked his way.

Hook blanched and froze.

Peter hesitated, then reached down carefully for Hook's sword, flipped it about and offered it back, hilt first.

"Curse your eternal good form!" Hook screamed.

He attacked without a word. They fought their way out of the blacksmith's and through the soup kitchen, Hook gasping and panting with every step.

"Peter Pan," Hook huffed in genuine despair. "Who and what art thou?"

"I am youth! I am joy!" Peter cried and crowed wildly.

Moments later they surged into Pirate Square. Swords clashed one final time, and then Peter zipped away to land in front of the crocodile clock. Jack and Maggie and the Lost Boys appeared at their heels, quickly spreading out to ring the combatants. Hook whirled guardedly, staring from face to face.

And suddenly there was the sound of ticking. Tick. Tick. Tick. Tick. Hook cringed. Jack and Maggie and the Lost Boys had pulled out watches and clocks of varying sizes and shapes and kinds, all ticking and tocking and chiming and beeping. The sound became a cacophony, and Hook shrank from it in terror.

Peter moved to stand before him. "Hello! Is this the great Captain Hook?" He glanced over his shoulder at the crocodile tower. "Afraid of a dead, old croc?" His voice became a child's. "Tick-tock, tick-tock, Hook's afraid of the old, dead croc."

The Lost Boys were quick to pick up the rhyme. "Tick-tock, tick-tock, Hook's afraid of the old, dead croc!"

Hook wheeled in fury, teeth clenched. He rushed at Peter to engage him, but Peter parried the blow easily and skipped away.

"No, it's not the croc after all!" Peter shouted suddenly. Then his voice lowered. "I think James Hook is afraid of time, ticking away . . ."

This was too much for Hook, who threw himself on Peter with a howl of anguish.

The battle was joined anew, Hook and Peter crashing together, swords ringing. Hook thrust wickedly, but Peter was too quick. He turned the blow aside, twisting his own sword so deftly that the captain's was swept from his hand. A second twist, so swift the eye could barely follow it, and Hook's wig and hat were flicked from his head through the air to land atop an astonished Too Small. Weaponless and hairless, exhausted and broken, Hook fell to his knees.

The point of the Pan sword came up to rest against his throat.

Hook glanced aside to see his hat and wig resting atop Too Small's head. "Peter, my dignity, at least," he pleaded. "You took my hand. You owe me something."

Peter stepped over to Too Small, retrieved the hat and wig, tossed aside the hat, and handed the wig to Hook, who clutched it before him in his hands in the manner of a disobedient child.

Peter's sword came back up to Hook's throat. His voice was stern. "You killed Rufio. You kidnapped my children. You deserve to die, James Hook."

Hook swallowed, then lifted his chin defiantly. "Then strike, Peter Pan! Strike true!"

There was fire in Peter's eyes as he beheld his enemy helpless at last, and a fierce rush of exhilaration surged through him. All about, the crowd held its collective breath—Lost Boys and pirates alike.

Peter's arm drew back.

Hook closed his eyes. "Finish it!"

But somehow Peter couldn't bring himself to do it. Neither the part that was Banning nor the part that was Pan could strike down a helpless enemy—even one as evil as Captain Hook.

He felt Maggie's hands on his arm.

"Let's go home, Daddy," she whispered. "Please? He's just a mixed-up old man without a mommy."

"Yeah, let's get out of here, Dad," Jack agreed, coming up to stand beside her. "He can't hurt us anymore."

Hook's eyes snapped open and tears welled up. "Oh, bless you, child," he murmured gratefully. He placed his wig back on his head. "Good form, Jack!"

Peter lowered his sword and stepped back, eyeing Hook coldly. "Okay, Hook—take your ship and go. I don't want to see your face in Neverland again. Promise?"

Hook swallowed whatever was threatening to choke him and with considerable effort managed a reluctant nod. Peter turned away, sheathing the Pan sword and taking his children's hands in his own. A cheer went up from the Lost Boys.

But they had missed the treacherous glint in Hook's eye. Something clicked within the sleeve of his weaponless hand, and a razor-sharp blade sprang forth from its concealment into his palm.

"Fools!" he cried. "James Hook *is* Neverland!"

Then he was on his feet, rushing to the attack. Peter

barely had time to shove Jack and Maggie out of the way
before the captain was on him. Hook slammed Peter back
against the crocodile tower and pinned him fast.

"You lied, Hook," Peter declared through clenched teeth.
He could not reach his sword. "You broke your promise."

There was a madness in the captain's red eyes. "Forever-
more, whenever children read of you it will say, 'Thus
perished Peter Pan!' "

And he thrust his claw at Peter.

But just as it seemed that all was lost, there was Tink,
darting out of nowhere to deflect the blow just enough that it
missed Peter and lodged instead in the belly of the crocodile.
Gasses and dust spewed forth in a cloud, blinding Hook. He
struggled to pull free and could not. The crocodile began to
shake and shudder, and the clock tumbled out of its jaws,
barely missing Hook as it struck the ground behind him with
a thud. The tower began to rock, then to teeter. A moaning
rose, as if a ghost had been awakened. The Lost Boys drew
back. The pirates who still remained began to scatter, fleeing
with wild cries. Peter pulled Jack and Maggie away.

Hook flailed, making the crocodile clock rock dangerously. He screamed like a madman. Finally he wrenched
free, but his efforts snapped the last of the crocodile's
fastenings and it began to fall toward him. Hook tried to
run, but ended up stumbling over the fallen clock. He lay
thrashing, horror mirrored in his red eyes. The crocodile
was descending, its jaws cracked wide.

Hook gasped. Down came the crocodile with a crash.

And Captain James Hook disappeared down its throat
with a gulp.

After the dust had settled, they all walked forward to peer
into the crocodile's jaws. One after another they bent down
for a look, amazement on their faces.

Captain Hook was gone.

"Where'd he go?" Maggie wanted to know. But no one
had an answer.

Then the cry of "victory banquet" went up again, and
everyone began to parade about the fallen crocodile, shout-

ing and cheering, "No more Hook!" and "Hurray for the Pan Man!"

Peter led the procession, caught up in the celebration, unaware that time was catching up to him once again.

"Let's go sink some mermaids!" Don't Ask suggested. "Wouldn't that be fun?"

"No!" Latchboy said. "Let's draw a circle in the ground and dare lions to cross it!"

"I want to bake a cake and feed it to the Neverbird!" No Nap said.

"But we've got to dress up like pirates and sack the ship first!" Ace declared.

They all joined in, each with his own suggestion for what they should do next. Peter began shouting suggestions of his own, a little boy himself again for just a moment.

But then he glanced over to where Jack and Maggie stood watching, Tink hanging in the air above them, and he knew that his adventures were over for now and it was time to go home.

He held up his hands and the cheering died. Lost Boy faces peered up at him.

"I can't stay," he told them. "I've done what I came to do, and now I have to go back." The joy faded from their faces. "I have to go home."

"But Peder, this is your homb," Pockets insisted.

"Yeah, this is where Peter Pan belongs," Thud Butt agreed.

Peter smiled. "No, not anymore. You see, I've grown up. And once you grow up, you have to stay that way. You can keep a little part of what's inside a boy; you can remember what it's like. But you can't go all the way back."

He turned from them and walked to where Jack and Maggie waited. He knelt before them. "Tink, dust them," he ordered. "A little traveling magic." He took their hands in his. "All you have to do is think one happy thought, and you'll fly like me."

Tink flew past in a sweeping arc, scattering pixie dust as she went. It settled over Jack and Maggie, who closed their eyes.

"Mommy!" said Maggie, and she smiled.

Jack's eyes opened, and he looked at Peter. "My dad, Peter Pan," he whispered.

Then up they went, all three, as light as feathers on the summer air. Tink led the way, a bit of spinning brightness in the sunlight. Below, the Lost Boys stood gathered, staring solemnly skyward. A few hands lifted tentatively, waving good-bye.

Peter glanced behind, hesitated in mid-flight, then placed Maggie's hand in Jack's and called Tink back.

"You know the way home, Tink. Take Jack and Maggie on ahead. I'll be right behind."

He watched them fly away, then settled down once more amid the Lost Boys.

"Don't leave us, Peter," Thud Butt pleaded. "Stay in Neverland."

He saw the confusion in their faces. "I have a wife and children who need me," he said quietly. "I belong with them."

"But we need you, too," Too Small sniffed.

Peter picked him up and hugged him. "The Lost Boys don't need anyone," he told them. "You have each other and Neverland, and that's more than enough."

"You'll forget us again," Ace declared solemnly.

"Not this time," Peter promised. "Never again."

"But you're our leader," Thud Butt insisted.

"Not anymore," Peter told him. He handed over the Pan sword. Thud Butt gasped. "You're the Pan now." He tried a comforting grin. "At least until I come back."

"Will you comb back?" Pockets asked in a small voice.

Peter met the sad, dark face and nodded, "One day," he whispered.

He went to each of them then, to Latchboy, Don't Ask, No Nap, Ace, Thud Butt, Pockets, Too Small, and all the rest, giving each a handclasp and a hug. Some cried. It was all Peter could do to finish.

"Thank you," he told them. "You helped me save my kids from Hook. You helped me to become Peter Pan again. I won't ever forget."

Then he lifted away into the cloudless blue sky. He rose, dipped, and swung back again, passing one final time over the gathered Lost Boys. Thud Butt raised the Pan sword in salute. Ace blew the antler horn. Don't Ask, No Nap, and Latchboy raised their hands and waved.

Too Small was crying. "That was a great game, Peter!" he called.

Peter gave a crow in reply, long and piercing, then turned toward the setting sun and flew away.

Thud Butt put his arm about Pockets and gave him a quick hug. There were tears in the other's eyes.

"Imb miss hib alreddy," Pockets whispered.

Farther out, close to the mouth of the harbor and facing back toward the smoking *Jolly Roger,* Smee looked up from the dinghy he rowed. Resting his oars momentarily, he watched Peter Pan fly past and disappear into the distance.

"Aye, doesn't it jus' send ye o'er the moon," he said, and sniffed. "Poor Cap'n Hook, he alwus 'ated 'appy endings."

He shifted to a more comfortable position amid the piles of treasure he had appropriated. The trio of mermaids settled at his feet smiled up at him, playing with the gold bracelets on their wrists and the silver rings on their fingers. A fish tail lifted and tickled his chin, causing him to blush.

"Ah, well." He sighed, picking up the oars and beginning to row.

As he did, one of the mermaids found the spare concertina he had scavenged and began to play. Smee sang.

"Yo, ho! Yo, ho! Yo, ho, for a pirate's life!"

An Awfully Big
Adventure

And so we come to the final chapter of our story, the one in which we tidy up all the loose ends much in the manner of mothers who straighten up their children's thoughts while they sleep. Traditionally it is not a chapter in which a great deal happens, all the excitement having taken place earlier, but is instead a time for settling back and reflecting. It is also a time for coming home from wherever one has gone, for taking delight in the simple pleasures that ends to journeys bring. So while some would skip on to the beginning of a new tale, those who understand the truths that embody Peter Pan will want to stick around to share in the Banning family's well-deserved garnering of warm fuzzies.

Peter and the children flew all night through the stars that led homeward, guided by Tink's small light pulsing like a beacon. Once or twice Peter was tempted to deviate from his course just long enough to sneak up behind a star and attempt to blow out its light (for old times' sake), but it would have meant staying his homecoming that much longer, and he was too anxious to suffer further delays. He spent his time holding his children close and telling them all the stories he had never shared, the ones that had disappeared from his life over the years, locked away in the adult that had no time for such nonsense. He hugged and kissed them frequently, as if afraid he might never get the chance again, and they laughed at silly nothings and foolish looks. At times they spoke of where they had gone and what they had seen and done, but yawns and the wind's lullabies made recollection difficult, and the words seemed to stray off by themselves like sheep from an untended flock.

Toward dawn, with most of the stars disappeared into the brightening sky and the moon dropped below the horizon, Kensington Gardens came into view, steepled roofs and brick chimneys shrouded in tattered winter mist. Peter's eyes grew so heavy then that he could no longer keep them open.

The last thing he remembered was letting go of Jack and Maggie's hands.

Shadows lay over the children's nursery at number 14 Kensington, layered patches of black that only just now were beginning to recede as morning neared. The china-house night-lights burned steadily above the empty twin beds, casting their small glow bravely into the dark, outlining the soldiers that stood guard before the fireplace, the rocking horse that waited patiently for its rider, the dollhouse where Ken stood ready to serve Barbie, and the books and toys that had given voice to the dreams of the children who played with them.

Moira sat sleeping in a rocking chair at the center of the room. She stirred at times, her fingers brushing at her gown, her lips whispering her children's names. She looked very alone.

Then a breeze blew open the latticed windows, brushing the lace curtains so that the figures of Peter Pan danced as if alive. A scattering of leaves swirled into the room. Then Jack appeared, floating through the opening and settling to the floor like a feather. Maggie, heavy-eyed with sleep, rode piggyback. Together, they stared at the sleeping Moira.

"Who is she?" Jack whispered finally, eyes blinking against his own need for sleep.

"It's Mother," Maggie answered with a yawn.

"Oh." Jack studied the sleeping woman carefully—the lines of her face, the way her arms crooked just so, the hint of kisses hiding at the corners of her mouth.

"She looks just like an angel," Maggie sighed. "Let's

not wake her, Jack. Let's just be there for her when she's ready.''

They tiptoed across the bedroom floor and eased silently beneath their covers. Perhaps it was their movement on the floorboards, perhaps simply their presence, but Moira awoke almost at once. She blinked, brushed at a stray leaf that rested upon her shoulder, and glanced at the open windows, aware of the breeze blowing back the curtains; then she rose and walked to close them, twisting the lock into place.

When she turned back, she saw the twin lumps in the beds (cast by shadows, she was certain), and it was almost as if the children had returned. The look that came over her was sad and wistful, and for a moment she could not move, afraid to break the spell.

Then the door opened and Wendy appeared in her robe and slippers, walking slowly, gingerly, leaning on a cane for support.

''Child?'' she whispered to Moira. ''Have you been up all night?''

Moira smiled and shook her head. ''I see them in my dreams so often, just like this, bundles in their beds, that when I wake I think they're really there. . . .''

But Wendy wasn't listening. She was staring wide-eyed at the lumps. Moira turned, a frown creased her pretty face, and one hand reached out tentatively.

Abruptly Jack sprang out from beneath the covers. ''Mom,'' he cried, and would have said more except his throat closed up and nothing came out.

Maggie threw back her covers as well. ''Mommy,'' she called, and Moira collapsed to the floor.

The children sprang from their beds and ran to her. She gathered Jack in her arms, holding him so tightly he thought he might break in two. She took Maggie in as well, crying freely now, sobbing as she hugged and kissed them.

''Oh, my babies, my babies,'' she murmured.

''Mom,'' Jack said, breaking away, anxious to tell everything. ''There were all these pirates, and they put us in a net, and—''

"But Daddy saved us," Maggie interjected. "And we flew! Great-granny, we—"

But Wendy cut her short with a warm squdge and a laugh that silenced the doubtful words that Moira was about to voice. "Pirates?" she repeated. "And you flew as well? How lovely, child. Gracious, it reminds me of the days when Peter and I flew."

And she hugged them again and gave Moira a hug as well.

Not far away dawn's light was just cresting the roofs of the houses, casting pearl streamers on the air and sunspots on the earth. Peter Banning lay sprawled in a snowbank. He was sleeping, his breathing slow and even, his arms and legs cocked in positions he never could have managed in waking.

Tink, tink, tink, sounded from somewhere close at hand.

He blinked and awoke, sitting up sharply. He had no idea where he was or what he was doing there.

"Jack, Maggie, we're going to fly. . . ." he began without thinking, and trailed off doubtfully.

He took a deep breath and looked around. He was in a snow-covered park. A river snaked its way past not fifty yards off, an early-morning mist rising from its waters like smoke. Hardwood trees towered overhead like sentinels, bare-leafed in the winter season. The air was crisp and bracing and full of breakfast smells.

"And how be ye this fine mawnin', Peter Pan?" a familiar voice asked. "Into some mischief, 'ey?"

Peter whirled in shock to find Smee standing not a dozen yards away, hands on hips and a bag across his shoulder. Except it wasn't Smee—it was a groundskeeper making his rounds collecting litter. And he wasn't addressing Peter at all—he was addressing a statue. The statue was the one of Peter Pan placed in the park near the Serpentine River by the writer J. M. Barrie in the year 1912—Peter Pan crouched ready for his next adventure, playing his Pan pipes, forever the boy who refused to grow up.

Peter came to his feet, stepped out of the snowbank, and

walked toward the statue. The groundskeeper finished
gathering up the stray papers he had attributed to Peter
Pan's mischief and moved on. Peter reached the statue and
stopped.

He was shaking as the memories flooded back.

Neverland. Hook. Maggie and Jack.

A tiny figure appeared on the statue's shoulder, small and
delicate in the soft morning light, gossamer wings beating
gently.

Peter blinked. "Tink?"

She smiled. "Say it, Peter. Say it and mean it."

He smiled back. "I believe in faeries."

Tink's whole body brightened as if a lamp had been
turned on inside. Her face shone. "You know that place
between asleep and awake? That place where you still
remember dreaming? That's where I'll always love you,
Peter Pan. And that's where I'll wait for you to come
back."

Then a streamer of sunlight crested the Pan statue's
shoulder right where she was standing, and she disappeared.

Peter squinted to find her again, shaded his eyes with his
hand, and took a step forward. But she was gone, and already
his memory of her was beginning to dim. A bit farther down
the path, the groundskeeper was gathering up a pair of empty
bottles thoughtlessly discarded the night before.

Tink, tink, tink, they said as they knocked together in his
hands.

"Tink?" Peter said one final time, and then the memory
was gone, tucked back away into a drawer within his mind,
safely stowed for the time that he would need it again.

Sudden exhilaration flooded through him. He was home!

"Jack? Maggie?" he called out anxiously. He stared
around. They had been right there with him when he had
returned from . . . He frowned. From wherever. But they
were safe, he was certain of that, and that was what really
mattered.

"Moira! I'm home!" he shouted.

Then down the park pathway he raced, hailing the
groundskeeper and everyone else he passed with cheery

hellos, chipper good days, and bouncy greetings of all sorts.

It took him only moments, it seemed, to reach number 14 Kensington from the back side. Disdaining to go around to the front gate, he vaulted onto the terrace wall and began to dance along it like a high-wire artist, leaping and bounding when he tired of that, springing down finally to rush to the front door.

It was locked.

He reached for the brass knocker and stopped.

No, not today.

He dashed around to the back, vaulting still another fence, singing and humming gaily as he went. He was almost below the nursery windows when he heard a phone ring. He stared about in an effort to locate the source and determined that he was standing on it. Kneeling, he dug away the snow and fresh earth and pulled out his holster phone. He let it ring one final time, then clicked it on.

"Hello, this is Peter Banning," he greeted. "I'm not in right now—I'm out deliberately avoiding your call. Please leave a 'you know' at the 'right now' and I'll 'do it' when I'm good and ready. Happy thoughts!"

He dropped the phone back into the hole and covered it up again.

Then he started to climb the drainpipe. Up he went, hand over hand, his face flushed and eager. He would not have dreamed of doing such a thing four days and a lifetime of adventures earlier, but things had changed for Peter Banning, even if he wasn't exactly sure what they were or how they had come about.

He reached the nursery windows and tried to push them open. Locked. He tried again. Still locked. He put his face to the glass and peered inside.

There was Wendy embracing Moira, Jack, and Maggie. Something within Peter threatened to break apart, and a memory of another time, long ago, was triggered by what he saw. He couldn't get in to them! He was shut outside once more! His breath fogged the windowpanes as he hung there on the balcony railing, terrified that somehow he was once again too late . . .

And then he began to pound on the glass, no longer caring what it took, desperate to be inside.

"I'm home!" he cried. "I've come back! Please, let me in!"

They heard him, of course, and Jack bounded to the window. There was a hint of mischief in his elfin face (did it seem suspiciously like Peter's own?), a grin on his lips, and the beginning of tears in his eyes. "Excuse me," he said. "Do you have an appointment?"

Peter grinned back. "Yeah, with you for the rest of my life, you little pirate."

Jack released the latch and swung the windows wide. Peter stepped inside and faced him. They stared at each other for a moment in silence.

Then Peter whispered, "What did I tell you about this window?" He snatched Jack up and hugged him. "Never close it! Always keep it open!"

He whirled Jack about, flying him at arm's length, both of them laughing and shouting.

Maggie bounced up on the bed. "Fly me, too, Daddy! Fly me, too!"

Peter snatched her up and swung her about. "Your wish is my command, Princess!"

Then he set them both down, picked up a startled Moira, and whirled her about as well, lifting her off the floor as if she were a child, his face alive with happiness. She clung to him, shrieking, and when he finally put her down again she threw her arms about him and held him close.

"Peter, oh, Peter," she gasped in relief. "Where have you been?"

But Peter suddenly caught sight of Tootles, peeking around the corner of the bedroom door. He broke from Moira and went to the old man. Tootles smiled shyly and started to leave.

"No," Peter said quietly, and embraced him, drawing him into the room with the others.

"Hello, Pedur," Tootles greeted uncertainly. "I missed the adventure again, didn't I?"

Peter shook his head and smiled back. Then he remembered something. Reaching into his shirt, he pulled out the bag that Thud Butt had given him, loosened the drawstrings, and poured the contents into Tootles' frail, shaking hands.

"I think these belong to you," he whispered.

Tootles's eyes went wide with disbelief. Tears started down his cheeks as he turned to Wendy.

"Look, Wendy. See? I have them again. I didn't lose my marbles after all."

Wendy went to him and hugged him, one hand coming up to smooth his wispy hair. Tootles took the marbles and moved over to the window to view them in the sunlight, murmuring about lost memories, caressing his happy thoughts. A moment later, to everyone's astonishment, he began to rise. He had found a trace of pixie dust at the bottom of the pouch and poured it over himself. Buoyed by his happy thoughts he flew bravely out the window, calling back, "Good-bye! Good-bye!" as he disappeared from sight.

Wendy moved to Peter and took his hand in hers.

"Hullo, boy."

Peter swallowed. "Hullo, Wendy."

"Boy, why are you crying?"

He smiled. "I'm just happy . . . to be home."

Wendy moved to embrace him, and as she did she remembered anew what it had been like all those years ago to fly away with Peter Pan to Neverland, to roam the island of pirates and Indians and mermaids, to live beneath the Nevertree and tell stories to the Lost Boys, to be a part of the dreams of childhood and youth and be free of the cares and responsibilities that growing up brought. She wanted to go back in that instant. She would have gone if she could.

"Peter," she whispered. "What of your adventures? Will you miss them?"

He shook his head. "To live," he replied, "will be an awfully big adventure."

And as he said it the last of the night's stars—if that is what it really was—flashed away into the darkness and was gone.

About the Author

Terry Brooks was born in Illinois in 1944. He received his undergraduate degree from Hamilton College, Clinton, New York, where he majored in English Literature, and his graduate degree from the School of Law at Washington & Lee University, Lexington, Virginia. He was a practicing attorney until recently; he has now retired to become a full-time author.

A writer since high school, he published his first novel, *The Sword of Shannara*, in 1977, and the sequels *The Elfstones of Shannara* in 1982 and *The Wishsong of Shannara* in 1985. *Magic Kingdom for Sale—Sold!* began a best-selling new series for him in 1986; Brooks presently lives in the Northwest.